P9-EMQ-020

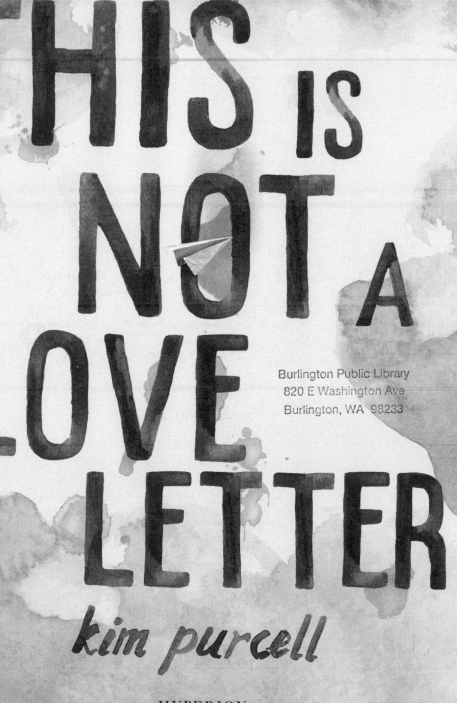

THIS IS NOT A LOVE LETTER

kim purcell

HYPERION

LOS ANGELES   NEW YORK

First Edition, January 2018
1 3 5 7 9 10 8 6 4 2
FAC-020093-17349
Printed in the United States of America

This book is set in 11-pt. Adobe Garamond Pro, Arial,
Bodoni 72, Helvetica Neue/Monotype
Designed by Marci Senders

Library of Congress Cataloging-in-Publication Control Number: 2016058454
ISBN 978-1-4847-9834-8
Reinforced binding

Visit www.hyperionteens.com

To my mom, Marion

This is not a love letter...

So don't get all excited for nothing. Maybe I should write you one, to go with all the letters you've written me and folded into perfect little airplanes. But I never wrote you one before, and it would be seriously bad luck to start now.

Chris. Where are you? How did you not come home last night?

I don't care where you went or what you're doing; I just want to know if you're okay. We all do. I mean, who does this? I'm starting to feel kind of weird. Desperate, if you want to know the truth. It's like when I get a mosquito bite. You're always telling me to leave it alone, but I can't stop itching until it bleeds. Right now you're my mosquito bite. Isn't that romantic?

I thought I'd write and let you know what we're doing to find you. Maybe it'll help me figure out where you are. So until you turn up, this is an account. I know. That's the unsexiest word ever. But if you want a sexy love letter, you're going to have to come back home and get it.

7:01 AM Saturday, my house

I'll start this account with first thing this morning.

I wake up to someone banging on my back door. I open my eyes. The pale light of early morning is drifting through my small basement window.

Of course, I think it's you at the door and I got to admit, I'm kind of pissed. I don't know why you'd knock when you have a key, but it can't be anyone else. I tug on my jean shorts and put on a bra under the tangerine T-shirt you bought me to match my hair. I wore it to bed. Yes, I admit—I was missing you, just a little bit.

More knocking. "For god's sake, I'm coming."

I open my bedroom door, step into the hall, and bump into a stack of magazines, which tips over, blocking the hallway. I climb over them. Seriously, if the big West Coast earthquake ever happens, I'll be buried alive under a pile of *US* and *People* magazines.

"Jessie?" My mom is making her way down the stairs in her old pink bathrobe, gripping the railing like her knees hurt. "What's going on?" She sounds groggy. Probably because of the sleeping pills. She looks worse than normal. Greasy hair. Dark circles under her eyes. Her tired, sagging face. I'm worried about her at the moment, not you.

"It's okay, Mom," I say. "Go back to sleep. I got it."

"Okay," she mumbles, and heads back up the stairs.

I navigate around the piles of laundry and random towers of my mom's stuff, and finally arrive at the back door, which I swing open. Nobody's there.

I stand with the door wide open. Really? Did you really wake me up and leave? I dig out the corners of my eyes for what you call "sleep surprises" and think about how we both get the same sick pleasure from morning crusties. You told me you love the feeling when you dig them out and they scrape against the corner of your eye, and right away, I realized that's what I like too.

This break is really stupid. In so many ways, we're perfect for each other. Anyway, it's a week before graduation and we should be together. I decide to stop being so stubborn and go make up. Give you a big old wet kiss. And forget about needing some "perspective."

I slide into my flip-flops, step out into the yard, and walk to the side gate. There's a strong pulp-mill smell in the air, like a stew of farts, rotten eggs, and used athletic socks . . . and yes, plus a little sugar.

The gate squeals as I throw it open. I expect to see you walking up the incline along our house to the front lawn, but nobody's there.

I listen for your truck. All I hear are the neighbor's dogs going crazy, barking inside her house. Are you in your truck already? Are you going to leave, again? I take off, running up the path, my flip-flops slapping against the gravel. I catapult myself around the corner of the house, ready to throw myself at you. Only you're not there.

Instead, I see Josh, pushing his bike past the giant tire in the middle of our lawn. The back of his white T-shirt is soaked with sweat.

What is he doing at my house at this time in the morning? Were you running with him? Did you fall? Are you hurt?

"Josh?"

He turns. Sweat is dripping down his face. His blue eyes are rimmed with red, like he's been crying.

He pulls off his helmet. His curly blond hair is so drenched, it falls down like an air mattress without air. He runs a hand through it and swallows. "You hear from Chris yet?"

I say something like why or what.

"He's missing," he says, as if he's reminding me, like that's something I'd forget.

"Missing?" The word *missing* echoes inside me, reverberates against the internal walls of my body, like an empty chamber. A guy like you doesn't go missing. You're responsible, smart, athletic, sexy, funny, sensitive, kind—you are hundreds of words, but you are not *missing*.

"Didn't Chris's mom call?" he asks.

I shake my head.

"Chris went for a run last night around nine, and he hasn't come home yet. His mom said she called you."

The phone rang in the middle of the night, vibrated on my nightstand. I was still mad about how you acted at the mall, so I grabbed it and mumbled something like, "Chris, I said a week." Then I turned it off.

I slide my phone out of my back pocket. There are two texts from Josh. And a drunken text from Steph about winning some money at poker. No text from you, but there are two calls from your home phone. Why didn't I see that? You never would have called from your home phone at two in the morning.

I listen to the voicemail. It's your mom. "Hi, Jessie. We're trying to locate Chris." Her voice is calm, not angry. "Can you call me?" She pauses, as if she's going to say more, but then simply adds, "Thanks. Bye."

"His mom called," I tell Josh. "I didn't know it was her."

He looks away. He's pissed. And I can't blame him.

I call your number, but it goes straight to voicemail: "Hey. This is Chris. You know what to do." There's a beep.

I can count on one hand the number of times that I've heard that message. And that beep. You always answer. My heart flips around in my chest. My arms buzz. I feel electric, like I'm guarding at the pool, and I'm about to jump in the water for a rescue.

"Hey, Chris, can you call me? I'm worried. Josh is here, and he's worried too. Please let us know you're okay." I pause. "I miss you." I don't say I love you because Josh is standing right there and I don't know why, it's dumb.

Then I send you a text: Call me!! XOXO

Josh is looking at his phone, like he just got a text.

"Who is it?" I ask.

"Tim and them. They're out looking too."

I wonder who "them" is. "Didn't you have a big meet in Seattle this weekend?"

"Yeah." He shakes his head like it doesn't matter. "I ran the two hundred yesterday. I came home in the middle of the night, soon as I heard. I've been riding the trails looking for him since I got back."

I cannot believe I've been sleeping this whole miserable night. "You check Matheson trail?"

"Yeah, we go there all the time."

"How about the Pitt?" Of course, I'm thinking about how those guys from the Heights beat you up there.

"I looked everywhere, Jessie. Been riding down every friggin trail, calling his name." He bends over and wipes his sweaty face on the bottom of his T-shirt. "There's nothing. No sign of him anywhere."

I have more questions, but I don't know how much Josh knows. Did he search the ground? Was there blood? Did he look for broken branches?

"That route is only twelve miles," I say. "He should have been home in just over an hour."

7

Josh frowns. "I headed out when it was dark, but the light on my bike's not great, maybe I missed something."

Down the street, a truck roars. We spin around to look. We're both hoping it's you, but it's not.

7:25 AM Saturday, the gang

Tim's red truck is speeding toward us. It's a raging beast of a vehicle, a grizzly bear bellowing through the quiet of the morning.

Tamara and Becky are sitting in the front. No idea where the rest of the guys are. The truck lurches to a stop and Tim jumps out. Tamara and Becky follow him. Josh pushes his bike down the driveway toward them.

"What's up?" Tim says to Josh, then lifts his chin at me. "Hey, Jessie." He's real serious, for once, instead of goofing around, speaking a mile a minute. His dark eyes hold mine.

"She hasn't heard anything," Josh says.

"I just found out," I explain.

"I've been calling everyone, waking them up. No one's seen him yet," Tim says, "but they want to help."

I feel a tiny swell of relief. People listen to Tim. Maybe it's something he learned from watching his grandpa, when he was the chief of the Lummi Nation tribe. But it's no coincidence that Tim's the captain of the basketball team and the valedictorian. I always wonder how he does it all.

Tamara and Becky walk up slowly. They stop next to Tim. Becky slouches over Tamara, like a willow tree giving her shade. They stare at my old house with its peeling paint, the big tire in the front yard, the long patchy grass we never mow. The curtain stirs. Mom is there, watching. Tamara glances at Becky and smirks, which makes me feel like crap, even though I know it shouldn't. Who gives a rat's ass what Tamara thinks, right?

At least she isn't wearing her little workout shorts, wiggling her butt in everyone's faces like normal. Today she has this huge black hoodie on; the sleeves are so long, the fabric curls around her hands. Her hair is pulled into a messy ponytail, and she's not wearing makeup. Looks pretty harsh. Just saying.

"I told you this is a waste of time." Tamara jams out her hip. "They're broken up."

"No, we're not," I say. "We're on a break, for a week. We just needed some—" *Perspective.* Yes, I was going to say that word again. You laughed when I said it to you.

She cuts me off. "Whatever. Did he come by your house in the middle of the night or not?"

Like I'm your booty call. "No," I say. "Not that it's any of your business."

Tamara glares at me and I glare right back.

Josh turns to me. "Chris stopped by Tim's house last night before his run."

I look at Tim. "Yeah?"

"Around nine thirty. I was having a barbecue." Tim lifts his Seahawks cap and pulls it back down over his straight black hair, the brim curled up tight like a small n. "It was almost dark. We should have made him stay."

"We tried, remember?" Tamara wraps her arms around herself, tucks her fingers under her armpits. "He looked over your fence at me and said he'd see me later."

It bugs me how she takes possession of you with those words, like you were coming back for her. Did you really say that?

"He even gave me his hoodie," she says. "He asked me to hold it for him."

What the hell? That's your hoodie?

Breathe. I got to pretend it doesn't bug me.

Tim shakes his head. "I don't know where he could have gone."

"Chris likes to go for long walks in the middle of the night." I hold up my knowledge of you like a trophy. "Sometimes he can't sleep. Maybe he went somewhere in town, like the doughnut shop or something."

"We just checked there," Becky says. "They didn't see him."

"We looked everywhere," Tamara adds. "He's not in town."

"Maybe he went for a drive, like to Seattle or Portland."

"He left his truck and his wallet," Josh tells me.

"What about his phone?" I say, thinking how maybe it's in your room and that's why it's going to voicemail.

"It's not at his house."

"That's weird," I say. It can't be dead. You're so good about charging your phone. You even plug in *my* phone so you can reach me.

"He didn't go home to shower or anything," Josh says.

"He would've showered," I say.

Tim nods. "Even when we go for burgers after a ball game, he always has to stop by home to change first."

"Has his mom called the cops?" I ask.

Josh heaves out a frustrated sigh. "Nope, she thinks he went somewhere for the night."

"Where the hell's he going to go with no truck and no money?"

"Exactly."

"Something could have happened," I say.

"Like what?" Tim asks.

"Maybe he got jumped."

"Who would jump *him*?" Becky says with a little laugh.

"He's a huge black guy," Tamara adds, rolling her eyes. I want to punch her.

"There are plenty of people who would jump him." The words whistle out of me. Before I can say more, Josh opens his eyes a little, warning me, and I stop talking. I don't get why it has to be a big secret. If you told your friends not to get revenge, they would have listened.

"Like who?" Tamara asks.

I kick at some grass sprouting out of a crack in the driveway. "I don't know. Some drunk assholes."

They're quiet for a moment.

"Nobody would do anything to him." Tim pauses, looks worried. "If they did, they're going to regret it." He pulls his keys out of his pocket and they jangle in his hand, a strangely happy sound, considering what he's just said. Even though Tim's normally a pretty easy-going guy, if he says someone's going to regret it, you don't want to be that someone.

"Why do you have a tire on your lawn?" Tamara says.

Everyone looks at it now, like it matters. That tire's been there forever. Dad changed it off his rig when I was little and I liked it so much, I begged him to leave it. We had so much fun on this tire, me and Steph. She'd come over, we'd climb on it and dance around, play queen of the tire, and then, when I got older, I'd take a blanket and read here in the streetlight, my butt in the hole, breathing in the night air, just to escape my hoarder house for a while.

How do you tell people that there's a good reason you look like white trash? I just shrug and look toward Steph's house across the street. "It's been there forever."

Tim looks down the street. "We should check out the bus station and Amtrak. Just in case."

"Good idea," Josh says.

"A bunch more people are out looking," Tim says. "We'll find him."

Josh presses one finger to the edge of his eye. "Yeah we will."

"It's going to be okay, Joshy." Tamara gives him a hug. The

hoodie's sleeve falls down. She's got a splotch of blue on her forearm, which seems strange. Never pegged her as the type to help with painting her house. Man, I really want that hoodie.

"Text us if you hear anything," Tim says.

Then they all climb in the truck and it roars down the street. Josh and I gaze down the street after them.

He sighs. "I'm going to keep riding the trails."

I follow him down the driveway. "Do you think he ran into those guys from the Heights again?"

"They were from the Heights?"

"You didn't know?"

"He didn't tell me who."

"Man."

He swallows. Never seen him look so worried before. That's what freaks me out more than anything. If you were just taking off like last time, you would've told him.

He jams on his helmet. "I'll let you know if I see anything." Then he rides off down the road.

He's already searched for hours, and now he's going back out—it's pretty amazing to have a friend like that. I can see you guys living next door to each other when you're eighty. Isn't that funny? The two of you on your separate porches in your rocking chairs. You wouldn't need to sit beside each other. You barely talk anyway. (I just heard you answering me in my brain. "Of course we'd sit next to each other." Okay. Whatever.)

At this point, I'm not sure what to do. I'm thinking this would be a good joke. Maybe you're trying to show me how bummed I'll be if you're gone. (I am! Come back! I'm bummed, seriously bummed!)

For a full minute, I stare down the empty street, toward the river, thinking you're going to show up, as if the powerful force of my mind could make it happen. I wait for you to run toward me, that dimple of yours diving into your cheek, your smile so wide it's like you've opened the cloudy Northwest sky and let the sun come in. You'll say you were joking. You'll pick me up and swing me around. Then, your lips will rest on mine, and we'll sway back and forth, and you'll dip me back, like in some old movie. I wait, hoping, but you don't come running down the street, and it's not a joke.

7:40 AM Saturday, your house

I have to tell your mom what I know. As much as I don't like cops, this might be the one time we need them.

I take off toward your house.

I'm breathing hard after two blocks. Should have grabbed my bike. I suck at running. It's the boobs, I swear. I know you're a boob guy, but most of the time, they're a damn hassle.

For the last block, I slow down to a trot. Tell myself not to panic. Maybe you're home. This is not the kind of day bad things happen.

There's not a cloud in the sky. It's the most beautiful day we've had in weeks. The guy on FM 101 is probably calling it a Blue Blazer.

Normally, on a day like today, you'd be waking me up with some cheesy thing like "rise and shine" and then you'd make me coffee and half an hour later, we'd be hitting the trails, me on my bike, you sprinting ahead, leaping over logs with your long, beautiful legs, like some goddamn gazelle, and I'd be chasing you down, panting like a hyena, carrying my bike over those same damn logs.

This is what I want to be doing instead of wondering where the hell you are.

When I get to your duplex, your blue truck is in the driveway, and I think, Thank god, you're home!! But then I remember you left your truck, and I feel this crushing disappointment like the damn truck started itself up and drove backward, over my twitching body. I guess I wouldn't be twitching until after my body was crushed. First, I'd scream. Then get crushed. And then twitch.

I slide my finger along its gleaming side. Not a speck of dirt. Inside there's no garbage and the dashboard is shining. You just cleaned it. For someone who doesn't really care about what he drives, you sure clean it a lot.

At your screen door, I pause. The cold metal handle rests in my hand. I'm worried your mom is going to be mad about this break. Maybe she'll blame me.

I open the screen door and knock, and then I step back and let it shut, like a door-to-door salesperson, or a kid who has to knock on doors for his religion. You never talk much about being a Jehovah's Witness, just that you decided it wasn't for you.

The inside door swings open. Your mom is wearing a dark purple skirt with a white blouse and a purple cashmere cardigan. Her short, dark hair is curled under. She always says a person should try to look her best. *Put your best face forward.* But she has huge bags and her eyes are all red—I bet she hasn't slept all night—and, baby, you got to know, today her best face isn't all that great.

"Hi." I cannot believe I hung up on her.

"Jessie!" She throws the screen door wide. I step into the house and she pulls me into a warm hug that smells faintly of cinnamon. "I was hoping you'd come by."

It is such a relief that she hasn't gone all cold on me. She's been like a second mom to me—I like her more than I like my own mom. Maybe that's bad to say, but it's true.

My hand rests on the back of her soft cashmere sweater. Her breathing is shallow.

"I just found out," I say. "Josh woke me up. He told me you called, but I didn't realize it was—" I suck in a breath. "Have you called the police?"

"Not yet. I talked to the elders at the church and they say there's no point panicking for nothing. He'll be home soon."

I can't believe she's asking the elders for advice at a time like this.

A buzzer rings in the kitchen. "I made some chocolate cinnamon bread for when he gets home. Have to take it out of the oven. Come on in."

Your house feels different. It's too quiet, too dark. Then I realize that the television is off, and that's why it's strange. Instead of light bouncing off the flowery wallpaper and the constant sound of a ball game or one of your mom's shows, there is only the quiet tick of your old grandfather clock.

Out of habit, I glance up the stairs, expecting to see you lumbering down, your kneecaps bobbing, your head ducking so you don't hit the ceiling. But the stairwell is empty.

I slide off my flip-flops and follow your mom toward the kitchen. My bare feet press into the Persian carpet you brought all the way from Brooklyn. It's strange being here when you are not.

All I can think is, man, I can't believe I have to tell her about those guys. She always goes on about how nice people are in Pendling, but you were beaten up bad, and we both know underneath lots of people aren't all that nice.

You said they didn't beat you up because you're black, not really. Those two words. *Not really.* You said it was about baseball.

It was a Saturday night, three weeks ago. Your voice on the phone, all pinched up: "Can you come? I'm hurt." I ran all the way to your house. Your sister and your mom were at the Jehovah's Witness hall. You said to come right in, you were in your room. I ran up the stairs, threw open your door.

You were laid flat on your clean blue sheet. The fact that you hadn't showered or changed was what made me realize it was bad. Your legs and arms had mud caked on them from being kicked on the ground, and your face was swollen on one side. You squinted at me when I came in, said you needed ice. Even then, your dimple danced on your cheek.

I flew down the stairs and grabbed an ice pack from the freezer and then hurried back up. Your mattress sagged as I dropped down beside you. When I lifted up your T-shirt, the movement of the fabric across your skin made you wince. Your ribs were so swollen, right away I knew something was broken. I placed the ice pack on them. You let out a moan and your eyes rolled into the back of your head. I ran the tips of my fingers over the goose bumps on your arm.

You told me what happened.

"You have to call the cops."

"It's nothing," you said.

"It isn't nothing! They could have broken your pitching arm. That's not a normal fight."

"Don't be mad."

But I was mad. "If you don't call the cops, they'll do it again."

"I'm not calling the cops."

No matter how many times I begged you to report it, you wouldn't. So I made you promise you'd never run down there again alone.

You. Promised. Me.

When your mom and sister got home, you told them you fell. Your mom went on and on about how you had to be careful on those trails, how it's easy to trip, all those branches and logs. Raffa stood, watching, her skinny eleven-year-old body curving into the door, scared, like she knew.

And now I'm in your kitchen and I have to tell your mom that you lied and I lied for you. Which I hate. Because if there's one thing I know about myself, maybe I can be brutal, maybe I tell it too straight, but I'm no liar.

Your mom taps the top of the bread with two fingers and glances at the large pendulum clock on the wall. That worry line you tease her about is forming between her eyebrows. "It's almost eight."

"I think you should call the police," I blurt out.

She frowns. "Maybe they picked him up."

"For what?"

"Maybe they saw him running and thought he was running from something. They could have arrested him."

This did not even occur to me. "But he'd get a phone call, right?"

She shrugs. "Maybe. Maybe not."

"Cops here are different from Brooklyn cops."

She gives me a look down and up. Fair enough. How do I know they're different? You and I did get pulled over for nothing more than once.

"He's probably going to come home any minute," your mom says. "He did this right after we moved here, too. Didn't show up all night."

"But he texted Josh that time."

"Fifteen years old! I was fit to be tied."

"Please call the police." My voice cracks. "It's different this time."

She frowns. "Jessie, do you need to tell me something?"

"It's not safe where he was running."

"How's that?" She folds her arms in front of her body and gives me that look she gives you when you come home with an A- instead of an A.

The words fall from my mouth like nails out of a bucket. "Remember his black eye a few weeks ago? Some guys from the Heights beat him up. He was running down there, in that same area, at that same time."

"Chris was fighting?" From her face, I see she doesn't believe it. She knows how you feel about violence.

"He didn't fight back. I wish he had. Then, they wouldn't mess with him again."

She frowns.

"He promised me he wouldn't run down there by himself again, but he was mad at me, so he did it anyway. And now he's missing." Sharp slivers of sadness cut at my insides. If you were here, you'd calm me down, speak to me in your low, steady voice, rub my back, tell me it's going to be okay.

"Well, let's not overreact." She sighs. "I'm sure he's fine."

"It wouldn't hurt to call the police."

"I called the hospital," she says. "I thought maybe he'd been hit by a car. But he wasn't there. I never thought about fighting. I didn't figure that kind of thing happened here."

Not here? Fighting's our town's favorite sport. If there's a week without a fight, it's a goddamn miracle. "People fight all the time. Just not Chris."

"He's a good boy." She turns to dump the chocolate cinnamon bread on a plate and then takes out a knife and slices it. Steam cuts into the air. The smell of chocolate fills the room.

"Please call. Just at least report him missing."

"He's eighteen," she says. "We may have to wait twenty-four hours."

"You can tell them he's in high school. Please?"

She gazes at me, worried, then picks up the phone and dials 911. On the other end, the operator answers and your mom says, "I'm sorry if I should be calling another number, but my son didn't come home last night." She sounds uncertain now. I wonder if she's ever called the police before. "He's eighteen, but he's in high school. His name is Christopher Kirk."

I can hear a high-pitched female voice on the other end, but I can't hear what she's saying. I take a bite of the chocolate cinnamon bread. The chocolate chips are hot and melty.

"Oh yes?" your mom responds to the woman. "Isn't that something?" Then, she explains that you went for a run last night. Another pause. "Yes, well, I thought he was at his girlfriend's house, but it turns out he wasn't." She gives your height and weight and what you were wearing: six foot two, 180 pounds, black shorts, blue T-shirt, Nike running shoes.

She doesn't mention your dimple. Or the way your eyes sparkle when you look at me. Or how you like retro candy. And of course, she says nothing about that sexy line of muscle by your hip. Or how you're a really good kisser.

"Thank you. Good-bye now." She hangs up. "Can you believe it? The dispatcher knows Chris. He coached her son on that Little League team."

It doesn't surprise me. There are thirty thousand people in our little town in the Northwest, but everywhere we go, people are always slapping you on the back, saying hi. After three years, you know more people than I do, and I've lived here my whole life.

"She said they'll put out an APB for him. All the police officers in the area will be looking."

"You should tell them that he has a dimple."

"I'll tell the detective when he calls." She rolls her eyes and shakes her head. "You watch, now that I called the police, Chris is going to walk through that door."

I look toward the door of the kitchen. You don't walk through.

She adjusts her smooth pearl necklace. "Last night he was studying for his exams. I brought him a peanut-butter sandwich. He ate it and told me he was going for a run. Said he had to burn off some steam. Said he'd be back soon."

"See? He's not going to say that and not come home."

"You're right." Her jaw quivers. I'm scared she's going to cry, but then she turns away and wraps the chocolate bread in tin foil.

I don't know whether I should ask if she's okay. "Where's Raffa?"

"Upstairs."

It's strange that Raffa didn't come down to say hi.

"Josh is riding the trails right now, looking for him," I say.

She's quiet for a second. When she speaks, her voice is tight, like an elastic stretched too far. "That's good."

"Do you want me to stay and talk to the police?" I admit it, I hope she'll say no. I really, really, really don't want to talk to the police.

She reaches her hands up to her eyes. I think she's crying, but there's no sound. "Don't you have to work at the pool today?"

"I could call in sick."

"No, you go," she says, turning around, her eyes shining. "It's best I talk to the police alone."

I'm relieved for a second, but then I wonder why. "I'm sorry I hung up on you last night," I blurt out. "I thought it was Chris. I didn't know it was you. We're on a break for a week and—"

She cuts me off. "You've got nothing more to tell me about. You're a teenager. You're doing what teenagers do."

Does she mean it's okay for me to do stupid things just because I'm a teenager? "He wants to turn down that scholarship and stay here with me."

"He's going to turn it down?" She presses her lips together, and I can tell she's mad. If you walk in the door right now, I'm going to regret this.

"I told him he's going. I'm not letting him give up his dreams."

"Good."

"I'm getting back together with him, though," I say. "Soon as he comes home. I can't live without him. I love him."

Those three words come, unexpected, little birds that decided to fly out of my mouth right at this minute and spin their way into your mom's ears.

You say *I love you* to me all the time. It's as easy for you as saying *pizza*. But the few times I've said it, I've had to force the words out of my mouth. It's like I'm getting a tooth pulled. No joke. It's painful. We don't say that in my family. It's not normal for us. But now, I've said it to your mom, like it's nothing.

She squints at me, kindly. "I know you do, Jessie."

"Can you let me know if you hear anything?"

25

My throat feels all clogged up, like I've swallowed a big chunk of crusty bread. Did you know that we release a hormone when we get sad that actually causes the throat to swell up?

"Of course I will." Her brown eyes crinkle and she forces a smile. "I'll make sure he calls you as soon as he gets home."

8:35 AM Saturday, Steph

I walk to Steph's house and try to see if there's any light coming through the brown bedsheets covering her window. Doesn't look like it. She'd want me to wake her up for something like this, but if I knock on the glass, her mom's boyfriend might freak out. You never know when they're on a bender—it's always best to call.

Besides, I have to pee. Badly. I know that will make you smile. You always tease me about being an inconvenient pee-er. Right when we have to leave for school. Or when the movie's about to start.

Back in my house, I dodge piles of laundry, step over newspapers, arch my body around what looks like Mom's old collage stuff. I'm pretty desperate now and only thinking, Toilet.

That's when my toe slams into something hard, something that was not there yesterday. Pain shoots through my body. I scream, grab my foot, and fall into a pile of old sheets. I search the floor for the offending object.

It's a cast-iron frying pan, nearly hidden, buried under laundry. We have never once used a cast-iron pan. It must have been bought online and dropped on the floor like everything else. My mom used to be an artist, but now she's a collector of projects she'll never finish, a buyer of useless items online, a builder of precarious piles.

I limp along the pathway to the bathroom, sit on the cold toilet seat, and count. My pee lasts for 32 seconds. My record is 107. I wonder if you count your pee. We never talk about this stuff, but we should. Bathroom habits are fascinating. When you get back, I expect answers about all things bathroom-related. You're such a gentleman that you probably won't tell me, but I'm going to pin you down and tickle you until you do.

I look at my phone. Why aren't you texting me? I read the text from Steph. It's a picture of a stack of one-dollar bills, along with: Made a hundred dollars in poker. Eat it!

No thank you.

I text her back. I know she's sleeping and what can she do to help, really? But she needs to know. Chris is missing...Call me

Then I leave you another voice message: "Hey. It's me again. Can you call? Please? Everyone's worried. I'm worried. I love you."

When I stand up, the phone vibrates in my hand. Of course, I think it's you and I nearly drop the damn thing in the toilet. But it's just Steph. She hasn't turned off her phone, unlike some people I know.

"Hey," I answer.

"Chris is missing?" She's slurring. Maybe she's still drunk.

"He went for a run down by the river last night, and he didn't make it home." I sob and grip my mouth tight. I can keep it together for everyone else, but not her. Okay, not you either.

"Hold on. I'll be right over." The phone goes dead.

I put the phone on the edge of the sink and blow my nose in a wad of toilet paper. "He's okay," I murmur at my reflection.

My tears draw wet lines down my dry skin. It's hard to say why I like looking at my sniveling self in a mirror, but I do.

My brain is foggy. I need coffee. You always come over in the morning and make me coffee.

Someone bangs on the back door. It has to be you! No way it's Steph. She takes forever to get out of bed.

I run out of the bathroom, leaping over the magazines. "Chris?"

9:06 AM Saturday, Steph

It's Steph, bursting into my house. "Oh my god," she says. "Are you okay?" She's rushing toward me, around a pile of Mom's crap, arms out, like a zombie girl in a red robe and giant puffy pink slippers. Her long brown hair is all bedhead, and she's wearing thick ugly glasses instead of contacts, and her makeup is smeared under her eyes. No idea what's under that robe.

Suddenly, she screams out and doubles over. "Ow. Ow. Ow." She hops on one foot and grabs her slipper. She's hit that same damn cast-iron pan.

"Oh man, I'm sorry. I did the same thing. My mom—"

She waves her hand. "I'm fine." She limps toward me, exaggerating, as usual. "I just broke my toe. No big deal."

She gives me one of her power hugs. Squeezes the air right out of me. I swear, she could bottle those up and sell them. You always ask if she's trying to break your ribs, but I know you like them too.

If she were missing, I don't know what I'd do. It would be more obvious that something awful had happened. With you, I don't know.

She loosens her grip and pulls her head two inches from my face. "He's fine. You hear me?" She breathes all over me. It's nasty.

I try to smile through my tears. "Your breath smells like ass."

Of course she gulps in a bunch of air and blows it into my face, dragon-breath–style, right from the gut. I gag and she laughs, releasing me.

"Seriously, you okay?"

"I'm worried." I sigh.

"He's going to show up, goofball."

"I know."

She heads over to the mini-fridge, pulls out two strawberry yogurts and spoons from the utensils box, and then hands one to me. "Here." Like it'll make everything better.

I shove a pile of my mom's unfolded laundry from our sagging brown sofa and we sit cross-legged next to each other. The yogurt is cold on my tongue. It feels nice.

"So he went for a run and disappeared and then what?"

I fill her in on what I know, circling my spoon in my yogurt so the red mixes with the white. "I keep trying to think of something that's not totally horrible. It's not like him to go AWOL."

She rubs her eyes under her glasses, further smearing her mascara. "Maybe he found someone else."

"While he was running in the woods?"

She shovels a heaping spoonful of yogurt into her mouth, sucks off the top, and pulls the half-filled spoon out of her mouth. She's never eaten everything off a spoon, not once in her life.

"Maybe," she begins, raising her eyebrows, "there was some rich seductress lady in a skimpy red dress, sitting on a log, and he couldn't resist her." She flings her hand to the side, still holding her spoon. The remaining yogurt wobbles in the air. I wait for it to go flying. "And now he's just hanging at her fancy house, sipping a latte, relaxing on her chaise lounge."

You would never go with someone else, but the thought of your lanky body trying to get comfortable on a chaise lounge makes me smirk. "He hates lattes."

She grins. "Hey, you hear about that forest fire?"

"No, why?"

"People were talking about it at the restaurant last night. That's why it smelled smoky yesterday. I guess it's taken over a ton of forest."

"Do you have a point?"

She shrugs. "Maybe Chris ran into the fire."

I gape. "That's a great image, Steph. Thanks. I really like imagining my boyfriend's body on fire."

"I don't mean that—I was just thinking he could have got lost out there in the woods. Maybe it was smoky and he couldn't see and he got lost."

"It's not smoky today."

"Depends on the winds." She takes another bite of her yogurt. "But he would've had to run, like, twenty miles to get that close."

"He doesn't run that far." Not normally.

"Okay, well, didn't you say he missed Brooklyn?" she says. "Maybe he took off for Brooklyn."

"Without his truck?"

She purses her lips, thinking. "He could've hitchhiked."

"Hitchhike across the country? Chris?"

She laughs. "Maybe he wants to live on the wild side. It's about time."

I give her a mock glare. "He's wild enough for me."

Then, I feel this rush of sadness. I think about how you saw me at the mall, dancing with Michael, like a big weirdo. It was fun, you know? It was just goofy, stupid fun. You took it all wrong.

"What?" Steph says.

"I was at the mall yesterday with Michael. Before work? And then I saw Chris." Each new bit of information drops out of my mouth, suspended in the air. I don't know why I didn't tell her. Why I didn't call her. Especially after I saw you.

"You went shopping with Michael?" she says. "I didn't know you guys were hanging out. Isn't he, like, twenty-two?"

Michael and I don't usually hang, except on the pool deck, so I get why she's confused. "He's like an older brother," I say. "We were guarding on Thursday night, and I told him about Chris, and he thought I could use some retail therapy, so he said we should go after school on Friday."

She frowns. "You could have asked me."

I shrug. "It's fine. Michael offered. He picked me up after school."

"In his Mustang convertible?"

"Yes."

"Do you think Chris followed you?"

"Oh god, I hope not. No, he wouldn't. He's not like that."

She gives me a look like, really?

"He's not," I say.

"Does he know that Michael likes guys?"

"Yeah, I told him. One night, he was watching me guard, and after, he freaked out about how Michael was massaging my shoulders and flirting with me, and I told him, but it was like he didn't believe me."

"Chris was watching you guard?" She says it like it's weird.

"He was waiting for me to get off."

"I can't blame him, really. Michael's like a friggin model with those blue eyes. That body." She smirks. "I'd do him."

"You and every other girl in our town."

In the convertible yesterday, Michael was playing with my hair. Maybe, if you saw the hair touching and the dancing, I can get why you'd be upset. "We were dancing. Maybe it didn't look good," I say. "I probably should have run after him, but it was insulting, you know?"

"Yep. He's gotta mellow." She rubs her eyes and the mascara streaks lengthen. Then she stares at the pile of laundry by her feet. Looks bummed.

"What?" I ask.

"I can't believe you didn't call me," she says.

"You were at work."

"Not till six." That's all she needs to say. The truth is I didn't think of calling her. That's how bad it's gotten.

"Sorry," I say.

She gives me a quick smile, but I see the hurt in her eyes. It's something she and I don't talk about, how we've been growing apart. She's always with her restaurant people, and I'm always with you.

"Well, what do you think happened to him?"

I decide to tell her the truth about that night. "I'm worried some guys beat him up," I say.

"Why would anyone beat him up?"

I hesitate. You didn't want anyone to know, but that's stupid. You told Steph you fell, and she teased you, said you'd joined a fight club, called you "Gandhi" with quote fingers, but she believed you, I could tell she did.

"Remember the black eye a couple weeks ago? He got jumped. Bunch of guys from the Heights, down by the Pitt."

"No way! I friggin called it!" She slams her palm down on the sofa cushion. "What the hell, Jessie? I can't believe you didn't tell me."

A year ago, I never would have kept any secret from her. "I'm sorry. It's just, we haven't been hanging out alone since then."

"We have to fix that."

I nod. "I'm sorry. He didn't want anyone to know. He said Tim and them would want to get revenge, and it would start up a whole thing. You know him. He's such a pacifist."

She's mad. I can tell.

"Don't be mad."

"I'm not." She smiles briefly. "I can't be mad at you."

"Steph, it's just, I'm so worried. What if they threw him in by the rapids?"

"Holy shit, Jessie." She lifts her hands palms up, telling me to stop. "Don't be such a drama queen. Those rapids are dangerous. They could kill someone. Nobody swims there. They'd know that."

"Maybe they grabbed him and thought he could handle it. Maybe it was a joke." In my brain, a bunch of blond guys, like the one you pointed out to me in the bakery, are holding your arms and legs and flinging you into the water, laughing, loving it, yelling "Yeah!" The rapids. Sharp rocks. The tunnels under them. Those boys who drowned, that's what happened to them. They got sucked under.

Oh god, I hope I'm not psychic.

"He'd fight," Steph says. "If he was having trouble, they'd get help. They're not going to let him die."

"Why isn't he answering his phone, then? He always answers."

"I don't know, maybe he got wasted somewhere and he passed out."

"He doesn't drink," I remind her.

"He probably does now. You couldn't blame the poor guy after this week."

I stare at her, all wide-eyed, give her "the look." I really love her like a sister, but man, sometimes she can be so thoughtless. *After this week?* What the hell does that mean? She never thinks before she says shit.

I didn't tell you this, but right after I told her we were going out, she started dancing around the piles in my rec room, twerking, singing in a country voice, "My man is hung, and I like to ride him, ride him, ride him." I got pissed at her and she told me to relax, she was just joking. I told her it wasn't funny. I guess she thought she could say anything to me, but she can't say shit that's racist. That's not okay. She never said anything like that again, but I've wondered if she thinks it and if other people do too. Guys stare at me more, for sure. They look at me differently than they used to, and I wonder what they're thinking. Do you know that people say you only went out with me because you thought I'd put out? I know that's not true. But why did you go out with me, anyway?

In my brain, you say, it's obvious—because I'm beautiful. That is just what you'd say if you were here. Man, why you gotta be so sweet to me? Nobody ever said I was beautiful before.

"He's going to show up, J," Steph says. "Don't worry. He's fine. Maybe not fine-fine, but he's not dead, for god's sake."

"Maybe I should call in sick and head down to the river to look for him."

"In the woods? When there might be some assholes down there?"

"Maybe he's waiting for me in our spot."

"Then he should answer his friggin phone," she says. "Go to work. If he wants to talk to you, he should man up."

"If we hadn't gotten into that fight, he'd be here right now."

"You guys are always fighting," she says. "Nothing's happened before. He gets all needy, you yell at him, and then he goes off and pouts, and finally he comes back and begs for forgiveness. Stop worrying. He probably ran into some other friends and went to Seattle or something. Maybe he lost his phone. Wasn't there a protest in Seattle last night?"

"I don't know."

"I saw something on the news." She gives me another super-powered hug. "I'm going to sleep. Call me later, okay?"

After she stumbles out the door, I sit there for a while and think about what she said. We are not always fighting. Are we? I guess what she said is kind of true, at least lately. You never used to need me to be around all the time, just the last few months. It's been kind of driving me crazy. But besides that, our relationship is damn near perfect.

Our first day was the most perfect day ever.

Except I lied.

I'm Not a Wild, Naked Girl

Ever since that first day in mid-October, you thought I was a wild girl who swam in the river naked all the time and did all kinds of other crazy things, and I let you think that because it's sexy, but it's not true. I'm not wild; I'm scared all the time, and even though I'd gone swimming in the river tons of times, I'd never taken my clothes off before.

This is the truth about how I ended up nearly naked.

It started out first thing in the morning. My house was a mess, like always, and I couldn't find a stapler, and I got crazy mad at Mom because everything disappears in our house. I freaked right out, like a goddamn stapler is the biggest problem in the world. On a scale of 1 to 10, I was a 9.5. I called my mom a disgusting pig. Said I hated her. Her green eyes blinked like I'd slapped her. I will never forget that look on her face.

Of course, I felt bad, but I ran out of the house, jumped on my bike, and rode for a long time down by the river, wavering between feeling mad at my mom and then guilty for being a jerk, until finally, I found myself at this hidden, grassy spot by the riverbank that Steph and I discovered when we were kids.

I was dripping with sweat and knew the river would make me feel better. Only I didn't have a suit and I didn't want to ride home all wet T-shirt contest.

Then I had a brilliant idea—I should swim naked. It would be daring and fun and so not like my mother. The thought of it made me laugh. Mom would scream in terror if she knew; she'd say I was going to be raped. Maybe I should text her a picture of myself naked next to the river with the message: This is how you live!

I peeled off my sweaty leopard-print T-shirt and then my black leggings and finally my bra and hung them on the bush. I was about to remove my pink underwear, but I couldn't do it. I wasn't scared of rape, exactly, more that someone would see me and take pictures and text them to everyone at school. So I left them on and took a giant leap into the river.

My body plunged underwater. The water was freezing but exhilarating. The current tugged at my feet. The weeds below waved at me. Beckoned. Bubbles flowed out of my mouth, downstream, sucked my anger with them. The water tasted of silt and some other faint chemical, probably pollution from the mill.

Above, through the bubbles in the water, the blue sky gleamed. Weeds tickled my feet. I kicked to the surface. My face burst out. I sucked in a breath of air. Then I put my face back under and floated on the water, kicking slowly to keep from drifting downriver.

My breasts floated to the sides like balloons. The icy water streamed under them. It felt so free, compared to wearing a bathing suit. You don't know what a bother these puppies are.

I vowed: I'm never wearing a suit in the river ever again.

Then I started to count, just to see how long I could float without taking a breath. You know how much I love counting.

Probably at that same time, you spotted my bike by the trail and came into the clearing and saw me in the water, facedown, the sun shining on my white back and pink underwear. I looked dead, I see that now.

At the count of fifty-three, something sharp jabbed in my back. I screamed and jumped up, trying to stand on the slippery rocks, spitting out water.

You were standing above me, holding your pointy stick spear, waving it around. Your face was twisted with fear, unrecognizable, not the normal face I saw at school, the guy with all the friends, laughing, joking around, Mr. Jovial, Straight-A Student, Super Athlete, Mr. Popular.

I screamed as loudly as I could. You dropped the stick in the water and waved your arms in the air. "Stop!" you yelled. "It's me, Chris, from school."

"Holy shit." I crossed my hands over my boobs, even though it was too late and you'd seen it all. I sank down in the brown water.

You glanced toward the trail, like you were afraid someone was coming. Later, you told me it wouldn't have looked good, a black guy with a white girl who was nearly naked and screaming. I thought it was silly at the time, but now I know you always have to think about that stuff.

"Why are you stabbing me with a stick?" I said.

"You weren't moving! I thought you were dead."

"I was floating."

"You looked dead. You had no top. And I recognized your red hair."

"Tangerine," I corrected. "The box says tangerine."

You gave me a funny look, like who cares if the box said tangerine. "I thought someone had..."

"Raped and killed me?" I had to point out the lack of logic in your imaginary killer's story. "And weirdly put my underwear back on?"

You grinned. That's when I noticed your dimple. "I wasn't thinking straight." You glanced toward my T-shirt and leggings resting on top of the bush and my bra hanging down. It was a huge old-lady bra but really supportive. I didn't have the money to go to a fancy lingerie shop in Seattle, like the girls you hung out with. I figured all the bras you saw probably had lace on them and not one single hole.

"Leave my clothes alone," I said.

"I'm not going to touch them."

"Guys think it's funny to take a girl's clothes."

"I don't think it's funny."

I tried to see if you had a cell phone on you. I worried you might take a picture of me, and it would be all over school the next day.

"You shouldn't be swimming here alone," you said. "The river's dangerous. A couple weeks ago, two kids—"

"I know what happened," I said. "The rapids are a ways downstream."

Two brothers had drowned. The younger one was being pulled downstream and he panicked. The older brother swam out to rescue him, but he didn't get there before the rapids, and they both died. The search boat and the scuba divers were on the news. I watched, gripping my mouth the whole time. The TV reporter was a leech, asking the best friend all these questions.

"Aren't you worried?" you said.

"I'm a lifeguard. I always swim in the river."

You studied me like you were trying to figure out if I was a crazy person. "Do you always go swimming with no clothes on?"

"It's the best way." I shivered. "Except it's a bit cold right now."

"I'll get your clothes." You stepped toward the bush.

"No!" I said. "I can get them. Just turn around and go back to the trail."

"Okay, okay." You let out a low chuckle and I worried I couldn't trust you, but I didn't have a choice. You disappeared under the Sitka spruce you later named Saber after a saber-toothed tiger because of its sharp needles. I hesitated for a second, but you seemed cool, so I rushed out of the water.

It took forever to get dressed. I was dripping wet and my fingers were frozen and I couldn't get on my damn bra, and then my leggings got stuck on my wet legs.

You were so quiet.

"Are you still there?" I called.

"Still here." A little laugh.

I ran my hand through my wet hair, smoothed it back, and then grabbed my backpack and walked over to the trail, trying to summon a little dignity. You were holding my bike for me, with your back still turned.

"Did you look?" I asked.

"No way."

"You're a real gentleman," I said, sort of teasing.

"I try to be." You grinned back at me in the cutest way, like you were shy. That's when I noticed the way your sweaty gray T-shirt was clinging to your lean chest. You have one of those rare, perfect bodies, but you aren't arrogant about it. You don't strut. I don't mean that in a bad way. It's just, you're understated.

"I'm Jessie."

You shook my hand, softly, held it in yours, which felt unbelievably hot. I thought it was because my hands were so damn cold—I didn't know then that your body is a human heater. "I know," you said. "We're in bio together. You sit at the back. You always know

44

all the answers." You gazed at me in that soft, quiet way of yours. "Of course I know your name."

"Bio is okay." I tried not to smirk. Steph always tells me a guy says one nice thing to me, I'm his forever. "You should see me in French. It's a disaster."

"*Je m'appelle* Chris," you said, in the worst French accent ever.

"Okay, maybe not that bad." I grinned.

You grinned back, and we were silent; maybe it was a little awkward. I saw an old chip bag on the ground, so I bent down, picked it up, and stuffed it in my backpack to throw out later. You gave me a funny look.

"I like to clean up the trails. You know, if I see something, I think about the environment and it's so beautiful here..." I trailed off, thinking, Oh my god, I'm such a nature nerd.

You smiled at me. "Cool." Then you gulped, and it was that action, at that moment, which made me realize that maybe you liked me a little.

I glanced at the ridge in your chest, which I could make out through your damp T-shirt, and wondered what it would be like to run my finger along the curve of it. You saw me looking and you gave me this wide, little-boy smile, a yes-I-got-what-I-wanted-for-Christmas smile, and your brown eyes were so shiny, and bright and smart, and something about that smile, I don't know, maybe it was your dimple, but that was it for me.

This is how that first day went, and from that moment on, damn near perfect. You tease me because I think I have an audiographic memory and you say nobody can recount conversations exactly. But I can! I swear. Somehow, people's words attach themselves to me, like ivy. I remember everything.

9:45 AM Saturday, my house

After Steph leaves, I sit on my sofa downstairs and text every damn person I know. Feel frantic. Someone has to know something. Most people are still asleep, but a couple text back, say they'll ask around. I'm hoping you crashed at a friend's house and you're still sleeping.

I stare across the downstairs rec room, which looks like a thrift shop that's been ransacked. Would you rather live in a house filled with garbage or in a house with absolutely nothing, no furniture, no TV, no food, no dishes? Must choose. Oh man, I already miss playing Must Choose with you, the way your top lip quivers with laughter when you've made up a particularly hard one.

I text Josh: Maybe he went to Seattle to watch the meet

He doesn't answer. He's probably still riding the trails.

I text again: Maybe he wanted to surprise you

Text three: lmk when ur back

I don't want to go to work, but I need the money. So I pack my bag for the pool and I leave, without talking to my mom. You'd say I should tell her you're missing, but if she doesn't care enough to come down and ask me why people were at our house at seven in the morning, I'm not telling her shit.

In the backyard, good old Ella is leaning against the metal fence. On that first day, you asked what my bike's name was and I said it didn't have one, and you said, "All vehicles must have names." Like it was bad luck to be unnamed. You asked me who my favorite singer was and I hemmed and hawed, 'cause I thought you'd judge, but finally, I said Ella Fitzgerald. You said, no kidding, like it surprised you, and I said I liked singing along, and you laughed, and said, "So do I." But you still looked at me funny. I wondered if maybe you thought I'd be into country or rock and roll, or maybe you thought I was lying to impress you, but then you said I should call my bike good old Ella after Ella Fitzgerald and so I did.

I'm almost at the road with my bike when our meth neighbor steps out her front door and walks over to the metal fence. Her stringy blond hair looks like it needs a wash, but her eyes are alive, not all milky like usual.

"Hey," she says in a drawl. "You had some visitors this morning."

"Yep." I think maybe she's going to say I woke up her dogs, even though she hasn't said more than hello to me since she moved in, so I keep walking.

"Everything okay?" she asks.

I look back at her, sharply. How is she the one who asks and not my mom? "My boyfriend is missing," I find myself telling her. "He was running down by the river last night and he hasn't made it home."

"Shiiiit." She squints at me. Her eyes are little balls of amber—I never noticed that before, how pretty they are.

"He's a black guy, right?" she says.

"Yeah," I say. What does she mean by that? I get all stiff.

"I saw him." She takes a long drag on her cigarette, which I didn't realize was in her hand until that moment.

"What?" I breathe. "When?"

"Last night. He was standing there, at the end of your driveway, like he was going to come in, but then he kept running." She's acting like she hasn't just thrown a grenade at me.

"What time was that?" I manage.

She shrugs. "I was on my porch. Maybe around ten? It was dark."

That means she saw you last. Did you see her sitting there? Did you go to the river after or did you stop by my house on your way home? Did you run into someone else in the three blocks between my house and your house?

"Where are you going now?" she asks, like maybe she wants to come. Her cheek twitches.

"Work." I'm gripping so tightly on my handlebars, the rubber gives.

"You work at the pool, right?"

"Yeah." How does she know this?

"My boyfriend died a year ago," she offers. "Before my dad passed. That's why I moved back here."

"Oh. I'm sorry." Why is she telling me this?

She takes another long drag of her cigarette. "Thanks."

I wonder how old she is. Her face is druggy-wrinkled, not old-person-wrinkled. Maybe thirty? I heard she was a meth head, that her parents hadn't seen her for years, they sort of disowned her, or something, but she got the house when her dad died, so maybe not.

"Your guy will show up, don't worry," she says. "He's a good one."

"Thanks." I think of how you'd be reaching across the fence, shaking her hand. "I'm Jessie, by the way," I say, though I don't reach my hand out.

"Beth." She smiles. Her teeth are crooked and rimmed with brown, but she has a full set at least, so maybe she's not a meth head.

"See you later." I push my bike toward the street. I told you she's a walking advertisement for why you shouldn't do drugs, but she isn't really all that bad, just maybe hurting, like we all are sometimes.

1:58 PM Saturday, the pool

I'm teaching my last private lesson to this cute little kid named Tony. I'm like a scientist in my laboratory, looking at his little body, trying to figure out how to help him move forward. He's over-bending his knees and flexing his ankles. He holds on to the wall and I grab his feet. They twitch in my hands like little mice.

"Point your toes," I tell him. "Rub your legs like they're two sticks and you're making a fire." He giggles and kicks all bent-kneed.

He plays baseball, like you. Lots of ballplayers have a tough time swimming because their ankles are too tight. You need loose ankles for swimming. You told me the kick was the tough part for you and breathing to the side. Lots of people have lousy kicks and that messes up their body position, which makes it harder to breathe to the side. I think about how I should get you in the water to show you how the leg motion moves from the hip to the knees to the ankle, like a whip, the way the best pitchers throw a ball, only with the legs. I could definitely give you some tips.

And then it's like a siren going off in my brain: YOU ARE MISSING.

Is it possible that you're dead and I'm teaching a swimming lesson? This whole time, while I was teaching, I kind of forgot about you. That's something about my brain. I have this fabulous ability to block out shitty things.

But maybe you're back. Maybe you've called. Maybe it's all good.

I'm still holding Tony's twitchy little feet. The clock says I have two more minutes. Whatever. I let go of his feet and tell him he's done. We don't play popcorn like normal and he whines about it, but I leave him with his mom and run down to the change room to grab my phone out of my locker.

No messages from you. Lots from other people, asking if I know anything.

I text you a desperate, and slightly angry message: Look at your damn phone. If you've turned it off, turn it back on. CALL ME. Yes, I do know what a ridiculous message this is.

Then, something weird happens; it's like you're answering me. I see a flash of you in our spot. You're standing on the grass, your bare chest glistening, your face peaceful and your eyes closed, like you're enjoying the warmth of the sun. Why would your chest be bare? Maybe you're sending me a brain message to meet you at our spot. Maybe we can read each other's minds. I told you that if there was one power I wish I could have, it would be the ability to read minds.

I text Steph: Going to the river

Steph: Noooooo

Me: Don't worry

Steph: I'm at work. It's slow. Maybe I can leave…

Me: I'll be fine. Going right now

Steph: That's stupid. Don't go

Me: Whatever

Steph: Seriously

Me: I'll text you when I get there

Steph: You are so stubborn

I grab my bag and run out of the change room. Michael is at the top of the stairs, about to start his guarding shift.

"What's up, beautiful?" He smiles and reaches his arms out for a hug.

I fall into him, breathe in the smell of his sweat mixed with his day-old cologne, from his date after work last night with some new guy he wanted to impress. He doesn't teach swim lessons, so he smells like a normal person instead of a swimming pool. You say you like my smell, but half the time, I smell like a school bathroom after the janitor has come through. You appreciate every goddamn awful thing about me. It chokes me up, just thinking about it.

Michael jerks back and stares into my eyes. "What's wrong?"

"Chris is missing." When I say those words, it feels like someone has taken a needle and stuck it through the soft, fleshy part of my throat.

I tell him everything I know.

"You think he was upset after he saw us?" he says. "Maybe he took off."

My lip quivers, I can feel it, wiggling like a worm on my face. "It's not like him to take off without telling anyone. I think some guys might have jumped him down there."

"I don't think anyone's going to jump him."

"They already did. A few weeks ago," I say. "He didn't fight back. He doesn't believe in violence. He says it just causes more violence."

"Really?" He says it like he's surprised, like he's reevaluating you. And then: "I got jumped once."

"You never told me that."

"Yeah, well." He lifts one shoulder.

"I'm sorry," I say. "That sucks."

"Whatever." He makes a face. "I hope he shows up."

"I'm sure he's fine."

"If I can do anything—"

"Thanks. I'll let you know."

I turn and run-walk across the deck. In my mind, I see you, standing, glimmering, by the edge of the riverbank.

Maybe you're standing in our spot waiting for me. Or is this just wishful thinking? Oh my god, I hope you're okay.

Would you give up your nonviolent principles and fight if someone was going to throw you into the rapids? I don't mean to judge, but Pendling is like any other small town. Sometimes you have to fight.

Please tell me you'd fight.

2:10 PM Saturday, the trail

Good old Ella flies down the trail. My arms are loose, butt balanced above the seat, weight on the balls of my feet. I've never ridden so well, ever. No joke, I'm jumping my bike over fallen branches like they're nothing. I could probably lift a car if you were trapped under it.

My panting fills the air. "Chris!" I yell, every hundred feet or so.

I call to you in my mind, hope you can hear me, wherever you are.

I'm coming, baby!

ESP is the one magical power that I can't help thinking is real, that it's possible to develop, if you try hard enough. I've been trying all day. You claim you can do it. And there was one moment at that bush party in April, when I thought, Whoa, maybe he's right. But I didn't say anything.

Remember when I went to the other side of the fire to get some spiked hot chocolate from Steph's thermos? You stayed with Tim.

After a few minutes, I felt something jerk at my mind, like someone was poking my shoulder (with a stick, ahem). I smiled at you across the flames and we walked toward each other and left without saying a single word. We never talked about it, but I thought it was cool and a little freaky, if you want to know the truth.

Maybe we can get that mind-reading thing happening again. ESP, like you call it. Maybe if you're in great pain, you have more ESP power. Maybe if you focus real hard, and I focus hard, our thoughts will meet and you can tell me where you are.

It's possible you're not gleaming in the sun. Maybe you're bleeding to death, but maybe it's not too late and I can save you. I fly down the trail, hopping over fallen branches like they're nothing.

No response.

I yell out, "Chris!"

Two more turns in the path. I brake hard by our spot.

I leap off my bike. "Chris?"

There's a strange sound, a crack, like a branch breaking. I freeze. When I'm lifeguarding, I listen for sounds that are out of place, sounds of danger. Like a kickboard being slapped on the water, because it's usually followed by a kickboard being slammed on a head.

Maybe that was you, pacing back and forth across the grass, your shoe breaking a stick on the ground. "Chris?"

It's quiet. No more cracking wood.

Maybe it's your killer. Maybe you're a ghost and the message was you saying don't go down to the river and here I am. Maybe the guy is about to jump from the bushes. The good thing is if a killer ever tried to attack me down here, I have a plan. I know that won't surprise you.

I'd dive into the river, that's what I'd do. If he followed me, I could fight him off better there. I've been trained to fight off a drowning person and I could fight off a killer, too. As long as I was in the water. I'd use my feet to kick him back. If he grabbed my arm, I'd twist into the thumb. As a last resort, I'd swim to the bottom. It goes against a person's natural instincts to be pulled under, and he'd let go. If a murder is going to be attempted, I want to be close to water, that's all I ask.

I scan the woods, look at each large tree for a person hiding behind it. The wind rattles the leaves. The river rushes past.

I'm clearly being an idiot. You are alive and well. Probably in Seattle. Or on your way to Brooklyn. Or to the Grand Canyon, without me. But why would you leave your truck? And why aren't you answering your phone? The only thing that seems possible is that you ran into those guys. Or you're somewhere, pouting.

A high-pitched sound by my feet makes me jump. A baby crow is standing about six feet away, cocking its head to the side. He hops toward me and does a little flutter in the air and lands back on the ground.

He blinks his intelligent black eyes. He's a fledgling, still in that hopping phase. If you were here, you'd name him.

"Hey, Little Man," I whisper.

He cocks his head to the side, which I take as a yes, he likes the name, and then he turns and does a little hop toward our spot. Is he trying to tell me something?

My heart picks up. I imagine your body in the clearing, a mangled mess, crows pecking at it. Did those guys follow you here?

It's been a while since I've been here alone. I always thought it was stupid that girls have to be afraid in the woods, and I stubbornly came down here anyway, even when Steph stopped coming. But now I'm scared.

A gust of wind rustles the needles on Saber. Little Man jumps into the woods and disappears. More mysterious sounds. The moss looks creepy today, climbing up the cedar trees, an ancient plant from the days of dinosaurs.

The loud bark of a turkey vulture echoes through the trees. My heart beats faster. Turkey vultures eat dead animals. Right about now I wish I didn't develop a weird fascination with identifying bird sounds when I was a kid.

I listen. More birds. Some sparrows. Crows. No cracking wood. No footsteps. It's just my imagination.

I crouch down under Saber's sharp branches and dive right into a spiderweb. I scream and bat at my head and think, Baby spiders, and enter the clearing, gyrating.

I stop. You aren't here.

It's so disappointing.

You'd say we have to be grateful for every little thing. Life is a gift, you'd say. Every night, when we talk on the phone, you ask me what I'm grateful for. You make me say three things and I moan and complain, but you know what? I like it. I'm admitting to you right now that I actually like it. When I hang up, the world does feel like a better place. Most of all, it's a better place because you're in it.

For the sake of karma, here's my list at this moment: your body isn't being eaten by carrion, and our spot looks real pretty. Okay, that's just two things. My third: I don't have lice. That's random, but I am grateful for it.

I wish you were here.

If you were, I'd run up to you and kiss you all over your face and your nose and your dimple and your small ears. At least, that's what I hope I'd do. In reality, I'd probably look around for a burger to throw. No idea why I did that. I never threw food at anyone before. I'm so sorry.

I do a lifeguard's scan across the area, from the shadows under the trees to the light shining in the center of the clearing. I admit it, I'm looking for a paper airplane. I missed it when I didn't get one yesterday. I was thinking maybe you'd left one here and you were going to send me on a wild-goose chase to find you. But there's nothing. In this whole clearing, there are no man-made objects of any kind, no garbage, no paper—just flowers, moss, and leaves.

Why haven't you called? Couldn't you have left me a voicemail or something? You would have left me some kind of message if you were planning to disappear. Or you would have told someone. This isn't your plan. It can't be. Something's happened.

A breeze blows through the green grass. I look for flattened spots, signs you've been here, but I see nothing. Above, the sun beats down.

That Bill Withers song plays in my brain. *Ain't no sunshine when she's gone*... Only I change "she's" to "he's"... It's sort of funny that this song plays in my head at this moment, when there's an abundance of sunshine.

The river is rushing past, even faster than it was on that day in the fall. We've had a warm spring, and more snow melted from the mountains than usual.

My phone vibrates. I look down.

It's Josh: You still down there?

Me: Yep

Josh: See anything?

Me: No

Josh: Chris has a ball tournament today at 4

I totally forgot about your game! That's it. I'm kind of excited. Maybe you'll show up. Or maybe, I don't know, maybe we'll learn something.

Me: Want to go? Maybe he'll be there??

Josh: I doubt it

Me: We can talk to the guys who beat him up

Josh: You know who it is?

Me: He pointed one guy out. From the Heights

Josh: Let's go

His house is pretty close to the field, so I tell him I'll be there in ten minutes. I ride by the Pitt. It looks like someone had a fire there last night. The burned wood is dry, not wet, and it rained yesterday, so it had to have been after the rain. There are some empty beer bottles. The sofa is nasty, as usual. The wood stumps look normal. There's no blood.

Something mechanical makes a whir noise to the right of me, by the river. A boat? I push through the woods. A bunch of guys with weed cutters on the bank are spread about thirty feet from one another, clearing the riverbank.

I stop beside one of them and wave my hands.

He turns off the motor. Pulls off his mask. "Yup?" He has a deep voice and light brown hair, longer in the back, shorter on the sides.

"I'm looking for someone?" I say. "Um, my boyfriend? He's six foot two, and he's wearing a blue T-shirt and black shorts."

"I haven't seen anyone like that."

"He's African American."

"Oh," he says, then kind of looks behind him, like he thinks someone might be listening, but all the other guys still have their helmets and motors on.

"If you see any clothing or anything strange, like blood, when you're cutting the weeds, can you tell the police?"

"No problem." He drops his mask down and turns the weed cutter back on.

I ride away and wonder why I said blood. He kind of flinched when I said that. I guess I would have too.

4:10 PM Saturday, Thomson's Field

Josh and I head to Thomson's Field on our bikes, his dog running along beside. Josh would have driven, but he said Sam needed a run. I guess the dog needs to go out even when your best friend is missing.

The parking lot is so packed we have to get off our bikes. The hamburgers are driving Sam crazy, and his massive brown mutt body keeps tugging Josh from one side to the other. I can tell Josh is getting annoyed.

Around us, people are laughing and carrying coolers and blasting country music and wearing skimpy tops, even bikinis, not a pool in sight. It's like school is done and it's already summer. Normally, I'd be joining right in, wearing my own half top and jean shorts. But with you missing, I feel like the whole world should be on pause, people should cover up and there should be no music. Yep, you'd hate that. I can hear you saying, "No music?" You wouldn't say no boobs, but you'd think it, and you'd shake your head, like, no way.

A couple passes us, pushing their bikes. The girl gives me a big smile. "Nice day for a ride." She looks at Josh and I realize, Oh my god, she thinks we're a couple. Josh and I glance at each other. Awkward. I'm hoping no one else gets the wrong idea.

At the hill in the center of the ball fields, I scan the crowds. "Maybe Chris will show up," I say. "Maybe he hit his head and doesn't know who he is, but he'll be drawn here."

"That would be great."

It's the winning-the-lottery version of a missing person. The person simply banged their head and they don't know who they are and it's just a matter of time before someone spots them wandering the streets asking people where they are and who they are.

"You hear about the protest in Seattle last night?" Josh says.

"Yeah, Steph said something."

"They were protesting that police shooting last month," he says. "Some of the streets were shut down. We almost got blocked in. It was hard to get out of town."

"You think he went to the protest?"

"He would've called," Josh says.

"He could have been arrested."

"Maybe the cops aren't letting him call." Josh's blue eyes brighten up, like this is a good thing.

I think about the protest we went to in Portland. On the drive there, I sat beside you in the truck and watched the muscle in your jaw as you pried open the pistachio shells without using your fingers, which is harder than it looks, and spit them in the empty Coke bottle, all the while talking passionately about peaceful protest. I never heard you talk so much, honestly, not at one time. About Gandhi.

MLK. Malcolm X. James Baldwin. About the organizer you met in Portland, the guy who invited you to come and bring friends. Josh and I just listened. When you talked about the soul fight, you were so fired up, it was inspiring. You said that Gandhi believed peaceful protest helped the soul, that we all have our own soul fight toward inner peacefulness. I never thought of things like that before. I mean, this is Pendling. Nobody talks like that. It was cool, though.

At the protest that night, I saw the way you stood up taller, clapped that organizer guy on the back, and it made me sad. I don't know why. Maybe it was a window into your future life, away from Pendling, away from me.

I don't blame you for wanting to leave. This town was built on racism, for god's sake. African Americans moved here in the fifties to work in the mill, but they weren't even allowed to live in the goddamn town. Lots of people around here don't even know about that; they think segregation didn't happen in the Northwest, just like they think they aren't biased because they have one black friend.

Remember that old lady volunteer at the half marathon? When you ran through the finish line, your arms reached out toward me, like I was your prize, and I grabbed your face and gave you a big wet one. I'd normally go for the hug, but I didn't want to get your armpit sweat on me. Your sticky running mouth was kind of gross, but it was better than armpit. (I can just hear you laughing, saying, "Better than armpit, huh?")

That woman gave me an evil look, like I was the worst person in the world for kissing my boyfriend. Then, she turned to you, all fake, "Congratulations," she said. You thanked her, gave her your wide smile, dimple and all. Then she added, "Do you have Kenyan blood, sweetie?" As if you were a mixed-breed dog with greyhound in it. I wanted to shove her *sweetie* up her butt.

Josh and I were so shocked that we looked at each other like WTF. You answered her, though. You were all like, "No, I don't think so," as if that was a legit question. You're too easygoing about shit like that, or maybe you act like you are. When we were going to that protest, you were open about it for once. You said people say things like that all the time. They don't even realize it. That made me wonder if I did too. God I hope not.

Josh nearly trips over his bike due to Sam leaping toward the hamburgers cooking by the barbecue truck. "Walk," he says, sharply, pulling back on the leash. "All I know is he's not on the trails, not on this side of the river anyway. I looked for at least five hours, twenty miles in both directions."

Just think of that. He rode the trails for five hours looking for you. He's such a good friend.

"He never goes that far," I say.

"Yeah, and it got real smoky to the north, near the fire," he says.

"He would've turned around." It's just a guessing game right now. Neither of us have any idea.

"His team is over there." Josh points at the far field. They've got white-and-black jerseys, like yours. "I'm trying to find the Heights team, though. I think they're green and white."

I scan for green uniforms, and then, I look up the hill and see something that I immediately wish I could unsee. I let out one of my horror-movie gasps. Josh jerks to the side and drops Sam's leash.

I guess he thinks I spotted you. But that's not what I'm looking at.

It's this guy in his mid-twenties, scraggly beard, sitting next to his girlfriend, drinking a beer, wearing jean cutoffs, his legs sprawled open, his friggin junk hanging out. It's hairy and wrinkly and fat.

Josh sees it, says, "Oh no, that's just wrong." He bends down for the leash, but Sam's too fast—he takes off, up the hill, toward the guy.

Then Sam shoves his goddamn nose right in the guy's crotch. I'm not kidding. The guy starts laughing, but Sam's not done. He's rubbing around like he wants to clean the dude.

Josh screams out Sam's name. The guy's girlfriend calls Sam a perv dog. Josh's eyes are wild with panic. The guy is petting Sam, who's practically climbing on top of him, licking his face.

Josh runs up the hill, grabs the leash, says sorry, and drags Sam away. He stumbles back down the hill to me, his eyes wide, in shock. I can't stop laughing; it's so damn funny. Then Josh snorts and he's laughing too.

We stagger around to the other side of the hill so we can't see wrinkly-balls man, and we fall down on the grass, clutching our sides, rolling with laughter.

Sam starts licking Josh's face, he's so happy, and Josh lets out this little scream because he remembers where that tongue has been. You could say we're sort of hysterical. Maybe it's just the stress of you being missing. It's not even funny. I want to stop, but I can't. I can't breathe.

"Josh? Jessie?" A screechy girl's voice. "What are you doing?" Tamara is standing above us, hands planted on her hips. Her face is contorting into this evil witch monster mask and her head is spinning around. Just kidding. She's glaring at us though, acting like we're having sex in the middle of the ball field.

Becky and Tim walk slowly up behind her. We are instantly sober. Josh climbs to his feet. "We saw this guy..."

We try to explain why we're laughing, but it never works when you try to tell someone what's so funny and it especially doesn't work when your best friend/boyfriend is missing and you look like you're having a grand old time.

"What are you guys doing here?" Josh asks Tim, changing the subject.

Tim lifts his baseball hat and scratches his head, scanning the field. "I thought I'd come out, see if anyone's heard from Chris."

"We're looking for a guy," I say. "Someone who might have information."

"Yeah?" Tim gives me a funny look. I know I'm being kind of vague. "Who?"

"This guy from the Heights?" I glance at Josh. You've been gone too long to keep this to ourselves.

"He and some of his rich buddies from the Heights beat the crap out of Chris three weeks ago," Josh says. "Remember the black eye?"

"What?" Tim's jaw tightens. "Why didn't he tell us?"

"He didn't want to make a big deal of it," Josh says.

"He said people would want to get revenge," I add. "You know him."

Everyone knows about you and your anti-violence, love-preaching, gratitude-giving ways. Tim's eyes flutter shut. He stays like that for a moment. "Where?"

"By the Pitt. Same place he was running last night," Josh says.

"You know what they look like?"

"He pointed one of them out to me last weekend at the bakery," I say. "The guy was eating a cream puff. I wanted to shove the damn thing in his face. But Chris wouldn't let me. He wouldn't even go in. We had to go back later."

"I guess this guy's been giving him a hard time for a while," Josh adds.

"He was on the travel team with him," I say.

Tim's shaking his head, furious, like he wants to get revenge for you right now. "I probably know him," he grunts.

"I just want to find out what his name is," I say, "so I can tell the cops."

"We'll come with you," he says. Tamara gives Becky a look, but they come along too, walking slowly behind us, whispering about something.

We find the Heights team a few fields over. They all have their parents watching, of course. Nobody has to work on a Saturday in this crowd.

I scan the field for a blond guy. The Heights team has a ton of blond guys, which is weird, since statistically only 2 percent of the world has blond hair. I can hear you saying, "How do you remember shit like that?" I don't know. Numbers stick in my brain.

I point. "There." He's got the lightest hair out there, pale blue eyes. I'd remember those eyes anywhere, how he stared at me through the bakery window, all cocky, assuming I was checking him out.

"I know that guy," Tim says. "His dad owns the Honda dealership."

Tamara stiffens, like she's nervous.

"Dave Johnson," Tim adds. "Good pitcher, but he's an asshole."

"Oh man, I bought my car there," Josh says.

"That's his dad on that billboard by the highway?" I say. "It's the cheesiest billboard. It looks like a teeth-whitening advertisement. Buy low. Go fast. Come to Johnson's Used Cars."

"That's him," Tim says, nodding.

Tamara is oddly silent.

Johnson walks toward us. We're by the dugout and he's coming off the field, talking to a teammate. Tamara bites the side of her pinkie. Becky gives her a nervous look.

"Johnson," Josh growls out. It surprises me because it's not like him.

Tim grips the metal fence. His other hand tightens into a fist. Which is bad news for Johnson. One of Tim's fists in your face would probably feel like being hit by a truck.

Johnson gazes at us, cold. Maybe he's tied you up in his parents' cabin, and he's cutting off one of your fingers at a time. I mean, maybe he's a real sick fuck. I don't know why I have this thought, but I do. All day long, it's just one friggin horror story of a thought after another.

"We've got to talk to you," Tim calls.

Johnson takes a few steps toward us and then stops twenty feet away, like he's scared the guys are going to charge him, even though there's a tall metal fence separating us from him. "What?"

"You see Chris Kirk last night?" Josh says.

His jaw tenses. "No." And then, he spots Tamara. "Hey, Tam, what are you doing with these guys?"

She doesn't say anything, but I swear, she looks afraid.

"We heard you and some friends jumped him a few weeks back," Tim says. "Did you?"

The edges of Johnson's mouth twitch up like he thinks it's funny. "Who wants to know?" His voice is overly deep, like he's forcing it.

Tim grips the wire fence surrounding the ball field. "I do."

"He was a pussy," Johnson says, and then he walks away.

Was? Why did he say *was?* I look at Josh.

Josh never gets mad, but his eyes are as hard as river rocks and his hand's gripping on Sam's leash, making a fist so tight it looks like he can't wait to punch someone. Has he ever been in a fight in his life?

Sam, on the other hand, is pressing his wet nose against the fence, wagging his tail, for god's sake. He's not the kind of dog you can say "Sic 'em" to, but I wish we could. He'll just lick you to death. Which, I guess, today, would be pretty nasty.

"Hey," Tim says to Johnson, who looks back. "You want to go?"

"Anytime." Johnson keeps walking toward the dugout. Doesn't look back. I bet he's scared. And now, he knows we're onto him.

"Come on," Tamara says to Tim. "You can get him later."

"How does he know you?" he asks.

"We used to go out. It was a mistake." Her eyes go all watery, and she looks away.

Something happened. I think we all figure that out. Becky looks real sad for her, and I don't want to say it serves her right, but you got to be stupid to date a creep like that.

"Let's go," Tamara says, tugging on Tim's arm, like she can't wait to get out of here. She looks like she's about to burst into tears. It's real shitty of me, but I want her to cry. I want her to feel bad.

It's because of that time she said I wasn't good enough for you. It hurt, you know? Like, I must have thought back to it a hundred times. My brain put her words in a hamster wheel and spun them around and around.

She's probably right—I'm probably not good enough for you. But you asked her out first and she said no, so too bad for her. (Yes, I hear stuff, don't think I don't.)

Tim waves good-bye. "Text if you hear anything," he calls.

I think of how you said he has mad techy skills. "Hey, Tim,"

I call out. He looks back. "You think you could search for Chris's phone? I know his password and his login. Is there a way, you can, like, track it?"

"Maybe. I'll see if I can get in—he has AT&T, right?"

I nod.

"Or if he has the Find My iPhone app. But I'm sure the cops are doing that."

"I don't think the cops are doing anything," I say.

He sighs like the weight of the world is on him. "You're probably right. Text me his info."

"Okay."

He waves again, and they head off.

I stand there and glare at Johnson. He flits his eyes our way.

You always say I've got good intuition about things, and right now, I'm thinking his cold blue eyes look like the eyes of a killer. Or, who knows, he could be just a regular asshole who likes the fact that he beat you up. It's hard to figure out if someone is a regular asshole or if their asshole-ness is so extreme, they're capable of murder. It's probably something cops need to figure out all the time, which is why they're so suspicious of everyone.

But there's something off about Johnson. And I'm going to find out what it is.

5:15 PM Saturday, Scott's Donutes

Josh and I stop by Scott's. He wants to see if they know anything. Like, if you bought a bunch of doughnuts or you were with someone, it might mean you went to Seattle or Portland.

While he's tying Sam up by the tables outside, I look at the worn wooden sign that says *Scott's Donutes.* You always want them to fix the spelling of *Donutes,* at least cut the *e.* It never bugged me until you mentioned it, but now it does. Before, it was just this typical thing about living in a mill town with lots of people who don't care about spelling.

Inside, there's a really long line. When we get to the front, we ask the staff if they've seen you, but they say no, and the weekend manager says we should come in and ask the weekday manager on Monday.

Um, yeah, thanks. That's a little late. You'd better show up by Monday.

We order two cherry-filled doughnuts and two coffees, and we sit outside next to Sam, who licks my hand. I try not to think about where that tongue has been. I look through the window to our table. Today, it's empty.

"You know we came here for our first date?"

"Yeah?"

I tell him about how you saw me floating in the river and you poked me with a stick. Josh laughs and says you never told him about that. Which is sweet. I appreciate that.

I tell him how we emerged from the woods that day, me pushing my bike, you loping along beside me with that casual walk of yours that tricks everyone about how intense you really are. "You want a ride?" you said. "I can put your bike in the back." The only vehicle in the parking lot was a large, old blue truck.

I burst out laughing. "That's yours?"

"Yeah, why?"

"It doesn't suit you."

"It was cheap—a thousand bucks. Bought it from this guy who was having a kid. Guys around here like trucks, and I figured, when in Rome..."

It was odd that this was like Rome to you. "Do *you* like trucks?"

"Sure." You shrugged. "But there's only so much love I can have for a vehicle, you know? This seemed good enough."

I smiled at you, intrigued. Guys around here go crazy for their trucks, like they're an extension of their dicks. This was one of the first signs you were different, in a good way.

"His truck was so clean," I tell Josh, shaking my head. "It was crazy."

"He's a neat freak."

"Yep." It chokes me up a little. I bend down and rub Sam behind the ears.

The whole way to the doughnut shop, you blasted the heat. I was shivering. Guess it's kind of dumb to jump in the river in October.

When we got to the doughnut shop, I let you help me out of the truck, holding your hand to jump down, even though I'd been getting out of my dad's rig since I was a kid. We stood in the long line. At the cashier, you rested your hand on my back and asked what I wanted. "I'm paying," you said. Maybe you thought I'd be all empowered-woman and say "I'm paying," but nope, I like getting treated. I ordered a jelly-filled and an éclair and you smiled at me, that killer dimple diving into your cheek. "One jelly-filled and an éclair for the lady." It was funny that you called me a lady. Nobody ever called me a lady before.

An older cashier woman behind the counter stared at us, disapprovingly, which struck me as weird. It wasn't like we were making out. We took our coffees and sat down at a table with a crack running through it, like a river, separating us.

I drew my finger along the sharp linoleum. "So, why'd you move to this shithole town anyway?"

"My mom's best friend lives in Kelso. Winona wanted her to come out. Said we'd all benefit from the nature. Mom found a job here and we moved clear across the country."

I laughed and waved my hand at the dilapidated doughnut shop. "This is pretty damn far away from Brooklyn. In every way. I bet they have gourmet doughnuts in Brooklyn."

You started laughing. "You know it."

"What about your dad?"

A ghost passed over your face. Every now and then I saw it, a shadow, and then that smile would be back. The dark peach fuzz on your upper lip quivered. "He stayed." You sniffed. Maybe that sniff was to show me you didn't care, but it seemed sad.

"That sucks."

"My sister, Raffa? She was pretty broken up about it. She wanted Dad to come, but Mom said he had to finish off some stuff, and he'd move here when he was ready. I guess he's been going through some . . . medical stuff. But he's visited twice, and every time he calls, my sister asks if he's moving here. He just says not yet." You looked away briefly, then turned your lips up at me. Knowing you like I know you now, I figure you didn't want to get too heavy.

"You think he found someone else?" I asked.

"No way." You shook your head, vehemently. "Nope. He loves my mom. And he's still, like, really involved—he sends letters and money and he calls every Sunday."

I let out a long, slow sigh and thought about how nobody's got a perfect family. They're complicated—they can make your life hell, but you love them anyway.

You went on, "I just want to see his new apartment. Isn't that strange?"

I put my elbow on the table, cupped my chin in my cold hand, and stared into your beautiful brown eyes, waiting. You didn't put on an act, no superficial bullshit like most guys I knew. It intrigued me.

"I wish I'd just seen it once," you said. "But we moved and then he moved. Now I can't picture him anywhere, except with us in our old apartment, and that bugs me, you know?"

"Just ask him to take a picture of his apartment."

You shook your head and smiled a little. "That would be weird."

I took my éclair out of the bag and stabbed it into the air like a sword. "Okay, fine, right here, right now, we're going to make up a place for him."

You laughed. "What?"

I sucked out the creamy insides of the éclair and licked my lips. "We need to imagine his place and give him furniture and decorations and everything, so that you can picture him somewhere."

"I like how you suck out the insides first."

I raised my eyes at you. Were you being a perv? I didn't think so. That wasn't your style. "Don't change the subject. What town is he in?"

Your dimple twitched, maybe you thought I was funny, but you were definitely humoring me. "Brooklyn."

"How big is his place?"

"Probably a one bedroom."

"You don't know?"

"I never asked him. We used to have a three bedroom, half a brownstone, in a good area. He's a music promoter but it was too expensive for him to stay there and support us here. I figure he just got a one bedroom."

"Okay . . . what color are his walls?"

You paused to think, pressing your lips out. "He'd leave them white."

"White?"

"Why paint if you're renting?"

I shrugged. "I'd paint. Bright colors everywhere."

"I bet you would." You laughed. Every time I made you laugh I felt like I'd just hit a home run.

"How about a sofa?" I said. "What color?"

"I don't know."

"Let's give him a mustard sofa with brown flowers."

"He'd hate that," you said, grinning.

"It's temporary. He's coming here, so he found this sofa on the street and he's just going to make do with an ugly sofa."

"People do put perfectly good sofas on the street in Brooklyn."

"See?" A shiver ran up through my body.

"You cold?"

"Nah, it's just my hands, mostly."

"That's what you get for swimming in the river in October. Here." You grabbed my free hand. It was a pretty smooth move. Your palms were dry and hot. "Your hands are so small." You fit my hand in your two hands, cupped, enclosing it entirely, heating it in your hand box. "You have the kind of hands that could fit into those little white gloves that women used to wear."

"Mmm." I finished my éclair, licked some chocolate off my finger, and reached forward with the other hand. "This one too, please. She feels lonely."

"Your hand told you that?"

"Yes," I said. "We have ESP."

"ESP?"

"Extrasensory perception. Like mind-reading."

You held that one too and gazed into my eyes, and said, "I'd like to have ESP with you." Oh man, I thought, I am in serious trouble.

That's when Tamara and her friends sashayed up to us. I don't know if you dropped my hand first or if I pulled it away, but all of a sudden we were sitting all chaste, opposite each other.

"Hey, what's up, Chris?" Tamara said.

That girl could not keep her eyes off me. She couldn't believe it. I guess you'd asked her out just a week or two before.

"You all know Jessie?" you said.

Right away, you made me more important than all of them. But were you doing that to rub it in her face? I wish you were the one who'd told me you'd asked her out.

They chorused, "Hey," or "Hi." In varying degrees of disinterest.

"We just worked out at the gym," she said, shaking her hips, wearing her tight little workout shorts.

You nodded politely. Averted your eyes. I glared at her.

"You coming tonight to Fisco's?" she asked. "It's poker night."

"I don't know," you said.

"She can come," Tamara said. I stiffened. *She.* I'm right friggin here.

"Thanks," you said, raising your eyebrows at me. "I think we're busy." Like we'd been going out for weeks.

Now, I gaze at the empty table where we sat that day, and tell Josh, "He said we were busy. *We.* Pronouns matter, you know?"

He swallows, like this is a sad story. "Sure they do."

"So then Tamara turned around, her butt in my face, and walked away. Most guys would have checked out her ass, but Chris didn't."

"I don't think he's noticed anyone since you guys started going out."

He's right, I know he is. Your eyes light up every time I walk into a room. "Nobody has ever been that happy to see me, except maybe my dad." Josh is just staring at me. I feel bad that I'm blabbing on about you. "Anyway." Sam licks my hands and I scratch his ears. I think dogs can sense if someone's sad. I let out a laugh. "Your dog is pretty great."

A smile flickers on his lips. "Should we go?"

I nod and we stand. "Where do you want to go now?" I don't want to go home and do nothing, but I'm running out of ideas.

"I'm going to check the other side of the river." He shrugs. "Who knows."

"He never runs there."

"Yeah, but I'm thinking Sam might smell something."

"Sam does like to smell stuff."

Josh groans. "Don't remind me."

"Maybe I'll go to Chris's house. See if I can find out anything. Unless you want me to come?"

"Nah, it's okay." Kind of sounds like he wants to be alone.

He rides with me part of the way, holding Sam's leash. That

dog can run. By the highway, I wave and yell, "Let me know if you see anything."

"I will." Then he heads toward the river.

For some reason, as I watch him leave, I'm worried. I have a weird feeling that he's going to disappear too.

6:15 PM Saturday, your house

I'm sitting at your kitchen table, telling your mom about how we went to the ball field and we got the guy's name. I already texted her his name so she could tell the cops. "He's got creepy eyes."

She gives me this funny look and drops a plate in front of me with hot lasagna. "Eat," she says.

I take a big bite. It's amazing. If it weren't for your mom, I'd be seriously malnourished this year. I guess Winona dropped off a huge casserole dish of it when she heard about you being missing, and soon as I got here, your mom told me she "needs" me to eat it, no way they can get through it all. I'm happy to comply.

"I told the detective," your mom says. "He's a nice man. Name's McFerson. Irish." She tells me he still has an accent even though he's lived here for sixteen years. He's forty-four and played soccer professionally. Funny that she got all these details about him.

"Did he search Chris's room?" I ask her.

"He looked around a bit. Didn't see anything. I looked too. I thought Chris could've written me a note. Maybe he was heading on a trip and didn't want to tell me directly." Her mouth flickers up, briefly, like she's remembering something sweet you did. Then, she shakes her head. "There was nothing out of the ordinary."

"If he was planning on taking off, he would've let you know."

She nods. "Last time, he left a note."

From upstairs, a violin wails. I look up.

"How's Raffa?" I ask.

She clicks her tongue. "Not good. She won't eat."

"Do you think she knows something?"

She shakes her head. "I don't think so."

"Can I go look in his room?"

"You go ahead, but let Raffa come out in her own time. And don't tell her about those boys. It'll only upset her. She's worried enough."

I head upstairs. Your door is closed. So is Raffa's. The violin is playing faster now—sounds like she's sawing that thing—it's beautiful, violent.

I open the door to your room. It's pristine. Like always. Your bed is made, the bedspread tucked in, military-style. The sheer blue curtains are open and the large window makes your room about ten times brighter than mine. I scan the track and baseball trophies on your bookshelf—nothing out of place. Coming to my house must make you crazy.

Your school calendar has the correct month up, unlike mine. You've scribbled reminders under the dates: the baseball tournament today, finals next week, graduation on Saturday with pink happy face exclamation points that I drew for you. Above your tiny white desk, the corkboard is still filled with pictures of us, thankfully. If they were gone, I might have puked all over your floor. My favorite is the picture of us in the middle, when I took you camping at Bear Lake, by the fire with our marshmallows on sticks, cheeks mushed up against each other. Nobody prints photos out anymore. Just you. Every time you give one of your photos to someone, they act like you molded something out of clay with your bare hands.

Your keys and your old brown wallet are on the left side of your desk. I pick up your wallet and open it, out of curiosity, then glance at the door, because it won't look good if your mom comes in. Not that she'd think I'm stealing your money, but still.

You have twenty-eight dollars. One twenty, one five, three ones. Your driver's license is in the front, beside your debit card, and you have a receipt tucked behind the money for gas and a bag of pistachios. It's dated yesterday, at 4:55 P.M. After I saw you at the mall.

My heart beats faster. This receipt is the first bit of good news we've had.

You always buy pistachios when we're going on a trip somewhere, like to Seattle or Portland. But your truck is here. Man, this is confusing.

Every time we drive somewhere, you pop the pistachios in your mouth and spit the shells in the soda bottle, and you get this faraway look in your eyes. Sometimes I ask you what you're thinking and you say, "Not much." But I know you're thinking something.

I slip the receipt back inside and place the wallet next to the keys with your metal World Series keychain. Your backpack is leaning against your desk, all ready for school on Monday. I pick it up and unzip it. I look inside and try to leaf through your stuff, but I can't see anything, so I shake it out above your bed. The contents tumble down, and fall off your bed, crashing onto the wood floor.

The noise booms through the house. Oops.

The violin screeches to an abrupt end. Raffa's door bursts open. There is the sound of slippers on the wood floor, and Raffa flies into your room.

She's still wearing her pajama shorts and pink tank top. Her hair is messy, not braided yet, her eyelids puffy, nostrils raw-red.

"Oh!" she says, her face dropping. "I thought Chris was back."

"Sorry." I open my arms and she hesitates for a minute before her body buckles into mine.

She sniffs into my shoulder. "He was only going for a run."

"He's going to show up," I murmur. Her hair tickles my nose, but I don't scratch it, don't dare let her go. "We'll find him. He probably got lost in the woods. You know his sense of direction. You'll see, tomorrow he'll be making you popcorn with cayenne and watching the Nets game with you."

She steps back. "Why'd you dump out his stuff?"

"I want to see if he left something, some clue, like maybe he went somewhere and didn't tell anyone. I found a receipt. He bought pistachios. You know how he always likes them for long drives?"

Her eyes brighten. "Yeah?"

"Did he say he was going anywhere?" I ask.

She shakes her head, but then she bites her lip and looks away, like she's holding something back. I figured she'd tell me if she knew anything, but now I'm not so sure. "Raffa?"

"No, there was nothing!" she insists.

I gaze at her. "Want to help me look through his stuff?"

She nods, and silently sits beside me, her bare knee touching mine. She lifts up a pen covered in strawberries. "This is mine."

"That's weird." Why would you have her strawberry pen?

She reaches for a ball of paper and unfolds it. I hold my breath thinking it could be a crumpled note, but it's just a math problem.

I flip through your calculus workbook, since you have calculus on Fridays, last block. At first, all I find are doodles next to the math problems, airplane designs, and random shapes. But then, ten pages in, I find a note in the side margin. The date says October 18—it was the first Friday we started going out. "Jessie. Sunshine. Sunflowers." And I remember.

"Catch!" you yelled. I was walking around your truck in the school parking lot and I looked up, afraid. That word has always sent a wave of terror through me because the next thing I know, a ball is about to hit me in the head.

But that time, a graceful paper airplane sailed over the truck toward me. I grabbed it in my usual spastic way, like I had ants crawling all over my body, and of course, crumpled the airplane. You laughed and said, "Open it."

In your neat handwriting, you wrote that I reminded you of sunshine and sunflowers, which is sweet, but also kind of funny because sunflowers are so stinky that stink bugs love them.

I didn't keep that love letter, or any other letter, and I'm sorry. It wasn't that they didn't mean anything, but I'm not sentimental like that. I read them and threw them out, just like I throw everything out. I don't want to be like my mom.

I leaf through the book, find more sweet notes and then, I find something that's the opposite of sweetness. You wrote: *Does love have to end in heartbreak?* It's like a sharp knife held straight out. I run into it and get stabbed in the gut.

It's the only thing you wrote on that page—in the corner above the problems. And no answer to that question. This was right before my best Valentine's Day ever. Wasn't it your best too? I close my eyes. Everything was going great with us until late March. After you were scouted.

"What?" Raffa says.

"Nothing." I keep turning the pages, hoping she doesn't look at it later.

Near the end of the workbook, last Friday, at the top of the page, you wrote, *Marvin Gaye.* Weird.

You introduced me to his music. I can't believe I never knew about Marvin Gaye before you. Some things seem so obvious to me now, like when you know, you hear his music everywhere, or samples of it, and it's hard to believe that not everyone knows his music, but I didn't. You played his music for me in your truck in that first week. We sat outside my house, listening. You told me it was a shame he died so young, how his dad shot him after an argument, how in the months leading up to his death, he thought someone was trying to kill him, so it's kind of ironic it ended up being his own father who killed him. You said he was so paranoid, he wore three overcoats in the rare times when he left his house, and a few days before he died, his sister told police he was getting so freaked out, he even tried to kill himself by jumping in front of a car. It's crazy how much you know about every musician, even ones you don't listen to—guess it's cause your dad is a music promoter. In the truck that day, you played his music for me and we listened quietly. Finally, I told you that his emotion was so raw, that was what made it special. You smiled at me then and said, "You get it. Not everyone does." I gave you a long kiss then, Marvin Gaye singing his heart out in the background.

Why would you write his name in this math book? I flip absentmindedly to the back. Something falls out. Something paper. A paper airplane.

It makes a *whoosh* as it falls and then a tap as the pointy end hits the wood floor. I stare down at it, like it's not paper, but a real, living thing, a monster, on the floor, near my bare foot. Why would you write an airplane letter and not give it to me? What if it's something bad?

Your sister says, "Look!" like it's good news.

I reach for it, and my fingers pinch the paper, but Raffa rips it away and opens it with excitement, like it's a Christmas present. The paper clamors out a warning.

"Raffa, give it here." I reach for it again.

She scoots away on her butt. "Stop."

I hold my breath.

She reads it, her eyes widening, and then she sniffs it. "He used the strawberry pen," she says. "It's for you. Just dumb stuff." She thrusts the note back. "I'm sorry—I thought it was for me. He always writes me air notes."

I love that she calls them air notes, like music. You never told me you write her too. That's so beautiful. Even after eight months together, I keep finding out about kind things you do, things you don't tell me about, but that I learn from others.

I take it from her and devour it, like I'm starving, like every piece of information is my favorite burger with mushrooms and Swiss cheese.

Dear Tangerine Girl,

When you waved at me today in the hall, I could tell you missed me. You almost planted a big one on my lips. Don't deny it. I know you too well. You wanted me, as much as I want you. Stop being so stubborn, just because you said a week. I want to be with you. Let's end this break now. You're the most beautiful, AMAZING person. I'll

never find anyone else like you. We're perfect for each other
and you know it. So let's be like Marvin.

Your Lover Boy, Chris.
P.S. Smell.

Your Lover Boy, Chris. Always with the period. Like, end of story. I'm yours, you're mine.

I read it again, slower this time, savoring it. Be like Marvin? You mean, "Let's Get It On." Ha-ha. Nice.

You waved at me yesterday and gave me the cutest grin. I knew exactly what your look meant, that I hadn't said, "No waving." So I waved back, and then, I walked away. Steph said I was an idiot, which is fair enough. I am an idiot, clearly.

What I wanted to do was grab you, rip your shirt off, and run my hands all over you. When you get back, we are getting it on, baby.

I sigh. "I wish I knew where he was."

"I keep looking at his Instagram," Raffa says.

I didn't think of that because I almost never use it.

"The last picture up there is the two of you on our sofa."

Oh man. You said my hair looked soft. You took a selfie of us.

"Did you break up with him?" Raffa asks.

"I didn't," I say. "Oh my god, I would never. We're on a break, that's all. It's different. We just needed some time to think. He wants to get married before college, which is crazy. We're too young. And

I might want to apply for this environmental work-study program at UW in a year. Did he tell you that?"

She shakes her head.

"It's cool," I tell her. "You spend the summers in the field, and the rest of the year, you study environmental sciences."

You want me to apply somewhere in Raleigh, but they don't have a good program for what I want to study. We both have dreams. Stuff we need to do. I need a plan, a way to get out of here, just like you. The phone rings. Your mom answers in the kitchen. "Oh, hello, Officer. . . . Yes, sir. . . . Of course, sir. . . ." There are too many *sir*s. That's not good. I press my hands into your splintery hardwood floor, dizzy with fear, and listen to the sound of her sensible heels running up the stairs.

8:55 PM Saturday, your bedroom

Your mom appears in the doorway, looking disheveled for the first time in her life maybe. Now, her hair is all wonky. Maybe she was running her hands through it? She's got one chunk of hair at the front that's sticking out.

"That was the detective," she says.

Please don't let it be bad. "Did they find him?" I breathe.

"No, the detective's going to stop by in a bit, get more details. He said they suspect he's a— They suspect he went somewhere."

"They think he's a runaway?" I say, incredulous.

"Yes."

"Didn't you tell them about—" I glance at Raffa.

"I did."

"But they haven't even started searching yet?" I say.

"Well, they have been looking for him, but he's eighteen." That piece of her hair flops from one side to the other. "It's twenty-four hours now. But they did put out a bulletin for him. It takes a while to get everything sorted out."

"The detective isn't going to do anything?"

"He said he'll come over tonight and give me an update."

"Oh." It sounds lame. "I could talk to him."

"No, that's fine."

Again, I'm relieved.

"Mom, what's up with your hair?" Leave it to Raffa.

Irritated, your mom flattens it down. Then she sees the paper airplane in my hand. Her eyes widen, like she recognizes it. Did you write her too?

"I found this." I thrust it at her. I'm thinking if she reads it, she'll see that you were happy yesterday. You had no reason to run off to Brooklyn. Something's gone wrong. "He wrote it yesterday during school."

She takes it from me, reads it, and hands it back, fast. Like I just handed her a porno. "This is your private letter. You don't need to show it to me."

I thought she wouldn't get that Marvin Gaye reference, but she's not stupid. Yep, that's embarrassing. Can't believe I showed that to your religious mom. "I thought it might be evidence," I say.

She nods, briefly. Presses her lips together. Like she didn't know that we do more than just cuddle on your sofa watching sports, like she hasn't figured out where you go when you're out walking in the middle of the night.

"Guess I better go home," I say. "Can you tell me if you hear anything?"

"I sure will," she says.

I give Raffa another hug. "See you."

"Bye." She lifts her hand.

I leave your house, gripping your love letter in my hand, and ride my bike the three blocks to my house. Your love letter gets all crinkled pressed against my handlebars. I never wrote a single one back. That's pretty shitty, I know it.

You've written me one every Friday for the eight months since we started going out. You don't know what a bummer it was yesterday when I thought you hadn't written me. But you did. You did! Why didn't you give it to me? If you'd given me your damn letter yesterday, we would've gotten back together and you never would've gone running.

That damn song, "Let's Get It On," starts playing in my head. What if it's a message from you? Yes, please, I think. I would like that. In case you're sending that song as a message, yes!

I send you a message back. It's X-rated. A mind picture. Did you get it? If you did, I bet you're grinning.

As I get closer to my house, I hear the sound of kids yelling on my street, the angry, vicious sort of yelling. It scares me, and I ride faster to see what's going on.

9:05 PM Saturday, my street

A group of boys are surrounding a kid who's curled up like a sausage on the ground. Near the dentist's house. It doesn't look good.

A bigger boy is swinging his leg back and kicking the kid's side. Oh shit. Why are all those kids watching? Why is this entertainment?

I ride down the street and jump off good old Ella.

"Stop it! Goddamn it!" I shove my way through the crowd.

The bigger boy looks up. I know him. He's from the bad block, just like I am. I hear his mom screaming out his name all the time. Billy.

The boy on the ground lifts his head. His nose is bleeding, dripping all down his mouth, making him look like a zombie.

I don't know his name, but he just got a new bike. He's from the middle block, the one with carports—his house has that red fence. I was outside a couple days ago when his dad was taking a picture, and I told the kid, "Nice bike." And he grinned at me in this super sweet, dorky way.

"Get away from him." My words are pellets in a BB gun, shooting out of my mouth. Billy is almost as big as me.

"You going to make me?" He's got a lot of nerve. No kidding, I kind of want to punch him. But instead I help the younger boy stand up. The rest of the kids step back, and even have the decency to look guilty. The younger kid wipes at the blood coming out of his nose.

"Why are you doing this?" I sound unstable, screechy. "Why are you picking on a younger kid? What's wrong with you?"

"He's a mouthy piece of shit." Billy plants his hands on his hips.

"He wanted to steal my bike," the kid pipes up behind me. "I told him to get his own bike." He does sound kind of mouthy.

"I asked to take it for a ride, that's all," Billy says.

The lights go on outside the dentist's house. I'm worried he's going to come out and yell. He gives out full bags of chips every Halloween; everyone knows this. But he yells at any kid who tries to climb up his tree house, even though his own kids never use it. They're always inside, playing the latest video game on the latest video game system.

I pick up the bike and hand it to the younger kid. "It's over," I say. "Go find something better to do. Leave him alone."

"Or what?" Billy says.

"Or you'll have me to deal with."

"Oooh," he says, sticking his face forward at me so that his friends laugh nervously. The little shit.

I shove past him, clearing space for the younger kid, who gets on the bike and heads to his house and doesn't say a word of thanks.

Probably when I was his age, I wouldn't have either. I hate this town. I swear, I can't wait to get the hell out. If you've left early, before graduation, I really don't blame you. Actually, I do blame you if you took off without telling me. I mean, you could at least call. But I don't think that's what happened.

I turn to the other kids. "Go home! The show is over."

They don't move.

"Where are your parents? Don't they know you shouldn't be out after dark?" I rage. "My boyfriend just disappeared. We might have a killer on the loose. Do you even know that?"

The kids blink at me.

"One of you could be next! You could be dead," I say. "Go home."

They don't go home.

I turn around. One of the neighborhood's stray tabby cats is sitting there, watching me, from the curb. It's kind of funny.

I grab my bike and get on it, ride back down the street. Shit. I cannot believe I just said that. When you come back, you're going to laugh your head off at me, clap your hand on your knee in that way of yours, and say, "No! You did that?" I glide up to my house, smirking. Good god. Today has kind of got to me. Those kids probably think I'm a crazy person. But at least maybe now they won't go out at night. Maybe they'll be safe.

I want them to be safe.

You say you like that about me, how I care about other people getting hurt, how I can never walk away, how I always got to rescue people. But you're the same. You rescued me, didn't you?

When You Rescued Me

It was the day after you poked me with a stick. I was riding down the trail, alone, just like you said I shouldn't, heading for another swim. Didn't need any guy to tell me something was dangerous. Even if that guy was super cute.

I tried to jump my bike over a log, not even that big of a log. I'd done it before, but this time I spazzed out, the wheel caught, and I landed weird on my arm. It cracked. I actually heard it. The pain cut through me.

After gasping and swearing on the ground for a while, I pulled my phone out. I called home, but Mom didn't answer. Then I called Steph. Her phone went straight to voicemail. I could walk, but I'd have to leave my bike, and it hurt to move. I thought of you. You had a truck. You knew the trail. And I had your phone number.

"It's Jessie," I said when you grunted out a hello, but then you didn't say anything. It was weird. I mean, it wasn't like you'd forget me. How often does anyone see a naked girl in the river? "Jessie Doone?"

"Jessie Doone. Jessie from biology. Jessie from the river. Jessie with the tangerine hair. You think I'd forget you?" I could tell you were smiling. "My mouth was full. I was just swallowing."

You didn't hear the croaky way I was talking, didn't realize something was wrong. "I need help," I said. "I think I broke my arm."

You nearly shouted in my ear. "What? Where are you?"

"Matheson Trail."

"You want me to call an ambulance?"

"Can you just come?" I couldn't tell you it was too expensive. An ambulance would cost seventy-five dollars. I only knew this because my mom had a panic attack six months back, and we called for an ambulance.

"I'll be right there," you said. "Stay on the phone with me." I dragged myself to a tree and rested against it, clutching my bad arm with my good one. It felt like I was being stabbed with a jagged knife from the inside.

You talked to me the whole time and told me what you were doing. "I'm getting in my truck." "I'm driving past the mill." "There's an old lady driving slow in front of me. I'll go around her at the next light." "Passing a cop car, maybe I should slow down." "I'm at the parking lot." "On the trail now."

I listened to your heavy breathing as you ran. Every few minutes, you'd say, "Almost there" or "I'm coming." I heard you before I saw you, your running shoes tearing down the trail toward me. You skidded to a stop, sweat dripping down your face.

"Oh, baby," you said. That was the first time you said *baby* to me. We barely knew each other.

You wrapped your arm around my body, your hand under my armpit, and helped me stand up. You pushed my bike, and I walked slowly beside you, cradling my arm, trying not to cry out with each step.

We made it to the parking lot and you helped me into the truck, pushed on my butt because I couldn't grab on and pull myself up. It would have been sexy if I weren't in so much pain. You even put on my seat belt for me—I didn't have to ask. It kind of blew me away. Before you, I'd never had a single thoughtful boyfriend.

You ran around the truck and jumped in. When the truck started up, Etta James blasted over the speakers. "Who's this?" I asked.

"Who's this?" you exclaimed, and then you went off on a long history of all things Etta James. Said her mother was fourteen when she had her, she went out with James Brown, who was a real great singer, but he beat her up. She deserved more, you said, then you patted the dashboard, and said, "Named this baby after her."

"Your truck has a name?" I grimaced.

"Every vehicle should have a name. It's good luck."

When we picked up my mom, it took forever for her to open the door, and then she was standing there in her housecoat with greasy hair and I thought, Man, that is it, you'll see past her, into my garbage dump of a house and you are never going to want to hang out with me again.

You helped her into the truck. She asked if I was okay, and then she said, "Oh, I love Etta James." I looked at her, like, who is this woman?

She told you that she never opens the door to strangers. You chuckled, said that was a good idea, ma'am. I gave you a sharp look—ma'am? But that's how you are, always polite.

"I thought you were selling something," she said.

"Why would he be selling something?" I was horrified. If I hadn't been in so much pain, I would have told her to shut up. But you would have hated that.

She turned toward me to answer and bumped my bad hand with her hip. You'd been so careful not to touch my arm, even pressing yourself to the window to avoid it. I screamed in pain.

"Oh no! Are you okay?" she said. "Here. For the pain." She reached in her purse and took out some aspirin, and you handed me your water bottle to drink it down.

"Are you friends from school?" she asked.

"We are." You looked at me with a smirk, like you weren't sure what to say. Just because you bought me a doughnut and we held hands didn't mean we were a couple. Mom gave me a funny look like she'd figured it out.

At the hospital, you sat with us in the waiting room and even went to get us two Mountain Dews from the vending machine. Mom registered me and had to interact with regular people. Had to admire her a little, doing that for me.

I said you could leave us, we could take a taxi, but you said,

"I'm not leaving you, no way." You waited until I got my cast and my painkillers, and then you drove us back.

On the way home, I gazed at the side of your face, at your smooth skin, the whiskers above your lip, that killer dimple, and I thought, What if he really likes me?

At my house, I just decided, I was staying with you. I told Mom we were going out for a doughnut. You looked at me, surprised. "We are?"

"Do you have plans?" I felt nervous.

"Hell no." Then you glanced at my mom. "Excuse my language."

I snorted. Mom and I were way beyond language.

She got out of the truck and you waited until she was in the house to drive off. "So?" you said.

"I don't care what we eat. I just want to be with you." I smirked, all loopy from the drugs.

"Ice cream?"

"Mmm-hmm."

We drove to Dairy Queen and went through the drive-thru for ice-cream sundaes, and you parked at the edge of the parking lot by the wooded area where no one could see us. You had a Jack and Jill, which I learned was chocolate mixed with marshmallow, and I had strawberry and I did that thing where I'm jealous of whatever the other person ordered, and I kept tasting yours.

You held out your dish, grinning at me like you didn't care if I took it all. I liked you for not being mad that I was eating yours and not mine. Once I had this boyfriend who wouldn't share his food—major red flag. Sorry, I know you hate it when I mention old boyfriends, but I'm just saying, because of this, I knew you were different.

You had this smudge of marshmallow next to your mouth and I couldn't stop myself—I leaned over and licked it off. It must have been the drugs, because that was the weirdest first move ever. I mean, licking a guy? Most guys would be pretty turned off, but not you.

You gazed at me like it was normal and we kissed, and your lips were so soft and warm; I felt like I could sit there and kiss you forever.

9:35 PM Saturday, home sweet home

I close the basement door and breathe in the familiar, musty-mold-mice-poop smell of my house. There's a bang in my bedroom, like a drawer shutting. I'm thinking right away, it's you. "Chris?!"

"Jessie?" Mom steps out of my room into the hallway, peers at me over the piles of newspapers and clothing.

Disappointment sits in my chest, plops its legs out, gets comfortable. Mom never goes into my room. It's off-limits.

"What are you doing?" I demand.

"I was worried about you."

"You were worried about me?" I say, incredulous.

She blinks her murky-green eyes. You once said her eyes were just like mine, only dulled with sadness. She used to look like me in other ways, too. Her body was just like mine at my age, and her hair, too. We look like sisters in pictures. It freaks me out, if you want to know the truth.

"Did you find Chris?" she asks.

"No."

"Are you okay?"

I can't remember the last time she asked if I was okay, and all I can manage is a quick shrug. It really hits me, no joke. She hobbles toward me, in her flowery nightgown that she calls a housedress, and wraps her arms around me. I stiffen at first, and then I relax.

I've forgotten how much I like her hugs. It's like hugging a soft, squishy pillow. Plus, she smells like baby powder and flowers from spending all that time in the tub Dad installed for her arthritis and her fibromyalgia and her million other disorders. When she lets go, I miss it.

"How do you know about Chris?" I feel guilty I didn't tell her, though she could've come downstairs and asked me before I left for work.

"I heard the kids talking through the window this morning."

That's funny, right? Why didn't she come down to talk to me? I just stare at her. She's a goddamn mystery.

"Do you think the police are going to come?"

"No, Mom. For god's sake."

This is why I'm scared of cops. You always laugh at me every time we get pulled over. You ask what do I got to be worried about? You say I act like I'm being kidnapped. It's true. I freeze right up. And I don't have a good reason like you do; I mean, I'm a white female. But my whole life, I've always worried about our house being condemned, of being thrown into the streets, homeless, or even worse, into foster care. My mom's been in foster care, and she's told me horror stories. Even when I was little, she said we could never call the cops or the fire department, and we could never allow anyone to enter our house in case they called the authorities.

It was dangerous. I mean, sometimes you need the authorities. Like, one time, when I was just nine, we had a grease fire on the stove. The whole damn house could have gone up. Mom was screaming at me from the kitchen: "Fire!" I flew up the stairs. I was always worried that one of her big, flowy outfits would catch on fire when she was cooking. Mom was screaming on the dirty linoleum floor in her nightgown. A frying pan was shooting flames toward the ceiling. "Get the fire extinguisher!" she yelled. It was in the cabinet on the other side of the fire. I grabbed it from the shelf and the damn thing felt so heavy, I nearly dropped it, but then I shot the white stuff all over the stove and put it out. No fire alarm went off. I guess we didn't have batteries in them. "Tell the neighbors we're fine," she screeched. "Don't let them call the fire department." So then I had to run outside. Sure enough, the old lady neighbor across the street was standing on her lawn with her phone. "You okay?" she called. "Should I call 911?" From the lawn, I could see the upstairs filled with smoke. I told her that it was just toast, we were fine. (In my world, *fine* has always been an alternate word for *awful*.) I went back inside and told Mom nobody was calling the fire department, and she said I was a good girl. And I actually felt proud.

12:45 AM Sunday, my bedroom

I'm in my dark bedroom, and I can't sleep, so of course, I grab my phone and call you. Your voicemail clicks on, immediately: "Hi. It's Chris. You know what to do."

Why do you always have the same sick recording? I don't know what to do. Not now. Not like this. I DON'T KNOW WHAT TO DO.

I plan to leave a super sexy message. But the electronic woman's voice says that the voicemail is full. What?

I can't even leave you a goddamn message. I have to talk to you.

I stare at those star stickers you put on my ceiling and think about how I should write to you and tell you what's been going on. That way, I can give the letter to you when you get home. I have so much to tell you already. I've already been writing it in my head.

Oh god. What if you never come home? My brain keeps jumping to all the horrible, bloody, violent things that might have happened.

You're always so good at thinking up Must Choose options

that stump me with equally awful or disgusting choices. Okay. Here's one:

Would you rather have your boyfriend eaten by a bear, thrown in the river to drown, or beaten so badly he's brain damaged and drooling and he doesn't recognize you, but he's alive?

Brain damage. I'm choosing brain damage.

Maybe you won't be the best at conversation anymore, and there will be drool, but I still want you back. No matter what.

Maybe I can just take off your clothes, stare at your body, lie with you naked, and not do anything. It would be sick to do things to a brain-damaged boyfriend. But we could lie naked and do nothing, like that first time.

Just Naked

I made you wear a blindfold the first time you came in my house. You protested, but I said you weren't coming in unless you wore it. It was a scarf, leopard-print. I held your hand and you banged into pile after pile, and by the time we made it to my room, we were both giggling like little kids.

I closed my bedroom door. "Okay. You can take off the blindfold."

You ripped it off and surveyed my room, grinning, and turning in a circle. "Hey, it's not bad. It's cool."

I laughed because my room is immaculate compared to the rest of the house. You had no idea.

We were kind of awkward then. It was weird, I guess. I mean who has to blindfold their boyfriend to let him come into the house?

Then, you walked around the room looking at my collages from when I was younger, when Mom and I used to do art together, and she was only a little crazy. I told you my favorite was the one with the endangered animals. You said you liked the one with all the weird world records. You let out a howl when you saw the woman with the long fingernails.

"Okay, must choose," you said. This was the first time we ever played it. You lifted up one finger. "Either, you must have long fingernails like that woman." You held up your second finger. "Or you must have hair so long, it drags fifty feet behind you, on the floor. Must choose."

All I could see was the dirt my hair was gathering. "Nails," I said.

"Oh no . . . Hair," you said. "At least you could do things. Can you imagine?"

You hung your arms down in front of your body, weighed down by massive imaginary fingernails, and mimed lifting them up and dropping them on the desk. You're a pretty good actor. I laughed and fell back onto the bed, and as I was laughing there, I thought this might be okay, you being in my house and all. It might really be okay.

But then, before I knew what was happening, you strode past me, out of the room, with no blindfold. I jumped up.

"Stop!" I yelled.

You called, "Can't stop me, I'm the gingerbread man." You thought it was a big joke, and you loved calling yourself the gingerbread man on account of being a fast runner and loving gingerbread.

I was too late. You were rounding the piles in the hallway, like you were rounding bases. "Stop," I whimpered at your back, a whimper that you ignored.

You gazed across the garbage dump of our downstairs rec room area. Clothes. Newspapers. A bunny cage even though we never owned a bunny. Old art projects. A bunch of random cords that someone could use to choke themselves with, if they wanted.

"See?" I said. "It's a garbage dump."

You turned around and stared at me. Disgusted? I didn't know. "I don't want you to think you have to hide anything from me."

My arms wrapped tight around my body. I was shaking, I don't know why. Maybe I figured you were dumping me? You must have seen something in my face, or my eyes filling with tears. "It's okay," you said, waving your arms out at the mess. "This is all okay, you hear me?"

I nodded. But it wasn't okay.

You stepped with your long legs over the mess and reached me, resting your strong hands on my shoulders. "This isn't you, okay? And I'm never going to judge. Never."

Tears tumbled down my face.

"Come on." You guided me back to my room, steering me around the piles, down the pathways. It was so embarrassing. I gripped my mouth, sobbing. Could not stop. In my room, you wrapped your arms around me and held me there for a real long time. "Hey now, hey, hey, it's okay."

I felt like a young girl, crying like that.

Finally, I managed to get myself under control, and I just stood there, gripping you. I murmured into your warm shoulder. "I don't know why I'm crying. It's just hard, you know? I don't let anyone see this. I don't let anyone in here, ever. Only Steph. And she's known me my whole life. No boyfriend ever came here before. No other friends."

"Thank you for bringing me." You pressed me into your chest.

"I clean it up, but my mom fills it with more crap," I tried to explain. "I can't stand it. I hate her."

"Shh," you said. "It's okay."

You gave me small kisses all over my forehead, my ears, my eyelids, my nostrils, and then, I couldn't help it, I giggled. "What are you doing?"

"Kissing your sadness away. Is it working?"

Kissing my sadness away. Oh my god. "Maybe."

"Let's be naked together."

I laughed. "Nice change of subject."

"Just naked, that's all."

We hadn't had sex. We'd only got to second base. Tops off. That's it. No BJs, nothing. "You think you can just be naked with me?" I laughed. "No sex?"

"Definitely. I have control."

You believed I was this happy nudist girl. Why wouldn't I want to be naked with you? But I didn't know if we could control ourselves, and I didn't want to have sex, not yet. Maybe one day, I thought. "I don't think so."

"I want to worship your body, that's all," you said. "No touching allowed." You gazed at me with your deep brown eyes, your dimple playing at your cheek. "Please?"

You already saw me naked, really. So what would it matter? You thought I was wild and brave and experienced. So I acted like I did this sort of thing all the time.

"You have to be naked first," I said. "And then I'll decide."

A laugh. "Fair is fair."

"You stand over there." I pointed to the other side of the red shag carpet.

You took a few steps back. "Ready?"

I nodded.

It was hot. Not because you were a wild stripteaser, but because you were the opposite of that, shy, really. You pulled off your gray T-shirt first. Your chest rippled. Even though I'd seen it before, our rule of no touching made it sexier. Your gaze flicked up to me, then down.

You took off your socks. And folded them together. Which was funny. Even in this moment, you had to be Mr. Neat. The belt was next, slowly undoing it, and then sliding it through the belt buckles like a snake slithering through grass. You placed it carefully on the edge of my chair by my desk.

I swallowed—yes, I kept swallowing—I had a river flowing in my mouth, no joke, I was literally salivating.

You undid each button of your jeans, looked up at me, and let out a chuckle, like you were embarrassed. Your jeans slid down and you stepped out of them. You folded the jeans and placed them on the desk. You were wearing tight black boxers. I held my breath. They showed everything. Your trail of hair led from your belly button like an arrow. You slid them down your thighs. Stood there, lifted your chin. I tried not to stare, but I did stare. I couldn't help it. It wasn't my first time seeing a penis, just my first time seeing yours. It was regular. Not to put it down. But I was curious.

"Boing!" I said to ease the tension.

You laughed and then slid your boxers down the rest of the way to your ankles and stepped out of them.

"Leave them on the floor," I said.

You hesitated but left them there. "Your turn."

It was too serious, too intimate, I don't know, it freaked me out, and I almost changed my mind. You wouldn't have made a big deal if I did. But then, I just thought, Why not? You saw everything already on the first day. I slid my pink top off, dropped it on the ground, and then my black skirt. I stood there in my bright pink bra and unmatching white cotton underwear. I reached around the back and took off my bra.

"Boing," you said.

I laughed, then hesitated. You hadn't seen everything at the river. Though my underwear might have been see-through. You gave me a little hopeful smirk and raised your eyebrows. And that's what did it. That hopeful smirk. I slid down my underwear.

You gulped. "Wow," you said, just like you do when you watch the sunset, all breathy and astonished. "I want to touch you, but I want to look at you, too."

We stared at each other. Your gaze traveled down me. "This is weird," I said finally. "And I'm dying here."

You laughed. "I promised."

"We can just lay with each other," I suggested.

You frowned. "I'm going under the covers. You go on top."

"Deal."

So that's what we did, and we kissed, too. Your hands rested on my back, didn't slide down even—it was like a soft sticky kind of glue held them there. I was dying for your hands to move across my body, but they didn't, not that time.

10:55 AM Sunday, the pool

I'm sitting on the cold metal bench in the female staff changing room, trying to decide whether to bring my phone on deck. I'm too goddamn afraid of dead babies. If I look at my phone for one second, that'll be the moment a baby crawls across the deck and slides into the water. It's my biggest fear. It was during lifeguard training, when that got planted in my head. The trainer was this old lifeguard with a potbelly and a bathing suit malfunction—it kept slipping partly down and then he'd pull it up. Anyway, he was on the pool deck in front of all of us trainees and he said in this dark voice, "You look away one moment, and boom, there's a dead baby." For the rest of our training, it was a joke—boom, dead baby—but it stuck with me, entered my imagination, my dreams.

A text slides across the screen, from Steph: Where are you?

Me: At the pool

Steph: Did you talk to the cops?

The cops? Definitely call-worthy. She answers and tells me a detective came by her house, asked her some questions.

"Did you tell him anything about me?" I say. "I mean, anything bad?"

"There *is* nothing bad, J."

I love that she says that.

She goes on, "I told him how you saw Chris at the mall—I hope that was okay. And I told him you're working at the pool today," she says. "He might come by. He's a big guy, tall, weird hair, but he has a sexy Irish accent. It's yummy. Even if he is old, I wanted to lick his mouth as he was talking."

I laugh. Only Steph. We say bye. I tuck my phone in my pocket and head up to the deck, where Michael is texting on his phone.

"Hey, babe." He looks up. "Any news?"

"He's still missing."

He frowns. "Where did you say he went running?"

"Down by the river." I sigh. "At least that's what he said. He usually runs along Matheson Trail."

"Matheson Trail?" he says, a little louder, like it means something.

"Yeah, why?"

"Who jumped him before?"

"It was a few guys from the Heights. One of them was on his travel team—Dave Johnson? You know him?"

He blinks. "Yeah, I know who he is."

The roar of children sounds from within the change rooms,

and I glance at the office window to see them pushing through the spinning gate. "They're coming."

"You okay to guard?" he asks. "I could help you find a replacement."

"It's just four hours," I murmur. "It'll keep my mind off of it."

"You don't need to be the tough girl all the time," he says.

"You think I'm tough?"

"Shit yeah."

"I'm not that tough."

He squeezes my shoulder. It feels nice. I turn up the side of my mouth. He gulps hard, like he's worried for me. "It's going to be okay," he says.

I head over to the strip of pool deck between the kiddie pool and the dive tank that we call the island. He walks over to the deep end. Another guard, Jody, comes out of the office and gets into position in the shallow end. She's the blond one with the boobs—don't pretend you don't know who that is.

Kids swarm out of the change rooms onto the deck like a bunch of bees flying out of a beehive, except that bees fly straight and these kids are going all over the place, like drunk bees.

I pace up and down the island. My scan moves from the divers to the main pool, where I spot a young girl crawling along the wall to the deep end, all white-knuckled, like she's Spider-Man. Swimmers don't do this. They swim.

I stride toward her, signaling *talk* to Michael and Jody, making my hand into a puppet. "Hey, honey, can you swim?" I ask.

She blinks up at me with these long, beautiful eyelashes, her delicate face framed with wet scraggly brown hair. She's wearing an old, shiny pink bathing suit that sags at the front, revealing her chest. I always think it's sad when kids have see-through or really old suits that don't cover them. I wish we had a bathing suit donation bin.

"My name is Talia. What's your name?" A big grin. She's missing her two front teeth. She's stinking cute.

I smile back. "My name's Jessie," I say. "Can you swim, Talia?"

"Yes." She lets go for a second, starts to sink, and then grabs back on.

"How old are you?"

She doesn't say anything but crawls back along the wall toward the shallow end. A larger boy swims up, head above the water. He has the same big green eyes.

"You her brother?" I ask.

He nods.

"How old is she?"

"Eight."

No way is she eight. She's maybe six. Eight is the age a kid is allowed to be in the pool without parents. But if her parents drop her off at the pool when she can't swim, maybe home's not safer.

"You have to stay with her."

"No problem," he says real fast, like he's afraid of getting in trouble.

I return to my position on the island. My phone buzzes in my pocket. I want to check it, but I can't. What if it's you?

I glance over at Michael. His lips are pursed. Is he doing duck lips? It's kind of funny.

"Bump." It's Jody.

I rotate down the deck, toward Michael. At the diving board, I have a second to slide out my phone and check. It's Josh: Call me.

What the hell does that mean?

I slide my phone back in my pocket. Michael jumps off the guard chair and wraps a warm arm around my shoulder. "You should be a spy."

"Learned from the best." I sigh.

He gives me a sharp look. "What?"

"People keep texting me. I'm worried." I curl up the edge of my mouth in a half grin. "Maybe it wasn't the best idea to work today."

"I'm going to make some calls and try to find someone to take your shift."

"Thanks." I smile at him, grateful, and he heads down the deck.

The deep end is nearly empty. Just some older kids diving down for a plastic rocket.

A movement in the stands catches my eye. A blue uniform. A cop is sitting down. Watching me. Why is a cop watching me?

I scan the middle of the pool, where the deep end meets the shallow end—it's the cross-over zone for scanning.

And then I see them.

Talia and her brother are kicking on a mat into the deep end, where she can't stand. What the hell? Didn't I tell her brother to stay in the shallow end with her? She can't swim.

I jump off the guard chair and signal to Valerie and Jody that I'm talking to them, so that they'll cover my zone.

Michael steps out of the office and waves, like he has something to tell me. It can wait. I turn to Talia and her brother.

"Hey, kids," I call, in my nice voice, so I don't scare them. "Turn the mat around."

Talia's eyes widen, and she tries to turn the mat, kicking her feet real hard, with overly bent knees, twisting her body. But then, she slides down the mat, and grasps for the edge, but it's too slippery. She slides into the water.

Oh shit.

Her fingers are inches away from the mat. If her brother pushes it toward her, she can grab back on. Her arms are paddling a little—she's a weak swimmer, not a non-swimmer, and she could do it, but then, her legs sink, pulling her farther away. Her head swings back, chin tilted up—it's an automatic reflex, how the head does that—and she panics, flailing.

Her little head goes under.

Her brother lets out a yelp and flings himself off the mat, which goes shooting in the other direction. He grabs her like he can save her. She climbs him like a ladder.

A drowning person, even a skinny little kid like this girl, gets a surge of strength when they're panicking. A kid can easily drown an adult, and now, Talia is drowning her brother.

I start running.

His face comes up. Gasps for air. They're fighting to breathe, grappling with each other under the water.

My feet grip at the rough cement as I sprint toward them and realize I don't have my float. It's back at the guard chair. I'll have to do the rescue without it.

I dive off the side and fly through the air. My fingers touch the water first. And then there's a splash and I'm under the water, kicking hard. Something in my shorts pocket is banging into my leg—my phone. Shit.

I hear the sound of a muffled whistle blowing. It's my backup. I reach the surface. Michael is running across the deck. I race toward the drowning kids, doing head-up freestyle.

I duck under, grab the boy from behind, gripping around his waist so he can't grab me. And then I lift him with a powerful egg-beater kick. Talia is hanging on to him, so she's up too. They have their heads above water, but I'm still under. I do the hardest kick I can, but they're too heavy. I can't get my head up.

The surface of the pool glimmers. The mat is gone. My throat burns. Hurry, Michael. He's a slow swimmer.

If I let go, the kids will start drowning again, so I tug the kids toward the wall, and count, like I do in the river, letting the bubbles drift slowly out of my mouth.

My lungs are screaming. The wall is ten feet away. I might have to let them go. And then, the weight is lifted. Michael has grabbed Talia. My head is up, gasping. Air is beautiful.

Talia's brother is still choking, his skinny chest heaving against my arm. I help him to the side. He pulls himself up on the edge, coughing violently.

When Michael gets Talia on the side, he jumps out, I go under, use my shoulder to push her up as he pulls her onto the deck. Talia is coughing bent over, a long drool hanging from her mouth. I reach forward, wipe it off with my bare hand, and then, disgusted, reach down and dip my hand in the pool.

My supervisor, Valerie, and Jody are now both on deck, covering the pool, so Michael and I walk with the kids toward the office, along the length of the stands. My hand rests on Talia's wet, bony back. Her brother lumbers along beside us.

I look toward the stands. The cop's still there.

"Please don't call my dad," her brother begs. He looks terrified. I think he'd rather be drowning. "I'm going to get in so much trouble."

Michael raises his eyebrows at me, like he's actually considering it. Michael's dad was really harsh, used to beat him with a broom, call him a sissy. You'd be surprised what we tell each other when we're bored out of our minds, guarding a quiet pool.

"We have to," I tell Michael.

"Can't you call my uncle? He'll come get us, I know he will."

"Sorry, one of your parents has to come. It's too dangerous." I decide to tell him more in case the parents are total losers. "I need you to watch your sister tonight, okay? If she breathed water into

123

her lungs, she won't get enough oxygen. This could make her fall asleep, and then the water could cover so much of her lungs, she could suffocate and die."

He stares at me, wide-eyed, and Talia whimpers. Michael gives me a look, like mellow out. Maybe I said *die* a little too forcefully.

"Just watch her, okay?" I pull a thick red guard-towel from the stack by the office and wrap it around Talia's tiny shoulders. "In case she looks drowsy."

Michael tilts his head toward the stands. "Cop wants to talk to you."

"Whoa, what'd you do?" Talia's brother says.

"Nothing," I say.

You can't blame the kid for thinking I'm guilty. Cops don't normally come to someone's work. I'd think the same thing if I were him.

11:43 AM Sunday, the stands

Before I head to the stands, I move up beside Valerie, who's still guarding, and tell her you're missing and I have to talk to the cop in the stands.

"What?" She looks at me like I robbed a bank. "Oh my gosh, I'm so sorry. After you talk to him, take the rest of the day off. We can find a replacement. For goodness sake."

The way she says *for goodness sake* repeats itself in my brain as I walk toward the cop. *For goodness sake, what's wrong with you?* I don't know why I care. She's the one who works at the pool when she's forty and has three kids.

I stare down at my orange toenail polish. My bare feet press into the spotty blue cement deck. This is embarrassing. I spent my whole childhood hanging out here, and I never once saw a lifeguard talking to a cop.

At the stands, I force a smile onto my face and push on the gate. The cop takes large, gangly steps down the stands toward me. He's over six feet, for sure, almost as tall as you. His uniform looks small on him—the pants are too short. He has uneven blue eyes and large, bushy black eyebrows that hover over his face, like black caterpillars.

"Nice rescue." He smiles. "I'm Detective McFerson."

Oh! He's the detective, not just a cop. He reaches out to shake my hand, which makes me feel better. If I were in trouble, he wouldn't shake my hand, right? I know you're wondering why I'd be in trouble. It's an old habit.

"That was impressive," he says, tilting his head toward the pool.

"I reacted too slowly."

"Looked fast to me." He gives me a quick smile. "I have to ask you a few questions, Jessie. You want to come in to the station or do it here?"

"Here's fine." I shrug like it doesn't matter, but the last thing I want to do is get into a police car and sit in the back like a criminal. For goodness sake.

Not too many people are up in the stands, only a group of moms farther down. The back row is empty and that's where I lead him.

He sits beside me, his knees bent up awkwardly in his short cop pants. He has old gray socks that fall down his legs and it's kind of sweet, but I wonder why he's wearing a police uniform. Aren't detectives supposed to wear suits and ties?

"Tell me about Chris," he says.

"We're on a break, just for a week." I have to clear that up right from the start. "We aren't broken up. We're getting back together."

"Can you tell me about his personality, what he's like? Is he happy or—"

"Yeah, he's a happy guy, in a quiet guy kind of way. I mean, he's not laughing all the time, but he laughs, for sure." The words stream out of me. "He's got a great laugh." Your laughter is the most rewarding laughter of anyone I've ever met—it's like taking a gulp of cold water on a hot day.

The detective holds his pencil and pad up, waiting.

"He's real thoughtful, too, you know? If someone's having a bad day, he'll do something to cheer them up. Even people he doesn't know that well. And he gets me flowers all the time, writes these notes that he folds into airplanes, even for his mom and his sister. It's the kind of thing he does. Sometimes he prints out photos—nobody does that, right? He's a real good listener. And he never tells people's secrets, not even to me." I glance at the detective. He's staring at me. Yes, I miss you. I guess that's clear. I stop talking. If I'm going to be a babbling idiot, this is not going to go well.

He gives me a kind smile. "Sounds like a real solid guy," he says. "I've been talking to lots of his friends and they're all saying the same thing. Can you tell me about the last time you saw Chris?"

"I was with my friend Michael at the mall. He did the rescue with me? He's a guard friend." I'm repeating *friend* like I have friend-in-mouth disease. "I mean we don't usually do things outside of work."

"And?" He nods, urging me to go on.

"There was a goofy song playing, like disco? So we started dancing. And that's when Chris saw us."

He stares at me like that's a bad reason to dance. "What did he do?"

I sigh. "Lately, he's been getting jealous real easy. Even though Michael is gay. I mean, Chris took off running. I called out his name. He wouldn't stop." I sniff, weirdly, and wonder if he's trained in lie detection.

Why the hell did I say that? I didn't call out your name. You know that. I know that. Michael knows that. The salespeople at Foot Locker know that. It's an easy lie to figure out. But it just flew out of my mouth like a little blue bird, flipping and spinning and flapping its way into his ears.

"What time was this?" He scribbles away on a pad.

"Around four thirty?"

He raises those caterpillar eyebrows. "After that, you went to work?"

I'm nervous now that he's tracking my every move. "We don't work until seven on Fridays. We went to the food court and got some dinner. I had a burger." I don't know why I add that, but it seems like the kind of detail you should add if you don't want to look like a liar.

"Why'd you go on this break?" he asks.

Why isn't he asking me about the Heights guys? "He wants me to live with him while he goes to university. He knows I'm taking a year off before college to save, but I don't want to follow him around. I'd be this small town loser girlfriend from high school." That word surprises me. I don't usually think of myself as a loser. "He wants to get married."

He winces. Yep, everyone thinks that's a dumb idea, not just me.

"I don't want him to mess up his life over me." I wrap my arms around my body. "But it was a stupid fight."

The Burger Throwing Incident

We were in your truck, in my driveway, and I was finishing my burger.

You had your hand on the upper thigh of my jean shorts, and you were squeezing my leg, trying to make me listen. The hand was sexy, but I was just shaking my head, chewing the hamburger in my mouth. "I love you," you said. "You're my everything. If I don't have you, the rest of it means nothing."

All I could think was: Oh my god, I can't get married. Neither can you. No way do I want to end up like my parents.

I finished my mouthful. "You're going to college."

"Not without you."

"Then we need to go on a break." You tried to talk, but I held up my hand. "We need time to think. We need a little perspective."

The edges of your mouth turned up like I was being funny. "Perspective?"

It made me mad that you were mocking me. I know I sounded

like a mother. Not my mother. But someone's mother. You can't blame me—I've been the responsible one in my family for years, and that's not saying much. "One week. No texting, no calling, nothing. Or I'm breaking up with you for good."

Then I jumped out of the truck, still holding my burger, and slammed the door. You ran around the truck after me. "This is stupid, Jessie."

Even then I knew it was stupid. I stopped in the middle of the lawn, next to the tire. "One week," I repeated, and then I took a bite of my burger and turned to walk into the house.

You grabbed my arm and spun me around. "We are not taking a break."

I didn't know what to do with this different side of you—I've never seen you angry before. You never grabbed me before. Maybe, if I'm being real, I thought it was sexy. It was like you were finally tough, like every other guy in my town. I know that's messed up. But then, the burger lodged in my throat and I started coughing, right there, on my lawn.

It could have gone down differently if I didn't start choking. Maybe we would have gone into my room and started making out and I would have forgotten all about us needing a break. But you rushed to get me your Coke inside the truck and you thrust it at me and I drank it.

When I finally stopped coughing, you laughed and said—do you remember this?—you said, "You'd probably choke to death if you didn't have me around." Then you gave me that arrogant smirk of yours, and it just made me want to kill you—not really, it's just an expression.

"I would not." I was dead serious, even though you're right, I'm always choking on things. I swear, my tongue is too big.

You took a step toward me like you were going to grab me again and I flung the burger at you. It was an instinct, that's all, but I'll never forget that stunned look on your face. I'd never thrown food at you before. Or at anyone.

"Jessie, baby," you breathed.

"Don't act like you're the only good thing in my life," I yelled. "Mr. Perfect. I'll be fine without you. Fuck." You just gaped at me, but that didn't keep me from going on. "I feel like you're a friggin animal that's swallowing me whole."

Me, calling you an animal, I could see what it did to you. Your hand hovered in front of your stomach.

I don't know why I said that. You know how I get when I'm mad. I was a 9.5 on the Jessie Scale of Anger. I'm sorry about so many things, but most of all, I'm sorry about this. How could I call you an animal? I didn't mean it like that. But I should have said sorry right away. Instead, I tried to justify it. "You always act like you need to take care of me, because I'm so useless, and I'm sick of it."

Your arms hung at your sides like I was a vampire sucking all the blood out of you and you were just letting me do it.

"I'll be fine without you. I was fine before you. And I'll be fine after you. I don't need you to take care of me. Or anyone else."

You reached your hand out to me. "You don't mean that."

"Don't touch me," I shouted like a maniac. "You think I can't live without you for a week? I can. I'll prove it to you. Seven days. No calls, nothing."

You stayed very still. "Jessie, come on."

I wondered briefly how things could go so bad so quickly. An hour before we'd been laughing in the Dairy Queen drive-thru. But now you said I couldn't make it without you, so you wanted to get married? My parents married young and look at how well that worked out for them.

"I mean it." Then I stormed into the house.

You sat out there in your truck for ages, waited for me to come back, and then finally, you started it up and drove away. Soon as you were gone, I wanted to call you, but I didn't. Because I'm stubborn like that.

Every minute of every hour you're gone, I wish I could reverse time back to this moment. I'd beg for forgiveness. I'd tell you I didn't mean it like that. I'd say sorry, and you wouldn't be missing.

11:51 AM Sunday, the detective

I tell the detective the basics of our argument, but I don't tell him how I called you an animal—I honestly didn't mean it in a bad way, and it's embarrassing. I don't want him to see me like that.

He takes notes even after I'm finished talking, but finally, he looks up. "I got to tell you, Jessie. It seems like he took off. He has a history of this. His mom said he called friends in Brooklyn this week."

"He did?" I think about the pistachios receipt. Maybe you did go to Brooklyn. "But he wouldn't have taken off without his truck."

"His truck's been giving him some trouble lately. Maybe he took the bus. Or hitchhiked. There are many possibilities."

"He wouldn't make people worry like this."

"I bet if we give it a day or two, he's going to show up."

"You know about those guys who jumped him, right?"

He nods slowly. "A couple people mentioned something happened," he says. "It sounds like it was just a fight."

"It wasn't a fight—he got jumped," I say. "It was Friday night three weeks ago, same time, same place. They attacked him. He didn't fight back." I tell him about what they did, how they called you the N-word, about your ribs.

McFerson's staring at me again. Maybe looking for odd tics. I wish I knew what he was thinking. Those huge eyebrows are distracting.

"Do you know any of their names?"

"Just Dave Johnson. His dad owns the Honda dealership?"

I wait for him to write it down. Then I explain, "Chris wouldn't fight back. He has a policy against violence. He believes in peaceful resistance."

I look at him to see what he thinks about that. Most people in our town would say a guy in that situation has to fight. But the detective doesn't blink. "He seems like a pretty stand-up guy," he says.

"He *is* a stand-up guy." I've never said *stand-up guy* before in my life. "I'm telling you, we need to organize a big search for him. He could be real hurt somewhere, he could have broken bones. We need dogs, everything."

His gray eyes sparkle, like he's laughing at me. "Jessie, you think we have a canine division in Pendling?"

"You could borrow dogs from like, Seattle. And we have search and rescue here," I say. "They should be looking for him. Maybe he fell in a ravine."

He nods. "I understand you're worried, but it'd be hard to get lost off those trails. Too many roads."

"Anything could have happened," I argue. "People could volunteer; they could search the woods. He has a lot of people who want to be doing something to help. They keep texting me."

"I'll talk to search and rescue." He smiles. "You don't give up, do you?"

"No, I don't."

"We'll do what we can, Jessie."

I can hear you laughing, somewhere, saying, "Nope, she doesn't give up."

"Here." He writes down his cell phone number on the back of his card and flips it at me. "All right, if you think of anything, you call me, any time of the day or night." His thick eyebrows jump up. "We're going to figure out what happened. Don't worry."

And for now, I believe him.

12:02 PM Sunday, a new phone

After the detective leaves, I get changed and wave at Michael across the deck as I leave. He waves back. Valerie turns and waves too. It's weird to leave early. It feels like I'm getting fired in the middle of my shift, only everyone wouldn't be waving.

I check my phone. It's dead. And I don't got time to wait and try the rice method for drying out my phone.

I ride fast to the phone store and go inside to buy another one, even though it seriously drains my bank account. I cannot afford to be out of contact with you for one extra minute. The entire time I don't have a phone, I feel panicky that you're calling me or texting me, that you need me.

Outside, I lean against the glass on the store. A half-drunk beer bottle stands beside me, like it's my friend. Just down the block, I see two town drunks heading into Joe's strip club.

Text after text slides into my new phone. Nothing from you.

A bunch of people are asking if there's news. I guess everyone's finding out now. I text Josh about making a game plan to try to find you.

A text pops up from an unknown number. A wave of excitement washes over me. Maybe it's you. Then I read: Hi. It's Raffa

This is the first time she's texted me. So sweet. I'm becoming a big sap while you're gone, seriously.

Me: Want to come to Josh's? We're making posters

Raffa: Can't . . . Mum wants me here

I smile. She's started calling her *mum* because of her love of Harry Potter and all things British.

Raffa: Can you ask her?

I call your mom and she says no. I try, really I do, but she's firm. "Can I come over later?" I ask.

I can't hear your mom because someone's yelling at me. "There's the lifeguard!" It's a girl, pointing at me, like I'm a celebrity. Talia. I almost didn't recognize her without her saggy bathing suit, but those big eyes and long eyelashes are hard to miss. She's waving wildly. "Hi, hi, hi!!"

I wave back and smile at her. And then I look up at the guy she's with. It's Dave Johnson.

"This is my uncle!" She gives him a tight squeeze from the side like he's her favorite big teddy bear. "He picked me up!"

Johnson lifts his chin up in a cold hello. Eyes of a killer.

But that little girl Talia loves him. It's clear by the adoring way she's blinking up at him. Did Michael tell him about secondary drowning? Why didn't her parents pick her up?

"Jessie, are you there?" Your mom.

The phone is still on my ear. "Yeah," I say, "I'm here."

"You come by later, okay?"

"Yeah, okay." We hang up.

"She saved me!" Talia is yelling at Johnson. "I almost drowned!"

"Thanks," Johnson says, and grabs her hand. "Come on." Then, he ducks his head and disappears with Talia into the store.

Wow—so Dave Johnson takes care of his niece. I guess all kinds of monsters have people who love them.

My voicemails have loaded up. None from you. But my mailbox is getting full, so I delete all the ones from people I know. They're just calling to find out what's happening and I don't have answers.

I text you: Pleeeaaase call me. I love you

Now that you're missing, apparently I have no problem saying or writing *I love you*. And then, because I want to hear your voice on your voicemail, I call you. It doesn't go to voicemail. Not right away.

It rings.

My gut tightens. It hasn't been ringing. All day yesterday it went straight to voicemail. But now it's ringing. Five times.

Finally, the voicemail clicks on: "Hey. This is Chris. You know what to do."

Oh my god. Someone's turned on your phone.

12:15 PM Sunday, Josh's house

Josh is holding a yellow writing pad when he throws open the door.
A pencil is sticking behind his ear. His curly hair is bouncing from
his head, no product. Dark circles shadow his eyes. He stares at me,
kind of like a mad scientist who never sleeps.

"Guess what?" I say. "His phone rang."

"So?"

"Every time I called him before, it went straight to voicemail.
Which means it was off. But now it rings. So someone must have
turned it on. Someone has his phone. Or he does. Or—I don't
know."

"Call him again." He jerks his head up at me, like, hurry.

I put it on speakerphone and we stand in his doorway listening
to your phone ring. Five rings. You don't answer. It goes to voicemail.
The voicemail is still full.

"You have to tell the detective," Josh says.

When I call McFerson and tell him, he says, "It might just mean
someone else found his phone."

"Can't you track it," I say, "if it's on?"

"We're trying. We already requested cell tower info, but it's harder to get tracking on phones for adults."

"He's not an adult!"

"He's eighteen, so he qualifies as an adult." There's a pause. "Jessie, have you considered he might just not want to be found?"

"Oh my god." I hang up on him.

Josh gives me a look. "Maybe you shouldn't hang up on the detective."

"Whatever, he's not helping."

"Come on." He waves me in, and I follow him through his spotless house to the backyard. Holy crap his house is nice. His backyard too. On his patio, he has one of those fancy outdoor glass tables with comfy chairs and all-new white cushions under a white gazebo, and in the yard, there are yellow and white flowers planted in real flower beds.

We sit down at the table, where he's already got his laptop set up. I tell him about Johnson. "He couldn't even look me in the eye. He's totally guilty. I swear, he knows something."

Josh shakes his head angrily. "Here, look at this." He rotates the computer. "This is what I've been working on."

I look at the screen. FindChrisKirk.com. Your website's got a timeline, everything we know so far about where you were last seen. He's even written down my street. "Wow," I say.

His mom strides out the back door, dressed in her spin-teaching gear and carrying a pretty lemonade jug with cute little lemonade glasses. "I brought you kids something to drink," she says, and places it on the table.

"Thanks, Mom."

"I'll be back right after the class, sweetheart." She gives Josh a kiss on the cheek, closing her eyes, like she's thinking about him going missing, too. "Okay, bye." She strides back to the house.

Josh is already typing away, doesn't even notice. He has no idea how good he has it. Seriously, what would it be like to have that kind of mom? I get mom envy when I see shit like that.

I pour the lemonade. It's freshly squeezed. You'd smack your lips and say, "Wow, your mom makes great lemonade." And these cups! It's silly, but drinking lemonade out of lemonade cups is way better. When I get rich, I'm buying me one of these lemonade jugs with matching cups.

You're always telling me to be grateful for stuff, and I'm grateful for this lemonade in my mouth and the hot sun on my face. Right now, it seems pretty impossible anything horrible has happened. Maybe the detective is right.

Then Josh says, "So the first twenty-four hours are the most important for finding a missing kid. That's what it says on the National Missing Children website."

"And after that?" I say.

"After that, it says the chances go way down."

Which is excellent. Since it is now thirty-eight hours. Not that I'm counting.

2:45 PM Sunday, Josh's backyard

The doorbell rings. It's your mom—with Raffa.

Raffa's eyes are swollen and red. It looks like she and your mom got in a big fight so she could come. Which is strange for Raffa.

Your mom explains, "She wanted to come and help, but I didn't know if we could get the house ready in time." Raffa presses her lips together, fiercely, like she's biting back words, and your mom continues, "Christopher is flying in tonight, you know. He lands in Seattle at six and then he's getting a rental car."

For a second, I'm confused by Christopher—she calls you that if she's mad—but then I remember it's your dad's name. Holy crap. He's on an airplane to come here to find you. You haven't seen him in person for over a year, since his last visit. Meanwhile, you might be on your way to Brooklyn, chewing pistachios, spitting the shells into a soda bottle.

Your mom leaves and I wrap my arm around Raffa's bony shoulders. Is it my imagination, or has she lost weight? "Thanks for making your mom bring you, sweetie. We could really use some help with the posters."

We walk through the house to the backyard. She sits down on the chair next to me, resting her delicate violinist hands on the table. "Put me to work," she says in her British accent.

I grin at her and answer in my own lame British accent, intentionally messing up. "Oy will, don't you worry, lassie."

"It's not *oy*," she corrects me, squinting.

There's our Raffa. I laugh.

My phone rings from the table. Unknown number. I snatch it up. "Hello?"

"Hi, Jessie. How are you?" It's the detective. Every single time, I think it might be you. Most people text.

"Jessie, I have a question for you."

My chest tightens. "What?"

"Has Chris ever tagged anything?" he asks.

Tagged? "You mean with paint?"

"Yes."

"He'd never tag anything," I say. "He's not into doing anything that is remotely against the law. He doesn't even like being near people who are breaking the law. The one time we went to a party where there were drugs, we had to leave." I glance at Raffa, think about how careful we always got to be around her, no swearing, nothing "bad." She's so protected. You don't want her to be a Jehovah's Witness, but you say it's her choice; it wasn't an easy choice for you to make. You love your mom and the church has a lot of great people who helped all of you when times were tough. But you believe all religions have some truth and you couldn't practice any religion that said other people were wrong. I admire that about you.

"He doesn't drink?" the detective asks skeptically.

"Never," I say. "He follows most of the Jehovah's Witness rules still."

"There was some vandalism on Friday night at the Honda dealership owned by Dave Johnson's father. Someone spray-painted a bunch of cars. They left a couple beer cans."

I stare at Josh's face. There are no words. I look at Raffa. Her eyes are wide open, like a cat that's just been scared by a loud noise.

"You think he did it because the person used spray paint? Like tagging is the kind of thing he'd do?" I'm raging now. "That's so racist."

"Jessie, I'm only asking because someone said they might have seen him there, and he disappeared on Friday night *and* he had a motive of revenge. It makes sense."

"He would never do that!" I say. "Never."

"It would explain a lot of things. Why he's disappeared. He wouldn't want to bring his truck. Too easy to trace."

"It's impossible."

He sighs. "Okay, Jessie. Relax. I'm just asking the question."

"Well, you have your answer. It's unrelated. Or maybe Johnson did it so that it would look like Chris did it."

"Okay, thanks," the detective says, and he hangs up.

Josh is staring at me. "What?"

"You won't fucking believe it." I wince, looking at Raffa. "Sorry."

She lets out an *umph*. "Don't worry about it." She looks a little pissy, like maybe she's tired of everyone treating her like a little kid.

So I tell them what the detective said.

"He wouldn't do that," Raffa says. The English accent is gone.

"I know."

She bites on the edge of her pinkie finger. Josh can't stop shaking his head. He types away and finally turns the laptop toward us. "Should we use this picture for the posters?" It's your yearbook photo with your cap and gown. Remember how they only had a few of the gowns for the photos, and you were worried they didn't have one big enough? You and Tim were laughing about it.

You look so serious in this picture. The little bit of mustache on your top lip. You asked me if you should shave; you said you liked your stash. I said it was sexy and you kept it. Your mom went off about it later, and I felt kind of bad.

"I like this picture," I say. "Print it." Then, I get an idea. "Maybe Raffa, you could check on the printer?" I give Josh a look. "Can you show her where it is?"

He jumps up. "Sure. Come on." She follows him, and a few seconds later he comes back. "Okay, what?"

I speak in a low voice. "Rosemary doesn't want us to tell Raffa about this, but you should write on the website about how he was jumped down there," I tell Josh in a low voice. "You should publish Johnson's name."

146

"Johnson might not have anything to do with this. That's defamation."

"Defamation?" I hiss. "He's defaming Chris's name! He's saying Chris could have vandalized his dad's shop. If Chris doesn't show up in Brooklyn pretty damn soon, or somewhere pretty damn soon, I'm telling you, Johnson attacked him. I swear to god. Remember how he looked at us?"

Josh frowns. "Yeah, you're right, Jessie. He's an asshole, but I don't want to, like, ruin his life. Not if we don't know anything."

You'd say the same thing.

"I'll just say he was attacked without saying who," he adds.

"Okay."

Raffa comes back, holding a stack of your missing-person posters to her chest, like she's hugging you. She sits down. "I brought the phone numbers of some of his friends in Brooklyn."

"That's a great idea."

When she's talking to your ex-girlfriend, Latricia, I tell Raffa I want to hear. I press my head against hers to listen in. Latricia says you called her this week. On Wednesday. When we went on the break, you called your ex. Great.

Her voice is soft, musical even. "How's he been doing lately?"

"Okay," Raffa says.

"He sounded pretty upbeat. I was just worried, you know, about before?"

Raffa looks at me fast and then pulls back. "I think he's fine," she tells Latricia. "But, like, maybe he went to Brooklyn? Can you call us if he shows up?"

Raffa hangs up and I ask her, "What did she mean, like before?"

"I don't know." She makes a face.

After the website's done, we contact all the newspapers, TV, and radio outlets that we can find.

Then, I don't tell Josh, but I write an email to the organizer of that protest in Portland, Steve. Even though we live near Seattle, he knows you at least and he's got connections.

I tell him everything we're telling the media, but then I add: *I think Chris could have been the victim of a hate crime. The police aren't doing anything. There's a guy named Dave Johnson—he's from a rich family and he beat Chris up pretty bad a few weeks ago. We need help. Thanks, Jessie.*

Is that dramatic of me? I push SEND.

4:20 PM Sunday, a bitchfest, on Josh's driveway, in front of your sister

Josh and I are standing in his driveway, saying bye to Raffa, when Tamara and Becky screech up in a black Mercedes.

Tamara's got her bitch face on. Guess they're not just picking up posters like everyone else.

Your mom and Raffa are getting in your mom's car. Raffa's holding a stack of posters. Oh god. Please let them hurry. I don't want them to hear.

Tamara jumps out of the Mercedes like a panther ready to strike, nails out, ready to scratch bloody lines across my face. She's all done up today, lots of makeup, hair curled, expensive jeans, a tight T-shirt. I, meanwhile, am wearing a helmet, getting ready to ride down to the river to put up posters. At least she's not wearing your hoodie.

She marches up to me. "Jessie!"

"What?" I glance over at your mom and Raffa. They're in the

car now, but Raffa's window is open and she's craning her head back to look.

Tamara points at me and shakes her finger in my face. I want to bite it right off. "You were at the mall on Friday with that blond lifeguard from the pool."

"So?" I say.

Your mom drives her car away, kind of jerks it forward. She must have heard something was going down.

"So, Chris saw you." Tamara's chewing something in her mouth—gum maybe, or possibly her latest victim's finger. "Why didn't you tell us?"

"I don't have to tell you anything," I say. "Chris just overreacted."

"Overreacted to what?" Josh says, confused.

"Nothing," I tell him.

Becky is stooped over like Big Bird. She always looks awkward and uncomfortable when Tamara's being a bitch.

"People saw you and that lifeguard pawing all over each other," Tamara spits out.

"We were just dancing," I tell them.

"It didn't look like that to Chris." Tamara raises her eyebrows. "He was crying."

"What?" I think about that look on your face at the mall. Did you cry? Oh my god, that makes me sick in my stomach. I never saw you cry before. Would you cry in public? "He'd never."

"You broke up with him and then he sees you at the mall making out with some hot, older guy. How do you think that's going to make him feel?"

My face heats up with rage. "First off, I didn't break up with Chris. Second, I wasn't making out with Michael. That's disgusting. He's like an older brother to me; Chris knows that. And he's gay." I shake my head, fiercely. "We were dancing to a song that they were playing in Foot Locker. Michael was trying on shoes and we started dancing. There's no way Chris would've cried about that. It didn't even look like anything."

Okay, maybe Michael went a little overboard. He was disco-ing it up, being extra cheesy. He's a real good dancer, what can I say? He was spinning me around and around, and it felt so fun, so free, I let myself go. I felt like myself again, for the first time in a while. Then, I looked up and you were standing in the entrance of the store, your goddamn mouth open, catching flies, an odd look on your face. Your arms were just hanging by your side. Then you ran away. I couldn't have caught you even if I tried.

"He's been totally depressed ever since you went on this break." Tamara puts finger quotes around *break*. "I'm telling you, if he shows up in the river—"

Josh stops her. "I don't think this is helping anyone."

I am speechless. Why does she think you're in the river? Did she talk to Johnson? Does she know something I don't know?

But then, maybe it's how Becky swivels her head, like this has even shocked her, and I realize Tamara's not saying that.

She's saying you jumped in—and killed yourself?

"What are you talking about?" I say. "The bridge isn't high enough to do anything and he can swim."

"He could have jumped in by the rapids," Tamara says.

It feels like the hole that I call a mouth is a pinprick in my face. No air can get in. Or out. Pain climbs through my chest. "He'd never do something to himself like that," I say, finally. Sure, you get bummed out sometimes, but you're not a depressed guy. You're Mr. Gratitude, Mr. Think-Three-Happy-Thoughts. "He's going to college soon. He has this whole exciting life ahead of him." I look from Tamara to Becky to Josh. "Right?"

A hesitation. Or did I imagine it?

"No, he wouldn't do that," Josh says.

Becky shakes her head. "Not right before graduation." She smiles briefly down at Tamara, like she's sorry. "Not over a breakup."

Tamara's eyes flash. "You didn't see what he looked like when he stopped by Tim's barbecue. You were in the backyard, making out with Ian."

"I told you: I just don't think he'd jump in there," Becky says.

Instantly, my mind pictures you doing a big jump into the water by the Pitt. And then, your body bumping along down the river and then disappearing into the class-four rapids. My heart breaks into a million pieces.

"There's no way," I manage.

"He has tons of friends," Becky says. "He gets straight As. He has a full-ride scholarship to one of the best baseball colleges in the country."

Josh adds, "He might be a starting pitcher. That's what the scout said."

"I mean, why would he?" Becky says.

"Over her? No fucking idea." Tamara tosses me a disgusted look. "I swear, if he killed himself over you, a fat-assed piece of white trash—"

"Whoa," Josh says, waving his arms. "Not cool."

Yes, she really said that.

Tears are hammering at the backs of my eyes, but I don't want Tamara to see. "Fuck off, Tamara." Then, I jump on good old Ella and ride away.

Josh runs after me. He's sprinting. "Jessie," he yells, "you okay?"

I wave my hand. Don't look back. "I'm fine," I shout. "I'll call you after I put these up."

I ride harder and harder, holding back a sob. His footsteps stop. I'm guessing he turned around.

So, now you know how low Tamara can go, what she'll stoop to—even in the midst of all this, she's trying to hurt me. You always say to me: "You can't let her get to you." But she does. She really does. You tell me to ignore her, that she's just jealous, but she has everything. Why would she be jealous of me? If she wanted you, she could have just had you.

The truth is she's a horrible person with a shell of a heart. Some people are plain old mean. You said someone turned her mean. It makes me mad how you stick up for her. We all have reasons to turn mean. Everyone has crap that happens to them. Some people, like Tamara, choose to hurt others back, and some people, like you, choose to make others feel better. Tamara should be the one who's missing right now, not you.

7:30 PM Sunday, the river

I stick about fifty posters along the highway and leading up to the trail. I make sure not to get the tape on your face, even though there isn't really enough room at the top of the poster.

The river chatters on my right. Sounds so friendly. Harmless.

You'd never jump in the river. You won't come close to the water. You won't even put your damn feet in.

I gaze through the moss-covered trees, toward the dark and gurgling river, like a pot of water before it boils. All the action is happening below the surface, weeds tugging and swaying, holding and releasing, and always, always the undertow.

When I was a kid, I thought the undertow was everywhere in a river, like some monster waiting to grab your ankles and pull you down. But it's not. The pull is strongest on the outside of a turn in a river. Water is drawn to the inside of the turn, which is deeper due to erosion. It sucks water and debris... and bodies... from the outside to the inside. Up ahead, where the river turns to the right, that's where the undertow would be. If you were in the river, your body would be pulled toward the inside of the turn, toward our side of the bank.

I make my way to our spot and sit on the bright green grass. The Indian paintbrushes are blooming, bright red and yellow flowers stretching over the bank and down to the water, like wildfire.

I think about the time I told you the Indian paintbrushes were poisonous, and then I took a bite of the flower. You jumped up and screamed, and I laughed my head off. You told me to spit it out; I mean, you were really freaking out and I couldn't stop laughing to tell you it was okay. Do you think I'm so crazy, I'd eat a poisonous flower? When I told you it's just the stem you have to worry about, you dropped backward on the grass, spread-eagled, saying "Man" again and again.

Sorry I always freak you out. I can't stop myself. It's too funny.

Like when I jumped off that cliff a month ago at Bear Lake, I knew the water would freeze my ass off, but I did it anyway because I wanted to see that terrified look on your face. I can't help it. The urge is too great. Nobody ever worried about me before. It makes me so happy.

You make me happy.

My gaze hops across the water, leap-frogging from a ripple to a log to a clump of old branches and leaves. It's one of those happy summer days. The river is glimmering. It looks inviting, even.

You aren't in there, no way, no how.

It's the kind of day we might come here and spread our blanket,

Sunset, Last Thanksgiving, Making Love

I'm just going to say it straight out.

Here's the truth: It was my first time. Not just my first time with you. My first time ever. I'm so sorry.

On that night, we walked down the path along the river with our basket and you sang that Dobie Gray song, "All I Want to Do Is Make Love to You." I grinned at you, like it was no big deal, making love, even though it was.

I knew it wasn't your first time. We were seniors for god's sake. You assumed I'd had lots of boyfriends, loads and loads of sex, piles of it, so many guys I didn't even remember them all. Didn't people tell you I was a slut because I'd dated a couple older guys?

Maybe I didn't say anything because I didn't want you to make a big deal. I wanted it to be normal. I didn't want you to keep saying, "Is it okay?" every two minutes, or "Does it hurt?" And maybe, if I'm being real, I didn't want you to be able to say that you were my first if we ever broke up.

So we packed our cheese and our grapes and our cheap-ass wine lay down, get naked. I rest my head back on the grass, close my eyes, and sigh.

There's something I got to tell you. I tried to tell you before, but I couldn't.

It's about our first time. I should have told you before.

and our blanket and our two condoms in a basket, and we made our way down the trail at sunset. The sunset was all purples and bright orange.

The gnats were going crazy—they kept going up your nose. You kept pinching at it, making that funny gargle sound. And the mosquitos were feasting on you too. We kept having to smack at them. They loved your scent. (I do too.) Remember how we were giggling?

We pulled off our clothes, fast, kind of avoided looking at each other. It was really happening. I was nervous.

"Come over here," you said.

The way you kissed me. You pressed both hands on my cheeks. Your lips wrapped around mine. My whole body unzipped.

We dropped down onto the blanket, but it was all rough wool and itchy. I sat on top of your legs, so that only my knees were touching the scratch wool. You undid my bra.

"Boing," you said.

I slid off your boxers.

"Boing," I said.

You didn't know it was my first time, but you were slow and careful, kind of like how you are with everything, even when you wash your truck. You put on the condom, like you'd had practice doing it. Once it was on, you didn't go right to it. Instead, your fingers tickled down my body. And then your tongue. And you kept saying, "Is this okay?" And I kept saying, "Yes." Finally, I couldn't stand it. And I said, "Come on!"

So you did.

It was a little painful, I'll admit. And after, I hid the blood. Which is kind of shitty. You had this real soft look on your face, the tension drained out. You said it was the best Thanksgiving ever. Thank you, you said. Thank you.

I said, "Thank *you*."

And you know how you say we have to be grateful? I did feel grateful. It was real special, having that first time be with you. That's more than most girls can say. But I should have told you.

9:16 PM Sunday, the whistler

I wake up to Little Man pecking at my hand. I let out a scream and jerk back. Don't know where I am. Little Man jumps back a few steps and tilts his head at me, then flies away, into the bush. I sit up and rub my eyes. What am I doing here?

YOU ARE MISSING!

It startles me like a horn blasting. Shit. I drop my head back on the grass. I'm here because of you.

It's got to be late—around nine? The sun is down already and the sky is a beautiful blend of orange and pink and purple, the colors all twisting into one another.

If you were here, you'd say, "Wow." You act like every sunset is a goddamn miracle, even though it's just pollution. I sit up and stare at the sky. It's real beautiful. Are you seeing this sunset? Are you saying "Wow" somewhere?

People are going to be worried. Steph, especially, is going to be freaking out. I told her that I'd be back no later than six. I said we could order in pizza.

Normally, I could probably go missing for a day and nobody would notice. Definitely, nobody would get calls in the middle of the night. But it's different now. Nobody knows if there's a killer on the loose. Or if some sick freak has you tied you up in a cabin and is torturing you.

Okay, here's a super power message. *If someone has gagged you and tied you up, do what you need to escape. If you have to, kill them.*

Is it bad to send someone a mental kill message? I don't know and I don't care. I'd kill them for you if I knew where you were.

You've been missing forty-eight hours. We're heading into Night Three, and we know nothing. It scares the crap out of me.

It's getting dark. If I don't leave now, I'm going to be in the woods really late. I stand up.

A crunch. Someone is out there. Moving toward me.

My ears are alive.

The sound gets closer. Heavy boots are crunching down on old, soggy leaves. The crack of a branch. Someone is walking carefully through the woods, trying not to make a sound. Closer now. And then, a slow, airy whistle.

It's not normal whistling, it's more like someone who's learning to whistle, high-pitched and breathy.

I stay very still. Wait for the guy to walk by. But the footsteps stop. He must have heard me.

Some birds squawk in the trees. I hold my breath. They always say killers come back to the scene of a crime. And what's up with that whistle? Does he know I'm here? Is he trying to scare me?

Maybe it's Johnson. Maybe he followed you here the other night and he killed you and now he's coming back to make sure there's no evidence.

Another branch cracks. He's going to come into the clearing!

I grab my backpack and slide down the bank. I'm not quiet. Pebbles follow me, call out *plink*, *plink*, *plink*, which in rapist language means "Hello, rapist, there's a girl here, with a vagina." Oh god, I don't know why I'm joking about this. Maybe joking makes shit less scary. I'm on the verge of a panic attack. Baby, I need you.

I press myself against the crumbly dirt bank. Friggin dirt is dropping down into the back of my shirt. My breathing sounds like Darth Vader.

The birds are totally quiet. They get quiet when a predator is near. This is how I know it's still dangerous. He's listening, just like I am.

Maybe Little Man's mom and dad will take a dislike to the guy; maybe they'll start diving at him.

"Hello?" It's a male voice.

Oh shit. Does he sound familiar? Sort of. It's deep, but is it as low as Johnson's? I need him to say more. Hello is not enough.

I slide my head up to see. The bushes rustle. Hands appear through the brush. The guy is pushing his way into the clearing, right by my bike. I duck back down, way low, hiding behind the bank. My heart bumps against my chest.

The dark river rushes by my shoes. I could jump in, but I don't want to, not yet. I'm too scared. It's dark. Can't see anything. And it's cold.

His breathing is above me. The river screams past.

Does he know I'm here? Is he about to jump on top of me? I'm pressed to the dirt, the bank curving over my head. I look up so I can see what's coming. My body is shaking. I don't think I could fight him off. I don't think I could dive into that dark water and do my lifeguard moves.

Some rustling comes from behind me. What is he doing? A crack of another branch. A scream fights inside me, but I hold it there, and it echoes in my mind. Then the footsteps continue down the trail, squishing down on the moist leaves.

His airy whistling fades down the trail. I can't tell which way he went, to the left or to the right. I stay there for a long time.

He had to have seen my bike. He knows I'm here. Or that someone is here.

Why did he come in the clearing?

The smartest move now would be to swim down the river, just a little ways. But I'd have to leave my bike. And it's really dark now.

The brown water is rushing by my shoes. It's faster than normal from all the runoff. I can't do it.

I climb up the bank and creep across the clearing. Good old Ella is still leaning against the bush. I crouch by Saber and listen for breathing. The whistler knows I'm here. When I come out, if he's waiting, he'll just grab me.

It sounds like he's gone.

I take in a breath and climb under Saber and step out onto the dark path. The trail is quiet, peaceful even, which makes it creepier, like in those horror movies with children's music playing. Am I that girl in the movie who the audience is yelling at? "No, don't go that way, you stupid fool! Stay by the water, you idiot! You have a rape plan! Go back, go back."

I don't see anyone down the trail, not that this means anything. It's too dark to see. The sky is now that shade of blue right before it goes black.

I flick on my light, swing my leg over the seat, and then I ride as goddamn fast as I can. Maybe he won't be able to grab me.

Soon, my legs are burning. My breath is clawing out of me. I can see a yard or two in front and to the sides, but otherwise, the path is now totally dark.

At the big log near the end of the trail, I hesitate because if I were a killer, I'd be on the other side. I stop and lean over to look at the other side.

Nobody's there. I let out a sigh of relief, heave my bike over the log and ride the last bit of the trail before the parking lot. My tires hit the gravel. The highway is up ahead, all lit up like a Christmas tree. I'm starting to feel a little silly. You always say I'm dramatic.

Then, a bright light shines in my eyes. There. Is. A. Car. The killer is waiting to run me over. I ride as hard as I can. My tires spin out on the rocks. My bike twists, and I scream and crash to the ground. I fall on my bad arm. The pain is blinding.

All I can do is lie there and wait for his wheels to crush me. The last time I hurt my arm this bad, you were there to rescue me. But there's nobody here to save me now.

9:45 PM Sunday, the parking lot

"Jessie?" The killer knows my name. He's standing above me with a flashlight in my eyes. His body is in shadow.

"Don't hurt me." I'm cringing on the ground, squinting in the bright light. So much for the tough girl.

"It's Detective McFerson."

He pulls the bike off of me, and then slowly, I sit up. "Oh my god," I say. "You freaked the shit out of me."

"I'm sorry." He helps me up. "Are you okay?"

I stretch my bad arm out. It hurts, but it's just bruised. "I guess so." That's a relative term. "Why were you whistling like that? You freaked me out."

"What are you talking about?"

"You were whistling."

He lets out a perfect whistle. "Like this?"

"No."

"Did you bump your head, Jessie?"

"Someone was whistling on the trail," I say.

"I wasn't on the trail."

"What?" I breathe. "Someone was there. A guy. He was whistling."

"What are you talking about? Back up, Jessie."

"Okay, I was in this spot where Chris and I always go and I fell asleep and—" I pause, feel around on my back. "Oh shit, I forgot my backpack."

"Where?"

I'm panting hard, thinking about how maybe he's hiding out there, maybe he'll come back and see my backpack and then he'll find my ID and my keys and he'll hunt me down. The detective is staring at me. Like I'm a maniac. "There was this guy. In the woods. Whistling. I thought he was going to kill me."

"Because he was whistling?"

Maybe it sounds dumb, but he wasn't there. "It was creepy whistling."

"Jessie, what are you doing here so late?" he asks. He says it softly, trying not to act suspicious, but he definitely is.

I feel flustered. I can't help it. Cops freak the crap out of me. Even nice ones. Especially nice ones.

"N-Nothing."

He cocks his head. "Nothing?"

"I was riding the trails all afternoon, and then I went to this spot where Chris and I go? It's our special place. I missed him, so I went there and then I watched the sunset like we do and I stayed too late and fell asleep, that's all. Really." Why can't I talk like a normal person?

"Were you meeting someone, Jessie?"

It makes me mad. "Who the hell would I meet?"

"A guy. Maybe Chris."

"I fell asleep! I wasn't meeting anyone, and definitely not Chris. I wish I were meeting him. For god's sake, I would kill to meet him." Why did I just say *kill* to a police officer? Am I a crazy person? "Maybe you should try to look for a guy who can't whistle."

He studies me. "You shouldn't be out here this late."

"No kidding," I say.

"Jessie, I'm here to help you."

"Really?" I glare at him. "How about organizing a search? We don't even have dogs looking for him. I shouldn't have to be searching out here by myself."

He sighs. "I promised you I'd talk to the police chief, and I did, but he says we don't have the resources."

"You think he vandalized Johnson's car dealership and then took off, so you aren't even going to look for him."

"I'm trying. Believe me."

"You're not trying hard enough." I think of the blue paint on Tamara's arm. "You should talk to Tamara Bell. She had blue paint on her arm yesterday."

His eyebrows dart up. "Really?"

"Yeah, really." I grab my bike. "Thanks for the heart attack."

He gives me this funny look like he's trying to figure me out, or maybe he thinks that I'm guilty of something. Then, I ride off, acting like I really am guilty of something. Because that's what I do when I'm around cops.

It's true, I guess. I am guilty. I'm guilty of all sorts of things, but mostly, I'm guilty of being a bitch to you, the guy I love most in the whole wide world.

I don't know why I had to act like that, to you, of all people. If it weren't for me being a bitch, you wouldn't have come running down here, that's for sure. So I am to blame, no matter what's happened.

I ride fast up the highway. A carload of kids passes me, music blaring. I wonder if they're kids from school. One guy sticks his head out the window and yells, "Nice ass!" I don't know why guys think that's a compliment.

You would never say that to a girl, never. You're so different from other guys in our town, and not just cause you're black and from Brooklyn. When you showed up at school at the beginning of sophomore year, everyone assumed you were a tough kid from the streets of Brooklyn, but you grew up in an artsy part of Brooklyn. No street fights. No gangs.

You said it was three-quarters white, but most people didn't look at you twice. You said it was weird coming here, especially for the first year. You said the color of your skin was the first thing people saw. I even looked twice at you on that first day. I didn't tell you that. I'm not proud of it, but I remember thinking, What's a black kid doing here?

Ever since I hit puberty, my ass and my boobs are sometimes the first and only thing guys notice about me. They are body parts. I am not my body. I am me. And you are you. You've always made me feel that while you liked those parts, you liked me more. I hope I've made you feel the same. I hope you feel that I see you, your beautiful heart, your swirling soul.

I turn into our neighborhood and then I pass your street, and I can't help it, I look toward your truck sitting at the end of your driveway in front of your duplex.

"Hoo boy," I whisper to myself.

And a wave of sadness hits me. The first time you heard me say that, you repeated, "Hoo boy?" And then laughed, like you thought my hick expressions were charming. Thank you for that. Thanks for making me feel special. For making me feel like my insides were important.

As I ride down the street, I stare into people's homes, at shadows shifting behind curtains, at backs of heads watching TV, at all the houses with trucks parked in yards, duplexes filled with cigarette smoke, people who will fight to make sure things stay exactly how they are. They hate new ideas. They don't question anything. They see body parts and skin color, and they think what's on the outside is what matters.

But when people don't look at the inside of others and they don't look at the inside of themselves, they're missing practically everything.

10:20 PM Sunday, the news crew

When I glide down my street, I see a news van is parked in front of my house, *Komo 4 News* splashed on the side, and one of those satellite dishes stuck to the roof.

I jump off my bike and walk cautiously toward my driveway. Beth is sitting on her steps. Her porch light shines from behind. Her face is in shadow. She lifts up the hand holding her glowing cigarette. I lift my hand back.

Is the news crew inside my house, filming our disaster? Our windows are dark. Are they downstairs?

Then, the door of the van opens. A bleach-blond woman gets out, holding a mic. A sketchy, shaggy-haired cameraman follows right behind her holding a big-ass news camera. The streetlight shines down on them.

No way. She's the same damn woman who interviewed the friend of those brothers who drowned! Her hair is in the same perfect bob, and she's wearing too much makeup, especially eyeliner. It makes her look like a bloodhound. She takes short, purposeful steps toward me, in her tight suit. I could outrun her.

The cameraman turns on the light. It shines in my eyes. The reporter woman extends the mic toward my face.

"Jessie Doone? Are you the ex-girlfriend of Chris Kirk?"

Ex-girlfriend? The camera's little red light is on.

"No, I'm his girlfriend. Not ex-girlfriend."

"People were saying you broke up and then he went missing?" She keeps her mouth open, for dramatic effect. Her lipstick is bleeding into the wrinkles around her lips, giving her the look of someone who's been sucking on a bloody deer carcass.

"No, that's not true," I say. "We're together, I mean, we were taking a break, but we're still together."

Please don't put me on TV looking like this. I have no makeup, I'm wearing a helmet, and I'm not making any sense.

"What do you think's happened to him?"

I swallow. I could just walk right past her into my house. But then I think of the police, who "don't have the resources" to look for a kid like you. Johnson's cold blue eyes. How you winced when I put the ice pack on your ribs.

"I think he was attacked," I say. "He was jumped a few weeks ago in the same place, same time, same everything, because he's black."

She shoves the microphone into my face. "You really think this might be a hate crime?"

"Yes." My voice cracks.

Her fake eyelashes blink twice. "Well, why did those boys beat him up last time?" Like it's your fault.

"One of them, a guy named Dave Johnson, was jealous. He didn't get scouted, and he was mad at Chris because he did, so he beat the crap out of him." I'm trying to speak calmly, but all I can see is your swollen face that day at your house, and the words spill out. "It was five guys to one. They broke his ribs, beat his face up real bad."

"How awful." Her voice oozes fake sympathy. "But that doesn't mean it was racially motivated. Or a hate crime. It sounds like boys being boys."

"What?" No joke, I want to tell her where to shove that microphone, but I think of you, how you'd say that's not going to help, and I hold back. "That's not true. They called him the N-word. They've been harassing him for months. That's not boys being boys. That's racism, straight up. You can even talk to another guy, one of his best friends, Tim Pinochet? He's a member of the Lummi Nation? He said when he played the Heights, they were always saying things about him, too, when the ref couldn't hear. Guys like that, they want to put people in their place. Johnson couldn't stand it that Chris was better than him after playing for three years when he'd been playing his whole life. He told Chris he got scouted because he's black, not because he's good. He tried to tell him that he wasn't that special, even though he is." I blink away some tears. "He really is."

She makes sympathetic noises. "I'm sure he is, sweetie. But this is a pretty serious allegation. It sounds like they were jealous of Chris. You really think it was racism?" She's holding her breath, hoping I'll say something even more "shocking."

"Nobody ever thinks they're racist. Doesn't mean they're not going to lose their shit when a black guy's better than them in baseball, better at school, better in every way."

She's not buying it. "He's not exactly defenseless, is he?"

What the hell does that mean? Blood drips out of my eyes. Words shoot out of my mouth, like darts, as I rage at this woman about racism, about her racism in particular, about how she better not try and justify the horrible things they did to you.

Bloodhound Blondie waves her hands. "I didn't mean it like that."

I stop talking. Holy crap. *I didn't mean it like that.*

That's what I told myself when I called you an animal. I know about the history of black oppression, I know how white people treated African Americans like animals during slavery, and yet, somehow, this is the word that I grabbed. Like a kitchen knife resting on the table, I reached for it and I stabbed it into you. I should have apologized right away. I am so sorry.

I'm not better than this woman. I'm not better than anyone. In fact, I'm worse. Because I love you and I still called you an animal. I would have said it to a white guy—in fact, I *have* said it to white guys—but you aren't white, and I still said it. At that moment, it was the first word that entered my brain. Why was that? Why didn't I stop myself? Why didn't I say sorry?

If you come back, baby, I'll do anything to make it up to you.

"Phew," she says to my silence. "I'm just saying, logistically, could those boys have seriously harmed him, you know, because he's a physically large person?"

Beth walks up to the fence, grips it in her hands. "Jessie, you don't have to talk to them."

"He doesn't believe in violence. They could easily have thrown him in the river," I say, quietly, glancing at Beth.

Her eyes look sad. Her cigarette shakes in her hand.

"Jessie!" Steph is stumble-running across the street in her big-ass slippers. Yep. She's worried. "Where the fuck have you been?" Her hair is piled up on top of her head, and her makeup is a mess. "I've been calling and calling you," she says, ignoring the cameras. "I was so worried."

I hug her back and then look at the reporter. "I'm done."

"That's a wrap," she says, like *she* made the decision to stop. She turns to her camera guy. "We can still get it on the eleven o'clock if we hurry."

The scraggly-haired camera guy lowers the camera and looks in my eyes for the first time. "You take care." He gives me a quick smile, and then looks away, like he's embarrassed, and he follows the reporter lady, who's already taking fast steps back toward the white van.

"Thanks," I say to Beth, as we pass her. She nods and takes a drag from her cigarette.

We walk around the house. Steph wraps her arm around me. "What the hell were you doing down there so late?"

"Steph. I think he might be dead." That word is heavy.

She guides me toward the back door. "He's not dead."

"We have to find out if Dave Johnson can whistle," I say.

She looks at me like I'm crazy. "What are you talking about?"

11 PM Sunday, the news

Steph is pressed beside me on my old sofa, watching the television. The news is about to come on. We're scarfing down frozen pizza that I heated up in the microwave, and it's not bad. I feel like I haven't eaten in days.

"Lots of people can't whistle," Steph says.

"But it eliminates people."

That commercial you love with the babies dancing in the mirror comes on. I picture you dancing beside the TV, being a goof. You like to make fun of your awkward dance moves, your snaps, your stiff side to side. I love that about you. You say you love my wild dancing too. I hear your voice now: "Baby, you move your body in all the right ways."

The Komo 4 music plays. You're the lead story.

They have your graduation photo, probably from the website. The anchor, Betty Jenkins, is saying a bunch of nice things about you. You're a straight-A student, a popular kid, set to go to North

Carolina State University on a baseball scholarship. But she doesn't say what a good kisser you are.

My stomach is in knots. She cuts to a shot of our school and goes to that reporter woman who's speaking so fast, she sounds excited. "Christopher Kirk went missing on Friday night. He told his mother he was going for a run, but he didn't make it home."

Then I'm on that damn little TV screen with my helmet. You can't see my bike, so I look like the kind of person who needs a helmet.

Under my name, it says *Former Girlfriend* like a scarlet letter. Oh my god, I'm so mad. "Fuck you," I yell.

And then, I'm talking on that little TV screen—no, I'm raging on—about the racism in this town.

Oh my god. My eyes look wild. I wish I could put up a disclaimer that I haven't slept in forty hours. Maybe it's superficial of me—yes, it's definitely completely and totally superficial of me—but it's brutal watching myself on television. My voice is higher and I look fatter. They say a camera adds ten pounds, but it's more like thirty. I know you'd disagree, but the evidence is right there. My lip is quivering when I talk and truly, I can barely watch it. Do I really go around town looking like that? When it switches to Josh, I can finally breathe. My face is hot, no joke. He looks straight in the camera, calm and clear. "Chris, if you're listening to this, just call and let us know that you're okay."

Tamara is next. Telling her goddamn story about the fence. "He came by the barbecue, looked over the fence at me, and said he'd see me later." Her face screws up into a butthole, then she goes on, "Something must have happened."

Then it's Tim, and he backs me up, agreeing that people of color experience racism in this town. "I'm from the Lummi tribe." There's a cut, like they did some editing. "People call us names, sure." His face twists angrily. "No doubt Chris faced it too, worse even. Maybe he headed back to Brooklyn. I would have, if I were him. But maybe it's something else."

Then your dad is on that screen. He has the same jawline as you. Different eyes. I've always thought your dark eyes with those long eyelashes were just like your mom's. He says some stuff about how they're hoping for the best. If anyone has information, please come forward, and then he says, "Chris, son, if you're listening, we miss you. We love you. Please come home."

Oh man. You would have loved to hear your dad say that. You would have loved to be here to see him. I close my eyes and try to get some mind-reading action happening. *Get home fast. Your dad's here!*

Detective McFerson gives the number to call for tips and says anyone who wants to join the search tomorrow can meet at the parking lot out by Matheson at nine in the morning.

Now the reporter is talking into her microphone in front of my house, like they always do with the tragedy behind, only the tragedy apparently is our sad, ragged lawn with that damn tire.

"Police aren't saying they suspect foul play, but there have been accusations of racism in Pendling and he was recently attacked in the area where he went running." She finishes with some trite thing about how the search is continuing for one African American kid in this white community.

It bugs me how she said nothing about you, who you really are, how you're the best listener I've ever known, how you're kinder than most people deserve, how you have principles that you stand up to, even when it doesn't help you. She doesn't talk about how you smile every time I walk into a room or how you can run your hand along the curve of my neck and calm me down in the middle of a tirade. I need you to do that now. Oh my god, I miss you.

After you, there's a story about fighting in Syria. You were before Syria.

"You did it." Steph bumps me with her shoulder. "You got your search."

It's hard to feel reassured, though. I mean, we're searching for you in the friggin woods—after two days, you're either dead or nearly dead.

"Can you believe she said I was his ex-girlfriend?" I say.

"She's an idiot." Steph gives me a quick smile.

"Did I sound crazy? You can tell me. For real."

She takes in a deep breath and holds it. Then she says, "You sounded great. Don't worry. You did a good job."

I frown at her. Why is she acting like this?

"It'll help," she says. "I'm just worried, like, how people will react about the racist stuff. You know how people are about this town."

"Whatever." Maybe she thinks I looked like a freak, but if it helps, I don't care. I'd do anything to get you back.

Steph lets out a big old yawn, stretching her arms.

"You should go home," I say. "Sleep."

"Nah," she says. "I'm staying here."

She's the twelve-hour-sleep queen. "Go," I say. "You'll be miserable if you don't get your sleep. I'm fine."

"You sure?" She grabs my shoulders and stares into my eyes. I put on my most "fine" face. Finally, she says, "Okay, I believe you. I'm going." She throws her arms around me, squeezes my guts out. "You call me if you need me—for anything. I'm leaving my phone on." Then she steps over the mounds of crap to exit my house.

But when she's gone, I miss her. I'm not fine. It's too quiet without her. I look down at my phone and read a text from Josh.

He writes: Chris is going viral

12:11 AM Monday, trolls

Holy crap. I stare down at the screen. Josh is right. Social media is going crazy. All the online news sites are talking about you. You're trending.

I get another message from Josh: Our website crashed

Me: Oh no

Josh: Ok now . . . I had to up the hosting

The headlines are: "Missing Black Teen Athlete in Small White Town," "Superstar Athlete Missing," "African American Baseball Star Feared Dead," "Missing Black Teen Suffered Harassment."

I look at my email and the protest organizer, Steve, has emailed me back and he said he contacted everyone he knew. They're tweeting about you. He's going to come out and help search for you too.

Are you somewhere looking at the coverage online? Do you see #chriskirk? You're famous. But you got lots more moments of fame ahead of you. This isn't your ten minutes of fame.

I start tweeting all the amazing things about you, so there's more than you being the possible victim of a hate crime. You are so much more than what these people may have done to you.

I look at my notifications. It's exploding. I got, like, a hundred retweets, and a bunch of follows. I read through the notifications. My gut clenches. Some people are saying horrible things. About you. About me.

My heart hammers in my chest. I feel scared. I feel unsafe in my own home. I don't understand. How can they climb into my computer, say these things about me and you? They don't even know us.

Josh: You should go offline

Me: Why are people like this?

Me: They can fuck themselves

Josh: You can't win this

I type back to the trolls and call them racist pigs, horrible human beings, your-mother insults. I'm not really taking the high road, I admit it, but they are slimeballs. They type back. It gets more vicious. I think of how you said violence begets violence, hate begets hate.

My phone rings.

It scares me so bad, I let out a short scream.

Fuck. I reach for my phone. My hands are shaking. I look down at the screen. It's Steph. I push TALK.

"I was just thinking"—her voice is all high-pitched and scared, like she knows—"maybe you want to sleep over at my house tonight?"

I haven't slept at her house in ages, and it feels weird. Even when we were younger, most of the time she slept at my house. As disgusting as it is, my house has always been the good house.

I look down at my laptop, at people, mostly white men, who are writing all kinds of horrible racist and sexist things to me. If you read what they're saying, you're going to want to give up those nonviolent principles. Part of me wants to beg her to come back, spend the night here with me, but she sounds scared enough already.

"Steph, I told you, I'm fine."

"Okay," she says. "But I'm leaving my phone on."

We hang up and I look down at the responses. At one in particular.

Yur dead

If you were here, we'd laugh about the spelling, but you're not. So it's kind of scary. At least these people don't know where I live. I'm more worried about my backpack. If that whistler guy returns, he can see my ID.

Our home phone rings. I think it's Steph, so I pick it up. "I told you, I'm fine."

"Bitch." It's a low growl.

I slam the receiver down.

Holy crap. Our phone is unlisted. I jump up. My mom isn't much for comforting me, but she's here at least. How did he get my phone number? Is that the whistler? What if he's outside? What if he found my backpack, and knows where I live? The goddamn keys are in it.

I sneak up the stairs, into my mom's room.

My heart is thumping. I want to wake her up. I want to crawl in next to her, like I used to do, when I was little. I want to snuggle in next to her warm body and breathe in the smell of baby powder. I want her to tell me it's going to be okay.

"Mom?" I whisper.

She's not moving. What if she's dead?

My voice sirens out of me. "Mom?"

She groans, shifts in her sleep, rolling under her sheet. But she doesn't wake up. Must have taken sleeping pills.

Outside, a car alarm starts to beep. It's the neighbor's car on the street. Is someone out there? We live on a dead-end street. Why would anyone be out there now? What if the whistler guy breaks into our house? He'd probably kill himself trying to kill us. Well, he'd kill my mom. She's a sleeping duck. But I could just hide under a pile of crap.

Dad said he was going to leave the gun, that it would be in the closet, in the back, on the right-hand side. The closet is blocked by stacks of clothes and linens higher than my head.

It's hard to see in here. The light from the hall creeps into the room, but all these piles block it. I heave stuff away from the closet doors and finally crack them open.

I reach up to the top shelf of the closet. Around the back. To the far right side. My hand touches something hard and cold. It scrapes against the shelf. Slides into my palm.

It's heavier than I remember. Cold heavy metal.

I ease out of the room, holding the gun in front of my body, and close the door behind me. I look around for something to block the door. There are a bunch of my grandma's old pots at the entrance to the kitchen. I place the gun on the floor and bring the pots in front of Mom's door to block it, just in case. I make a mental note to move them in the morning.

The gun is back in my hand. I dodge the piles leading to the stairs, more of my grandma's stuff. I round some chairs piled up on top of a coffee table, keeping an eye on the floor. Don't want to trip and shoot myself by accident.

The stairs are blocked with large black plastic bags filled with old recycling and non-food garbage. The front door is still locked. But I don't know about the back door. If the guy found my keys, he could be here now.

The car alarm is still blasting outside—sounds like a fire truck.

I make my way, slowly, down the steps, holding the gun out from my body, this grizzly bear of mechanical things. Guns don't kill, Dad said. People do. It's just metal. Until it bares its metal teeth and rips your neck out.

Dad would want me to protect myself. But you'd hate it.

I slide around the mountain of stuff, half of it from my grandma when she passed away, over ten years old now. Mom didn't want to throw anything out.

Finally, I make it downstairs. I'm breathing hard.

That damn car alarm.

I climb over the magazines in the hallway and slide my way

through the living room, to the back door. Okay. It's still locked. Nobody's in the house, not yet. I examine Dad's gun. It quivers in my hand. Must have been two years since he took me out to the firing range. I have to find the safety. It's not the kind of thing you want to look for when the scary man is rushing you.

I lift it up. There.

Dad's deep voice grunts in my ear: "Click the safety off and hold the gun with two hands to steady it. It's about balance and control. Squeeze the entire gun, don't just pull the trigger, squeeze it like a chicken's neck."

I don't want to have to shoot anyone. Have you been rubbing off on me? I don't even want to look at this thing.

My huge black purse is hanging on the hooks you put up by the door. It's safe, relatively, and I'll be able to get the gun fast, if I need it. I lower the gun down inside the purse.

My heart is fluttering. I listen to the car alarm and stare at my purse. The gun claws at the insides, growls. It feels so alive.

And then, there's another sound, a real sound, the sound of gravel crunching on our walkway. It's too loud to be a raccoon.

I step back, trip, and then, I'm falling backward. My hand dives down onto a pile of rope mixed with some papers and the rabbit bottle from when we were going to get a rabbit but we didn't. I lie there, clutching the rabbit bottle, like it can save me.

Another crunch. Yep, that's the gravel. And there's a dragging sound too. It is the sound of a body being dragged.

I pull myself out of the ropes and rush at my black purse. The gate squeals open and slams shut. There is a definite dragging noise. I dive my hand down into my purse.

The gun climbs into my fingers. I grip it. Slide it out. Hold it with two hands. Move by the door. Dad's words: "Squeeze the trigger, don't pull it, squeeze it like a chicken's neck."

The dragging, oh god, the dragging. The doorknob rattles. Holy crap. They're trying to break in.

I unlock the safety on the gun. My hand is shaking. I raise the gun up. Point it at the door.

"Who is it?" I scream.

12:36 AM Monday, my back door

"Let me in!" Steph's annoyed voice.

"Oh my god." I put on the safety, shove the gun back in my purse, and blow out long and slow through my mouth. Holy shit. I open the door. Steph is clinging to her giant, heavy comforter and a big duffel bag filled with her stuff—that's what was dragging across the gravel.

"You freaked the crap out of me," I say.

"Why?" She marches past me with her comforter train.

"You're creeping around, dragging something. What do you think?"

She gives me a look like I'm whacked. "Okay, it was a bag?"

"It sounded like a body." I smirk. "What do you have in that thing? Are you moving in?"

She barks out a laugh. "Maybe."

"Did you set off that car alarm?" I ask.

She shakes her head. "Nope. That was going off already." She opens her mouth like she's going to say something else, but then she doesn't.

I let out a sigh of relief. "Okay, clearly, I'm freaking out here." I don't tell her about how I almost shot her through the door.

"I just looked online—people are such dicks. You think I'm going to leave you here by yourself, you cray-cray. You should have called me."

"I wanted you to get some sleep."

"I can't sleep thinking about all the hate you're getting. Anyway, I have to be here in case anyone eggs your house or something. I am a human shield!" She reaches her arms out and stands in front of me as if she's blocking bullets.

I smile. I'm grateful for Steph, that's my first thank-you for the night. Number two: grateful she wasn't a killer. Number three: grateful for the gun.

Steph glances at the door, like she's worried now too. The car alarm has beeped off.

"What?"

"Nothing..." Steph gives me her big old smile, showing all her teeth, which means she wants something. "Maybe you could make some cookies?" She blinks her big brown eyes and bats her eyelashes, bunching up the comforter around her waist.

"You came here for cookies?"

"Damn straight. Chocolate chip. And then I'm sleeping here. No arguing. Or I can make the cookies if you don't want to."

"No, I got it." It's something to do at least. I reach into my plastic box for the ingredients and send you a sugar-powered message: *Making your favorite cookies. Think: hot, melted chocolate chips.*

I dump the cookie mix into my bowl and reach into the fridge for eggs. "After this, I'm out of eggs." Sadness twists inside me, ropes around my intestines, squeezes them like a wet towel.

"You gotta go shopping."

"Chris always drives me. He better get home soon." I add oil and eggs to the dry ingredients. Don't tell her how the thought of grocery shopping makes me ill. We've been doing it together for the last eight months, like we're already married.

"You should have considered that before you went on this break."

"Yep, along with a lot of other things." Oh gosh. The lump in my throat feels like an orange shoved in there.

Steph winces. "I'm sorry, I keep saying the wrong thing."

I sniff. "Don't worry about it. If you can't say the wrong thing around me, who can you say the wrong thing around?"

"You'd never use a guy for his car."

"Nope," I say. "Would you?"

She laughs. "Um, yes."

That's so true. "It's nice having him drive me around, but sometimes I like to ride my bike. It's my only exercise."

"Cycling hurts my crotch."

"You need a better seat," I say.

"It's boring."

"Not if you dip in and out of traffic." I slide the first batch of cookies in the toaster oven and look over at Steph stretched out on the sofa. "Cycling makes me feel alive, you know?"

"Until you're dead."

I shrug.

"I like to sit on my ass and have someone else drive."

After the first batch of cookies are done, I put two on a plate for Steph, and then I think of how you always try to help people who are sad and the only person I know who's worse off than me is Beth and maybe she'd like some cookies too. So I put the remaining two on a plate.

"I'll be right back," I tell Steph, and take the cookies outside.

Soon as I'm outside, I think of the whistler. I hurry around the side of the house and open the neighbor's gate. Sure hope the dogs are inside. I knock on her door.

I don't hear anything inside. I'm thinking, Oh shit, this is a mistake, I mean, the lights are on, but it's after midnight. And what about the whistler? Then she calls in her croaky voice: "Hold on." She's unlocking the door. Then it's her head in the crack and the dogs are going crazy behind her.

"I brought you warm cookies." I feel like a goddamn Girl Scout.

"You brought me cookies?" Her prematurely wrinkled face twists, as if it doesn't know what to do with this news.

I hold up the plate.

"Thank you." She reaches a skinny hand through the door and takes the plate. "I can't—the dogs."

"No worries," I say. "Just dropping them off. Bye."

I hurry out the yard, feel kind of stupid. Don't know why I did that.

Steph is on the sofa, eating her first cookie. She's grabbed herself a glass of milk and put the next batch in the toaster oven. "You take them to your neighbor?"

"Yeah." I make a face. "It was weird."

"It was nice," Steph corrects me. She picks up a cookie from the plate and holds it out to me. "You want?"

I drop down next to her and take the cookie. I remember the last time I made them. You were on my sofa, stretched out, your feet over the end, saying you always wanted a woman who could cook, and I was telling you how sexist that was, that I wanted a man who could cook, and you laughed and said, "Done." It made me happy, you saying that.

I look at Steph and sigh. "I'm worried."

She nods and sucks her lip. A tear rolls down her face. "Fuck," she says, wiping it away. "I told myself I'm not crying, not in front of you."

"You can cry."

"I care about him too, you know?"

I hug her. "Thanks. All we can do is wait. Maybe he's okay."

Steph sniffs and then curls up on her side with her thick comforter and closes her eyes. I do not close my eyes. My brain is spinning. I'm thinking about Dave Johnson and your phone being turned on and those trolls and how I'm going to be a basket case tomorrow and I should sleep so I don't lose it and also how nice my best friend's feet feel on my leg. Sometimes what you need isn't always what you ask for, and it takes a good friend to know that.

8:00 AM Monday, the human flamingo

Josh is outside. He's picking me up in his old blue Toyota. When
I run out the back door, I pause. It's colder than I expected, and I
think about going back in, because all I'm wearing is a T-shirt, my
pink shorts, and my black hoodie that matches your black hoodie.
But Josh is waiting, and it'll warm up throughout the day—it is
June, after all.

I jump into the passenger seat, my running shoes bashing
against the empty caffeine drinks. In his car, the heat is hissing.
He takes off.

I've never been in his front seat. This is where you sit. Normally, I sit in the back, next to his smelly workout clothes, my knees
crammed into my chest, and I watch you, slouching like a paper bag
with the top folded down so your head doesn't hit the roof.

Your absence screams in this car.

We head down the highway. It's search day. Holy crap. It's real.

I gaze along the side of the road for any sign of you. I don't know
what I'm looking for. Feet?

I spot a black garbage bag filled with something, and it makes me think about the last time you let me drive your truck. I swerved on the highway because of a full garbage bag and you said I should have driven straight over it. Not worth hitting a car. But I said, "What if it's got a dog in it?"

You repeated, "Dog?" Like that was just crazy.

But I've heard people do that. They put the dogs they don't want in garbage bags and toss them out of their car on the highway, so I always think of that when I see a garbage bag with something in it. You shook your head, laughing, and said I was being dramatic.

Maybe this is *dramatic* of me, but what if someone put you in a garbage bag and threw you on the side of the road? You could be in that garbage bag we just passed. After I told you about the dog thing, you said you'd never look at a garbage bag the same way.

If you don't show up, I'm not going to look at anything the same way.

The Matheson Trail parking lot is blocked off with yellow tape this morning. Josh parks on the side of the road. We step over the tape. I'm worried, like why is this here now? It wasn't here last night. Did they find something?

A search and rescue vehicle is parked inside, along with two men wearing red jackets with SAR on the back. One of them is old and grizzled, and the other is around our age, tall, good-looking. We walk through the parking lot and they watch us. I'm worried they're going to stop us. I need to know if the whistler took my backpack.

Josh calls out, "We can go on the trail, right?"

The old guy calls back, "Go for it."

"We meet here at nine?"

"You bet," he says.

Josh waves and we head down Matheson Trail. I guess they're just blocking off the parking lot on account of it being the place everyone's meeting.

When we get to our spot, Josh strides right past it. You never told him? I told Steph. Not that it wasn't special, but that's how girls are; we talk.

"It's here," I say. "This is where we always go."

He stops. There's this flash in his eyes, like TMI. Maybe he thinks it's gross to come to our spot, I don't know. Did you ever notice how he looks away every time we kiss? It must be hard being around us all the time when he has no one. When you get home, let's start Project Girlfriend for Josh. If he wasn't so shy, he could get anyone.

"There's no trail," he says.

"It's hidden."

That whistler guy, who may or may not be a killer, found it. I made a noise, but still, it was like he knew exactly where to go. Did he follow you here?

I duck under Saber and hurry toward the muddy bank. I look over the edge. My backpack is resting on the dirt, a few feet from the edge of the river.

"It's here!" I jump off the bank and pick it up. Something in the water catches my eye. It's long and dark and floating just under the surface.

I scream.

Josh runs up. "What?"

It's a log. For god's sake. Josh's face is white. "Sorry," I say. "I'm just seeing things."

"What are all those prints?" he says.

A bunch of shoeprints huddle around where I'm standing. "These? I guess they're mine from last night."

"What about that one?" He points to one about twenty feet away. "It's different. Bigger at the front."

I didn't go over there.

There's a single half print, just the front of a shoe. Nothing around it. Which is weird. My shoeprints have made a mess in the sand. But the lonely print is set apart, and there's just one of them. A one-legged man. A human flamingo.

Could it be yours?

If you were pushed, you'd land with one foot and then the momentum would carry you forward into the cold, churning water.

I see Johnson shoving you. Your foot landing. Your body flying forward into the rushing water. Your arms reaching out to stop yourself. And then landing with a splash, the current dragging you away, pulling you toward the rapids.

I imagine you in the water and my own hand diving after you. For some reason, my arm is very long. My fingers tighten around your cold wrist. I try to pull you back, but I can't. The river is too strong.

"We should tell the detective." Josh slides down the bank, careful to go around the prints, even mine.

I blink, coming back to reality. Good god. "It can't be his," I say. "That print's too small."

"It's bigger at the front." Josh touches the edge of the print.

"Not as big as Chris's shoe," I say. "It's barely bigger than mine."

"It's not a complete print."

"Maybe it's from a fly fisherman. Or one of those guys cutting weeds. Any one of them could have left it."

Josh stares at it. "I think we should tell the detective."

"Fine."

He makes the call. The detective says he'll be here in twenty minutes. We sit down on the grass and wait. The river is flowing faster than normal. There's been more melt-off this year.

A high-pitched caw comes from behind. I turn to look. It's Little Man. He's cocking his head to one side. I caw back.

Josh looks. "Oh!" He jerks in surprise.

Little Man flutters toward the bush.

"Don't startle him. His mom and dad are probably around, watching. If they think he's in danger, they'll dive at us." I make another quiet caw. Little Man hobbles back. "You remember me, Little Man?"

"Um, do you know this crow?" Josh asks.

"I know his name, don't I?"

He turns up the side of his mouth, attempting a smile. "He's so small."

"He's a fledgling," I say. "The parents move them to different spots every night until they can fly. It keeps them safe."

Little Man hops closer. Blinks up at Josh. Cocks his head.

"He likes you," I say.

"He's beautiful," Josh whispers.

"Crows are one of the only birds that recognize human faces. If you get on the bad side of one of them, they'll hunt you down. But if you get on the good side"—I click my tongue—"they'll be your friend for life."

Josh gives me this strange look like he's trying to figure me out. Guess he doesn't know I'm a nature nerd. You're always surprised by what I know too.

"Did Chris tell you I'm going to apply for a program at UW to study conservation?"

"No way, really?" He sounds surprised. Maybe he doesn't believe me.

I like talking about the program, but will I do it? Sometimes I worry I won't.

We sit there for a while longer, and then we hear fast footsteps on the trail. Very different from the guy I heard last night. "Hello?" The detective's accent makes it more like "Hollo."

I'd feel so much better if I knew who the whistler was.

"We're over here," Josh calls.

We stand up and Little Man hops into the bush.

The detective moves into the clearing. He's wearing a big police rain jacket. I glance at the sky—looks like it's going to rain. Which is great because I'm just wearing a hoodie and my pink shorts. He claps me on the back. "You did a good job. Telling the media what you did. We got more resources now."

So it took a seventeen-year-old to do that? "No problem."

He gazes around our little clearing. "This is the spot where you and Chris like to come?"

I nod and look away, embarrassed. It feels odd showing it to an adult, like, Yep, we did it, right there.

"Where's the print?" he says.

I point down and he jumps off the bank. "And those?" He points at my mess of scared prints by the river.

"That's where I hid last night, when that guy was looking for me."

"You didn't go over by the other print?"

I shake my head. He bends down, takes a look.

"The print's too small to be his," I say. "He has a size eleven foot."

"I'll get someone to take measurements, maybe we can make a mold." He looks up at the darkening sky. "If we're lucky, before the rain." He sighs. "Let's just hope it's not a match."

"He's not in the river," I say.

He gives me a long, sad look, like maybe he feels sorry for me. "We'll figure out what happened, Jessie. Don't worry."

Ain't No River Wide Enough

The last time I was in the river was a month ago. It was flowing real fast, even then, on account of the warmer temperatures in the spring, and I knew that, but I was trying to impress you with how fierce and daring and wild I was.

You called, "Hey, tangerine girl, come out. I've got something for you." Like you were nervous. I loved making you nervous.

"I got something for *you*." I sprayed the silty water up from my mouth. "Why don't you come in and get it?"

You waved your hand in that patient way of yours, with that smile, like you were too cool to get wet.

"There's nothing better than doing it in the river," I said, even though the truth is I'd never done it in the river. Or in any other body of water. Only with you. On land.

"Too cold for the dude," you said.

"The dude?" I laughed, cause that was weird for you to say "the dude." It wasn't a thing you said. "Come on! It's warm." I splashed you. "See?"

"Aah!" you screamed. "That's cold." Your dimple twitched on your cheek.

I climbed out, half-naked, and grabbed your arm. "Come on! I dare you." Your foot slid on some mud, and your eyes flew open, a raw fear that I'd seen before, when kids are drowning. You were terrified.

"What? Are you scared?"

You let out an uncomfortable laugh. "Hell yeah."

"But you know how to swim," I said. You'd come to the pool a couple times. I'd seen you doing your head-up crawl. It didn't make sense.

"I don't like rivers," you said. "They're creepy. The current. The undertow. All those weeds." You made a face.

"I can't believe you never told me that."

You shrugged. "I didn't want you to laugh at me."

"I would never laugh." I grinned, unable to stop myself.

You pointed at me. "You're laughing."

"You are such a city boy," I said. "What if I was on the other side of the river and the only way you could get me is if you swam across?"

"I'd do it." You grabbed my hand then and you sang that Marvin Gaye song: *Ain't no mountain high enough, ain't no valley low enough, ain't no river wide enough, to keep me from getting to you, babe.*

It made me grin, I couldn't help it. You and your Marvin Gaye. "You'd probably go find a boat to cross that river."

And you laughed. "You know it."

9 AM Monday, Matheson Trail parking lot

Above, dark clouds are rumbling in. This morning when I left home, it was just a little cloudy, no big deal. I'm never much of a planner. You're the one who checks the weather. At least the weather finally feels appropriate.

Josh and I walk slowly up to the back of a huge crowd. You wouldn't believe how many people have shown up. I count over two hundred. And school buses are still driving up. Josh told me the principal said kids can skip school.

The search and rescue guys are huddled up in their red jackets beside the red SAR truck. There's an ambulance here now, and some cop cars too.

It feels surreal. Like one of your races, except nobody has on numbers and people are more serious. Josh's mom, dad, and brother slide in beside Josh—I say hi, but I feel kind of awkward. It's just so weird being around them without you here, too. His mom gives me a smile. "How you holding up?"

Her sympathy almost does me in. "Okay." My eyes heat up. Do not cry. I suck on my lip.

Most of the people here now are adults, but the buses are still arriving with kids from school. A lot of the people in their twenties look like Seattle/Portland types, nose rings and dyed hair, and all shades of brown and white, the kind of mix we never see around here, but I wish we did.

All your friends are here. Tim, Tamara, and the rest of them are standing at the front, like they want to win the race to find you. But Steph isn't coming. Spiders and all that—you know how she is. I told her it was fine, I'd be with Josh. She helped with the posters and she's been posting stuff online. It's not like she doesn't care.

I kind of thought Michael would show up, but he hasn't texted, nothing. Some people suck when times get tough. They just disappear. That happened when my mom got sick too. Her friends disappeared.

Your mom and Raffa are staying by the phone, in case you call. Your dad's coming, though—that's what your mom said—I don't see him yet.

The guys on your regular baseball team are wearing their white-and-black leather baseball jackets. But not all the guys on your travel team are here. Not Johnson.

I feel a drip of rain on my cheek. And then another. Why didn't I wear a rain coat?

A strong hand claps me on the back, startles me. I turn around.

206

It's Steve, full of that fiery organizer energy, even here. "Hey, Jessie. You got a good crowd."

My eyes tear up and I gush, "Thanks so much for everything."

"No problem." He holds out his arms, gives me the warmest hug, and then he clasps Josh's hand in this special kind of handshake. How do guys learn those things? They hardly know each other. It's like a special handshake club.

An older search and rescue guy moves to the front, facing the crowd. He plants his feet apart, like an old oak rooted to the ground, and raises an orange bullhorn. Anyone who was talking shuts up real fast.

"Thanks for coming, everyone. My name is Bill and I'm in charge of this operation. We believe Chris Kirk ran down here on Friday night. Dogs caught his scent here. We're going to head out in both directions, off the trail."

I thought I heard dogs yesterday. They caught your trail? Ugh.

He points a thick finger up at the dark clouds. "We're going to hand out some rain capes." Just as he says that, the rain starts coming down harder, not the normal wispy rain of the Northwest, but hard pellets beating on my head, my shoulders.

I almost wore your jacket today, but I didn't want people to stare. It's in my closet still. This morning, I smelled it, and man, it was nice, that deep salty sweet smell of you. But don't worry, I'm not going to turn into some smelling perv. Unless you don't come back soon. Then I might. The first thing I'm going to do when you get back is smell you. Or maybe kiss you and then smell you. You'll laugh that beautiful laugh of yours, my nose buried deep in your neck.

A familiar voice slides up next to me. "Hey."

My heart squeezes. My eyes cloud up. It's Steph.

"You're here."

"I wouldn't miss it." Steph gives me a big old kiss on my cheek, then wraps an arm around me, opening her jacket, so we can share. It shields my back from the pouring rain, and even though I'm still soaked, her warm body next to mine makes all the difference.

Can you believe she came?

Finally, the capes get to us. I slide away from the warmth of Steph's body and pull the cape over my head.

"Hey." Josh pokes me in the shoulder. "Isn't that Chris's dad?"

A lone African American man is moving up past us, at the far right, dressed in black in a sea of yellow. Must be your dad. He looks like you. Almost as tall.

He's wearing a long black trench coat over what looks like black slacks, and nice boots, now dirty with mud. Is he really going to search for you in those? Maybe he has all kinds of dressy boots.

He stops next to some kids from school who barely know you. Someone passes him a yellow cape, and he takes it, ducking his head under the plastic, says thank you. He has a quiet way. Reminds me of you.

I heard your mom talking to him on the phone once. She was in the kitchen and I was going in to get a drink, and I heard her ask him if he was taking his medicine. And then I guess he said he wasn't because she got mad at him and said it didn't matter if it made his brain fuzzy, he needed to take it, or go on a new one. And so, I turned around and didn't get the water, and I didn't tell you about it either. Maybe I should have.

Search and Rescue Bill lifts his megaphone and shouts out instructions. "We're going to walk straight through the low growth, off the trail. Everyone needs to walk two arm lengths from one another, like this." He stands next to the young guy, and they both reach their arms out so their fingers are nearly touching. "Be careful of where you step. We're looking for clothing. Fabric on a branch. Something caught on a tree. Anything. Even if it looks like garbage."

The rain is really coming down now and he has to squint through it. "If you see something, put your hand up and we'll come to you with an evidence bag." He waves a zipper-type bag in the air. "Don't pick it up. We will pick up the items."

He holds up a black iPhone, like the one I bought you for Christmas. It's getting wet, which bothers me. Is he about to say no listening to music? A bunch of people have their headphones in.

"We think he was holding a phone. This is really what we're most interested in finding. Even something as small as an ear bud." He lifts the headphones in the air; they swing around like a lasso.

I know how to spot stuff that's out of place. If there's one thing being a lifeguard has trained me to do, it's this.

SAR Bill shouts in his megaphone. "If you see some ground that looks disturbed, maybe some blood, or something dark brown on the ground, let us know. We'll check it out. But we're not searching for a body."

A dramatic gasp escapes out of my mouth, and a middle-aged woman in front of Josh turns around and squints at me, like she's waiting for me to freak right out. Steph pats me on the back and Josh gives me a worried look.

Did that man really say *body*? Yes, he did.

Steph whispers, "Nobody would blame you for leaving."

"I'm fine," I say.

The Search and Rescue guys put us into rows—each row is supposed to have twenty people, but they don't. I count them because I'm compulsive like that. There are eleven rows, each with between eighteen and twenty-four people.

The first row moves forward, into the woods, in the direction of the Pitt. The search and rescue people didn't tell people how to scan. It's a technique, the zigzag scan, and I worry people will miss something important. Search and Rescue Bill sends off the next row. There's a gap of about fifteen feet between each row.

Tim, Tamara, Becky, and their group are in the second row, behind your dad. I bet Tamara has already introduced herself and told him how you looked over the fence and said you'd see her later.

When it's our turn to go, I step forward into the woods, two arm lengths from Steph, two arm lengths from Josh. Soon we're passing our spot and I can see the cops in there. Blue uniforms flash through the mossy trees. Your dad steps out of the line to talk to them.

Josh pushes off his hood. "I can't see with this."

The rain flattens his curly hair. His parents plod along beside him, steady, glancing over at me every now and then. His brother, Billy, looks totally miserable, like he doesn't want to be here. I guess none of us do. But we're here for you, all of us. It's cool that you have so many people who care about you. I wonder how many people would show up for me.

The brush gets denser. Steph is avoiding anything spiderish. Walking around the creepy bushes with webs. She pauses to wipe her eyes—her makeup is dripping down her face, typical Steph, and I love it a little. She makes a face, then bends down and pulls her socks over her pants.

"Thanks," I whisper.

She nods and sucks in a shaky breath. It's scary down here for her, and not just because of the spiders. I never told you what happened.

We were thirteen.

We were walking along the path, past the Pitt, and we ran into some older guys drinking by their campfire. It was after school, not the kind of day you expect to see anyone. One of them grabbed Steph's arm and said she was pretty.

She tried to yank her arm away, but he wasn't letting go. I don't remember much about him except that he had a Hawks cap on and he was missing a tooth, but he wasn't homeless or anything, just randomly didn't have a tooth. Steph struggled like a little weasel, but she couldn't get away. He pressed her hard against a tall birch tree. She was so much smaller than him, but still, she spat in his face. He slammed her backward. That's when I knew we were in big trouble.

"Jessie, run!" she screamed.

I was a quiet kid back then, not really a fighter, but I wasn't about to leave her. I ran up and kicked the guy hard in the shin. That's what my dad always told me to do: kick him in the shin, not the balls, and then jab him in the neck. I didn't jab him in the neck. The guy doubled over, and we took off.

Steph and I hid behind a rotten log, wrapped around each other. The guy searched in the woods, calling us little bitches (that's why I hate that word). His friends were laughing, like it was hilarious. That's the thing I hear when I remember our terror.

As we were hiding, a spider crawled across Steph's face. She started to scream, but I gripped her mouth hard so he wouldn't hear.

Her face shook under my fingers. Later, she told me all she could think was *brown recluse spider* because I'd just told her that they were the only dangerous spiders in our area, that if they bit someone, that part of the person's body would rot off, but she shouldn't worry because they liked to hang out in rotten wood. I'd meant it to be reassuring. I didn't know we were about to find ourselves in a situation near rotten wood with a spider crawling across her face.

Eventually, the guy gave up, headed back to his fire, and we ran home.

She never came down here again. That's why she hates spiders. So it's a big deal she came today.

The rain picks up, bangs on my plastic-hooded head, like a little kid on a piano, random, incessant. We move through the woods. It smells of wet dirt and pine needles. Ahead, the people in yellow capes are spread out, bright flashes of yellow in a forest darkened by rain.

Steph takes a big step over a fallen log and swerves to avoid a web that looks like a spiderweb, but is not. She lets out a short scream. People turn to look. She waves her hand, like it's fine.

"Most of the webs are from tent caterpillars," I say. "Not spiders."

"Don't say that word." She shakes her leg like she has the heebie-jeebies.

I'm shivering. The skin on my legs is frozen. My running shoes are drenched. My teeth start to chatter.

"You want my jacket?" Josh whispers.

I shake my head. "I'm okay." That would be weird, right? Even though I'm cold, I don't want to be blanketed in another guy's smell, not even Josh's.

"Hey!" A man shouts out in the row behind us, sticking up his hand, victorious, finding something I did not.

A SAR guy puts the object in one of those clear zipper bags, which we normally use for sandwiches. Looks like the outside of a black iPhone. I wonder if they know your phone has your initials. I bought it for you for Christmas with my guarding money and I got it engraved. It was your first Christmas present; when I found out you'd never got one before, when you were a Jehovah's Witness, I wanted it to be special.

"What is it?" I ask Josh.

He shakes his head. Doesn't know.

We search for another hour and then there's lunch and Josh's parents leave and guess what? His mom brings me back some sweatpants before she goes to work. It's like she handed me a million dollars. Steph shields me with her jacket and I change. They are so soft, so warm.

We keep searching all afternoon while it continues to rain.

When the woods open up to the river, I do a lifeguard scan across the water. See your arm reach up. Your body pulled away fast with the current, the hand disappearing behind the trees, and into the rapids. Thanks, brain.

I keep walking.

A middle-aged woman with dark hair and a big-ass mole on her nose in front of Josh keeps sniffling and whimpering. I want her to shut the hell up.

She kicks at a pistachio bag, still half filled with nuts. My stomach clenches. The receipt in your wallet. I pick it up and half the nuts fall to the ground. Josh's eyes widen. I told him about the receipt.

I put up my hand to tell the SAR people, but then there's a shout.

Up ahead, in the middle of the yellow capes, a man with long hair yells, "There's blood!"

Everyone moves forward in this big surge, and Bill shouts out for everyone to stay in formation. The search and rescue guys and the cops huddle in a circle around the area, next to a mossy cedar tree. They look like they've found a body part and they're trying to hide it.

Detective McFerson slides on a blue surgical glove, bends down, and scrapes at the ground. When he lifts up his hand, I see something brownish red on the plastic. I clench the pistachio bag. It crinkles in my hand. Nuts dribble down around my feet.

The younger search and rescue guy takes this little shovel, like the kind you use to plant flowers in a flower garden, and he scoops the dirt covered in blood into one of the zipper bags. Are they digging you out?

My stomach twists. I gag.

"Jessie?" Steph's voice stretches toward me.

I have a brief, sure moment of knowledge that I'm going to puke. And then it comes. All my lunch. The ham. The cheese. The bread. The cookies.

People leap out of the way. I'm pretty sure I got the hiking boots of the man in front of me, but he didn't say anything. Mostly, it lands on the tall grass, and on the leaves of a nearby bush, steaming in the cool air.

"Are you okay?" Josh says.

I'm hanging my head down, trying to get my hair to cover my face. Are the camera crews still here? People are murmuring. Someone is sobbing, a woman.

"Jessie?" Josh rests his hand on my back. "Come on."

I wipe my slimy mouth with my sleeve and stand up, blurry-eyed.

"I can take you home," Josh says.

"No, I'm fine."

"Come on, hon." Steph's fingers curl around my arm. "This is stupid."

"I'm staying." I pull my arm back and she looks surprised, like she actually thought I might come. "You can go. I'm not going."

"Are you kidding me?" She plants her hands on her hips. "I'm not going if you're not going."

Detective McFerson tromps over the bushes toward us, through the crowd. The glove is off, thank god. He stops a few feet away. "Are you sick, Jessie?"

"Not anymore. It's all out of me—it's on the ground." And on that guy's shoe.

"You're certain?"

"Is it his blood?" My eyes fill up.

"No, I don't think so," he says, and then, softly, "I think you should go home, Jessie."

"I don't want to go," I say, a bit loudly. My voice squeals. Maybe I sound like I'm about to go bat-shit crazy because people turn to look. I make my voice even out. Steady now. "I need to be here. It's just the shock, you know? I heard someone say *blood*."

He gestures back at the SAR guys, who are digging up dirt and putting it in bags. "It's probably from an animal."

"Oh."

He glances at the pistachio bag crunched in my hand. "What's that?"

"I found it, right there. I saw he had a receipt in his wallet?" Maybe he doesn't know about the receipt. "He bought pistachios on Friday."

"That's right." He puts on a glove. "Good job, Jessie." He takes the bag from me and puts it in an evidence bag.

Above us, there's the crackle of lightning. Everyone looks up. The detective walks back to the search and rescue team and they talk in low, anxious voices.

3:34 PM Monday, Matheson Trail parking lot

Even though the lightning seems to be to the left of us, and it's not coming any closer, they call the damn search off. Everyone's back at the parking lot and buses are already taking kids back to the school.

I slosh toward the detective, the mud squishing through my toes in my running shoes. He looks up at me, raising those big eyebrows, spotted with beads of rain, like birds nesting on branches.

"We can't stop because of a little lightning," I say, clenching my jaw to keep my teeth from chattering. "We got lots of hours of light left."

The detective gives me a steady look. "We're not stopping; we just can't have a bunch of kids out in this weather. It's a liability issue."

"Oh," I say.

Josh moves in next to me. "You look cold, Jess."

The sweatpants are drenched, my shoes are filled with water, my hoodie is soaked, despite the rain cape, and I'm shaking. "Did you find anything else?" I ask the detective.

"Maybe." He frowns. Like he's thinking. "Jessie, I have a question for you."

It makes me mad, him and his questions for me. "Why do you always got to do that?"

"What do you mean?"

"Say my name and then say you have a question. It freaks the crap out of me. I don't mean to tell you how to do your job, but you should just ask the question."

"Fair enough." His eyes crinkle at me. "Do you have Chris's phone?"

"What? No!" I exclaim. "Weren't we looking for his phone all day?"

"Relax, I'm just asking."

"Why?" Josh says.

"We just got the phone records back," he says with a sigh. "His phone has been pinging all over the place. Last night, it was pinging by Jessie's house, around midnight."

"Midnight? That's when Steph came over. She saw a car there." What if your killer has your phone and he was outside my house? "And I got this call last night on our home phone?" I say. "Not from Chris's phone. It was this creepy guy. He called me a bitch. I thought it was just like one of those online troll guys who found my phone number. But it's unlisted, so maybe it's the guy who has Chris's phone."

The detective looks worried. "Okay, we'll get that call traced."

"Has his phone made any calls?" I ask.

"No, it's just on," he says. "Like you told me."

"If he has Chris's password, it means he did something to Chris."

"We don't know that, Jessie." He shakes his head. "It's too hard to guess. Anyone could have his phone. Maybe he gave it to someone."

"Well, I don't have the phone. And Chris wouldn't have given it to anyone else. I bought it for him." My teeth are chattering.

The detective looks back and forth between us. "You kids did a great job out there today. You should go get warmed up." He's trying to get rid of us.

I don't move. "Did you talk to Dave Johnson?"

"He has an alibi." He clears his throat. "He was down by the Pitt the whole night with his friends."

"But that's where they beat him up before," I say.

"I know, Jessie. Relax." He waves his hand, trying to get me to calm down, but good luck with that.

"That's not an alibi!"

"Actually, Jessie, it's a pretty good alibi, backed up by plenty of good witnesses, kids from nice families."

I glance at Josh, hurt. We all know I don't come from that sort of family, the kind that has a normal mom and a dad who comes home every night, the kind of family that has flower beds in their backyard where no one can see.

"Don't you think they could have lied for him?" Josh says.

"We interviewed everyone separately. The boys admitted the other incident, and some girls were there this Friday. We interviewed them too. They wouldn't have a reason to put themselves on the line for those guys."

I can think of a whole bunch of reasons. "Did you ask Johnson to whistle?"

He shakes his head. "No, Jessie."

"Then I'm going to ask him to whistle."

"You stay away from that boy. It won't do you any good."

I walk away and toss back over my shoulder, "Whatever."

Josh follows me, sloshing behind through a mud puddle. "Hey," he says. "They're trying their best."

I feel like crying, but I don't. We walk toward the car.

Someone behind us says, "You're Josh, right?"

Josh turns. It's your dad. "Yes, sir."

"Thank you very much." He shakes Josh's hand for what feels like a long time. "Rosemary told me all about you. You've been a good friend to my boy. I appreciate it. He's had a rough time."

It chokes Josh up. "He's a good guy."

What does he mean by *a rough time*? Because of me?

Your dad's face folds into a map of sad lines. "He sure is." He turns my way. "You must be Jessie?"

"Yeah."

He shakes my hand too, and I'm real grateful. I was getting worried he might just ignore me. He stares into my face with his serious eyes, taking an inventory of my tangerine hair with the ash-blond roots, my upturned nose with the ring, my too-small chin, the zit on my forehead. Yep, it's all there.

Is he trying to figure out what you see in me? Sometimes I don't even know myself. I stare back.

He reminds me of you. Something about his intensity, how he looks right into me. I wonder if he laughs like you.

"Thank you," he says.

Nothing about how I've been a great girlfriend. I don't blame him, though.

"Sure," I say, awkwardly.

Your dad says good-bye and strides over to the detective. We keep walking toward Steph, who's standing by the highway. She waves us over. "I want you to meet Pete."

A truck with huge tires pulls up, and the driver waves. Now that it's time to meet this boyfriend, I sort of don't want to. These guys never last long and they're always jerks and I don't want to think of Steph's boyfriend when you're lost and possibly in danger. But right off, this one seems different.

Normally, her dudes would beep and she'd go running. But he jumps out of the truck and lopes toward us.

Then, I'm like, Yep, he's her type. He's got the same longish hair, and he's wearing jeans and the standard black T-shirt with a heavy metal band on the front.

He grins at her. And Steph's smiling back at him real sweet, which is odd. She's usually anxious around her guys, but she's looking at him like she looks at me, only sexier.

When he comes up, she wraps her arms around him and gives him this long, inappropriate kiss, shoving her tongue down his throat. Which is classic Steph. But for once, the guy is embarrassed. He steps back with a cough. Steph introduces him and he actually shakes our hands. "I've heard a lot about you," he says to me. "It's so good to finally meet you."

Has she been hiding him from me because he's nice? "Same," I say.

He gives me a shy smile. I smile back, quickly, even though I'm weirded out. I was wrong. This guy is so not her normal type.

"You want a ride home?" Pete asks me.

Steph grins. She didn't have to ask him if he would drop me off. "I think I'm going with Josh?" I say, glancing at him.

I hope he says yes. I really don't want to be in that truck with Steph and her new guy, while Steph's groping him like a maniac. I want to grope you like a maniac. I want to give you a big old inappropriate kiss. I want to shove my tongue down your throat. I want to run my hands across your back, bury my nose in your neck. I want to smell you.

"Sure, no problem," Josh says.

We say bye.

I drop down into Josh's car, exhausted. Smash my shoes against those energy drink cans again.

Josh lowers himself into the driver side. Gives me a worried look. I hold it together long enough for Pete's huge truck to drive by and to wave back at Steph, and then it's just too much.

I drop my head down into my palms and sob.

Josh turns on the car so that the heat's blasting on me, but he doesn't drive off. We sit there. He rubs my back slowly in small circles. Just waits. Finally, when it's all out of me, and I feel exhausted, he hands me something. "Here."

It's a hand towel. It feels clean.

I wipe off my face, soaked with rain and tears, and then, I'm not even thinking, because I blow my nose in it.

"Did you just blow your nose in my towel?"

I look down at it and laugh. "Oh my god, I did. I'm sorry." I try to hand it back. "Here."

"Oh no," he says with a laugh. "You can just keep that puppy."

It's funny how we can still laugh, right? Then, he starts up the car, and we drive down the road.

4:10 PM Monday, Scott's Donutes

It's still early, so we decide to stop by Scott's. The manager will know if you came in—you're always talking to her. She even sits down with us sometimes. When I'm with you, she always says hi to me too, and remembers my name, which is nice, because most people don't bother.

There's a long line, but I see her up front, taking orders in her smiley way.

I glance at our empty table. I can see you sitting there with your shimmering eyes, your dimple sliding into your cheek. I wave at you, in my brain. But you won't wave back. You just stare at me. Like you hate me.

When we get to the front, Roberta looks at me in surprise, and then at Josh, like she's trying to figure out if we're together.

I speak fast, "We were wondering if you saw my boyfriend, Chris, on Friday after school? He's missing."

"I saw you kids on the news."

I hold my breath, scared of what she's about to say, like maybe that our town isn't racist, that everybody loves you.

"I'm so sorry, honey." She gazes at me with sympathy. Maybe she can see that my eyes are all puffy. "You and Chris are so sweet together. This must be hard for you."

I did not expect that. That's one thing about our town, sometimes people surprise me with their kindness.

"I wanted to join the search today," she says. "But I had to work."

"That's okay," I say. "We had lots of people."

"Did you see Chris on Friday?" Josh asks, like he doesn't want to know the answer.

She nods slowly. "I see him almost every day. On Friday, he came by around four thirty, sat in the back corner, ate a couple doughnuts, then left. Didn't talk to anyone. You know, usually he's so friendly. He asks about my kids. But not on Friday. He was spaced-out...." She frowns. "He had his headphones on, and he looked like he didn't want anyone to bother him. Left without saying good-bye."

I'm probably staring at her like I've just seen a car accident, but I can't help myself. This is not what I want to hear.

"I'm really sorry." She sighs. "I wish I'd said something to him. It wasn't busy. I could've gone up, brought him an extra doughnut on the house. I could tell he wasn't right. His eyes were—" She sees how we're looking at her and shakes her head. "Anyway, I sure hope he shows up. Most kids do." She manages a little smile. "What can I get for you two?"

I don't feel like anything now, not even my jelly-filled, but we order coffees and she hands us a bag of doughnut holes. I try to give her some money, but she waves it away. "It's on the house."

Josh thanks her and takes the bag of doughnuts. I pick up the coffees, and then I pause. "Why do you spell doughnuts wrong on the sign outside? Chris always wants to know."

Her eyes crinkle sadly. "I think it was a mistake at the sign shop."

"Oh," I say, sucking my lip. "I'll let him know, when he comes home."

So now you know, blame the sign people. I lead Josh to our table in the corner. He places the doughnuts between us. The fluorescent lights blare down from the ceiling.

Over the speakers, Norah Jones is singing "Come Away with Me." You sang that song to me a couple weeks ago, right here, at this table with the crack in the linoleum. They must have it on their playlist.

You begged me to come away with you and I said no.

I wish I could talk to you. I mean, I want to kiss you and run my hand along the sharp curve of your back where it meets your ass and do nasty things with you, but even more than that, I want you to be here with me at Scott's Donutes. I want to hold your hand across the table and tell you I'll come with you to North Carolina, or any other damn place you want me to go.

This song is so beautiful.

"I can't eat those," I say.

Josh swallows. "Me neither."

We get up and Josh grabs the bag, but when we're outside and Roberta can't see, he tosses it in the garbage.

4:45 PM Monday, Josh's car

Josh speeds through the streets. He's probably going to crash the damn car if you don't get back soon. We're heading into our fourth night. I fire a series of texts at your phone:

Me: Hello person who has Chris's phone

Me: Better turn yourself in, you sick fuck

No response.

Me: Hello?? Whoever has this phone, I dare you to answer me.

Me: Hey, small dick

Me: Puny tiny ball-less wonder

Me: The cops are onto you

No response.

I look back on our old texts, refreshing. I guess the cops have read them all by now.

There are about four times the number of texts from you to me than from me to you. Most of my recent texts to you are okay, a few are pissy. At least before the fight.

My last text before the fight is Nice elbow. Code for butt. You do have a nice elbow. It really bugs me that the person who has your phone might be able to read our texts. Especially my grumpy ones.

Our fight was on Wednesday. You weren't supposed to call or text, but that night, you texted that you were sorry and to please call. I didn't answer. On Thursday, you wrote a couple texts in a row about how you miss me and you needed me, etc. They sound desperate.

I told you: STOP.

And then you wrote: Please, let's meet.

Me: No.

You: Five minutes. We have to plan our trip.

Me: One week.

You didn't text again.

I glance at Josh. We're at a stoplight. "He hasn't texted me since Thursday. But he was talking about our trip, look."

I show him the text about the trip. His jaw flexes, and he drives forward, staring out the window. Rain is hammering the car now.

"Do you think he went on the trip without me?" I say.

Josh says sarcastically, "Have you met Chris?"

My chest aches. I speak in a low voice because I have to know. "Josh?" I say. "Did he say anything that might have made you think he'd do anything to himself? I mean, I know he was upset, but—I just want to know."

He is silent way too long. "There was one thing."

4:55 PM Monday, Josh's story

Josh turns down my street and pulls up in front of my house. The rain is beating down on his car. By my feet, the cans shift as he jerks to a stop. He swallows. His Adam's apple jumps like a little mouse stuck in his throat.

"Just fucking tell me," I say, gritting my teeth. I am not ready for this. I am not ready. Please don't.

"I keep thinking about something that happened last Thursday," he says. "I can't get it out of my head."

"What can't you get out of your head?"

"We were on a run and we were crossing the highway?" He glances at me, briefly, like he's not sure if he should say it.

Get it over with.

"There was this rig coming at us. I thought we had more time, but it was going too fast. I started sprinting. Chris didn't. He saw the rig, just like I did. I know he did. For Christ's sake, he looked right at it. Then he slowed down, like he didn't care. His face, I can't explain it. He was really out of it, like he wasn't even there. I shook him and yelled at him, asked him what the hell he was doing." He stops.

My face is flushing with heat. I wait, but he's silent. Is he saying what I think he's saying?

"And?" I burst out. "What did he say?"

Josh gulps and shakes his head. "Nothing." He doesn't look at me. "You know how his dad said I've been a good friend?" His voice cracks. "I shouldn't have gone to that meet on Friday." He lets out a heavy breath. "He didn't look good. You know how he gets?"

I don't say anything. But yes, I know. Lots of times, you just get quiet. You stare out the window when you're driving. Even a bad test or a bad practice can do it to you. But sometimes you get this funny look on your face. I've only seen it a few times, but it makes me wonder if you're okay.

"The whole drive to Seattle with my dad, I kept thinking about how he almost got hit by that rig and how, you know, how his face looked. I kept thinking I should've stayed home with him. But then I called him before my race, and he wished me good luck and he sounded real upbeat. So I didn't come home. But in the hotel? I couldn't barely sleep. Then, I got that call." He gulps. "Worst call of my life."

"It's not your fault."

"I keep thinking if I wasn't out of town, I don't know, maybe he'd be here now." He digs his nail in the old leather on his steering wheel.

"Are you saying you think he jumped?"

"I don't know," he says miserably. He hangs his head down and his shoulders start to shake.

10:35 PM Monday, your driveway

Did you jump? Those three words poke at me, internally, repeating again and again, until they are permanently there, tattooed on the inside of my skin. It's funny how words can do that.

I stop at your house and stare at your duplex from the street, like a creepo. Lights are shining from your living room. I feel this weird urge to touch your truck.

I should have told you that you were my first. It was wrong to keep that from you. If I'd told you, maybe you wouldn't think I'd go with anyone. My mind has been circling around this thought like a wolf. It won't leave me alone. You'd be here if I told you that one little thing. Right?

The streetlight shines above me, casts my shadow alongside the truck's shadow, like we're friends. I think of all the times you leaned me against this truck and kissed me at night, in the school parking lot, in front of my house, out in Bear Lake. We've had so many firsts with your truck. First date. First kiss. First time you saved me. First time you said, "I love you."

You said it too early. Maybe the first month? Before our first time. My whole heart stopped. It was like you'd said, "I hate you." It wasn't normal for me to hear this or to say it back—I don't remember my mom or dad ever saying it to me. The only person who ever did was Steph. And she's like a sister. I was physically incapable of saying the words back to you, but not because I didn't feel it. Instead, I said I love your dimple, and you said, "It's okay if you don't say it. I'm going to keep saying it to you." And you did. You said it right after we "made love"—you said, "I love you so much. You're my everything."

It's a lot of pressure to be someone's everything.

Finally, after Christmas, I said it. You made such a big deal of it. You yelled, "Yes!" and pumped your fist in the air. I was nervous to say it again. But I did. You don't know what a goddamn act of courage it was every time I said it. Then you told me you were leaving for college, that you got the scholarship, that they might be starting you, that pro teams wanted to draft you too. I could see your future, a future without me. Baby, I'm sorry. I got scared.

I think of all the times I stuffed those words back inside of myself over the last few months, how everything would have been different if I hadn't.

I stuffed another word inside myself too. I should have called you the day after our fight and said I was a jerk. But I was ashamed about that word I'd called you. I couldn't face it. It made me sick. And I thought if I apologized about it, and you didn't even think anything, then it would be worse. So I think that's why I avoided you. Isn't that shitty? If I'd just said sorry, we'd be together right now.

Your screen door opens. Raffa is standing in the doorway. "What are you doing here?" she demands.

She steps forward. The screen door bangs shut behind her. Her cheeks are flushed and she looks sick, like when she had pneumonia. Her eyes are dark with anger.

"Raffa—"

She marches across the grass in her bare feet and glares at me. Looks like she wants to hit me.

"You broke up with him and then you were dancing with that guy at the mall. People told me all about it. And he was crying, did you know that? I came out to help him clean his truck, and he told me to go away. He said he wanted to be alone, but he was crying. And it was your fault!"

I can't even speak. I think of all the times you and I were cuddled up on the sofa, watching a ball game, eating popcorn, and she'd come over and plunk right between us, wiggling her body to spread us apart, and how we'd both laugh because we didn't mind. It's true. I didn't mind. Seriously, I liked including her in our cuddle. I always wanted a little sister.

"Why are you even here?" she demands.

"I just want to be close to him."

She wraps her arms around herself. Her hair is glistening in the light.

"And I wanted to see you," I say.

She stares down at her bare feet with the chipped pink nail polish and then looks up at me, says, softly, "Why would you do that to him?"

"That other guy is a friend. I swear. He's gay—he's out, he likes guys, Chris knows this. I don't know why he acted like that. He was bummed out."

"He wasn't *just* bummed out."

"He didn't do anything to himself. He would never."

She won't look at me.

"Someone has his phone, Raffa. They've been calling me."

"I saw the news," she says. "I saw what you told them."

"Yeah?"

Her face flushes and her nostrils flare. "Chris told me he fell."

"He didn't fall, Raffa."

"He wouldn't lie to me."

"I— He—" What can I say to that? Yes, he would lie. Yes, he did lie.

Raffa's glaring at me again. "You didn't even love him." Didn't? Sweet Raffa, with the beautiful tinkling laughter, your little bird, she's given up.

"I *do* love him," I say.

The screen door opens and your mom is standing there, illuminated by the light coming from the hall. "Raffa, honey, come on inside."

Raffa turns away from me and marches past your mom. Your mom walks toward me in her brown slippers. "Did you tell her about those boys?"

My heart beats faster. "I'm sorry, I— She heard about it on the news." Is your mom going to tell me to stay away from Raffa? It would kill me. Seriously.

She stops a few feet away, takes a long, slow breath in and out. "This isn't easy for her," she says.

"I know."

"How you holding up?" she asks. I swear, your mom is the kindest person I've ever met.

"I'm okay."

"I heard you were searching for Chris all day in the rain."

I nod.

"Thank you," she says.

What does she expect? "Yeah," I fumble, "of course."

"You must be tired."

My lip quivers and my eyes fill up. Baby, I'm trying to keep it together. The last thing your mom needs is to try to make me feel better.

"Give yourself a break, Jessie. If he's meant to come home," she says, "he'll come home. You try to get some sleep now, okay?"

"Okay." I'm being dismissed, so I say good-bye and turn away from her, and Raffa, and the truck and the house, and you. And I walk the three blocks to my house pushing good old Ella. With each step, I think of Raffa's words: *You didn't even love him.* It's a drumbeat moving to the rhythm of my feet. *You didn't even love him, you didn't even love him, you didn't even love him.*

Maybe she's right, maybe I don't love you enough, maybe I don't know how to love, maybe there's some defect inside me that keeps me from loving like other people love.

I should have written you a love letter. It would have made you so happy.

11 PM Monday, the local news

"Today, the search continued for Chris Kirk, but police have found no sign of the high school senior who disappeared while going for a run on Friday night. Meanwhile, there are troubling signs that there may be more to this case than meets the eye. Channel Five spoke to the father of the boy who allegedly attacked Chris Kirk three weeks ago. On Friday night, the family's Honda dealership was vandalized and witnesses report that Chris Kirk was spotted near the scene."

What?!

The anchor stares out vacantly; her perfect blond hair and her makeup pasted on and her empty eyes. Like it doesn't matter that she's just thrown dirt all over you.

Then Mr. White Teeth himself is on the screen. "A number of our cars were vandalized on Friday night. I was in the office. I saw a girl and a tall black boy running away, and I think it could have been the Kirk boy."

The screen goes to a shot of cars sprayed with blue paint—looks like words, but they're blurred out. I guess they're swearwords.

Why would they put that on the news in connection with you? Now people are going to think you spray-painted the cars. Why would Johnson's dad say he saw a black kid? You'd never do that. Why would he discredit you like that? Just because he can?

My anger is like a wave crashing. I'm holding a soda can, half-full, and I'm filled with an urge to throw it at the goddamn television. I would, except then our TV would be ruined.

Johnson's dad looks like a white supremacist if I ever saw one.

The reporter says, "Did your son attack Chris Kirk on Friday night?"

"No, my son was with his friends." He gives the camera an arrogant smile. "They account for him the entire time. He had nothing to do with this boy taking off."

I swear at the television.

Back to the reporter: "Meanwhile, at the news conference today, Detective McFerson said they had no new leads on this missing person case. There are many people in town who are now wondering if this is in fact a missing person case, or rather, a case of a young man who got himself into some trouble."

How can she say that?

I see the flash of blue paint on Tamara's arm. The blue paint on the cars. Tamara did this. Were you with her?

I run out of the house, grab my bike, and ride fast to her house.

11:25 PM Monday, Tamara's house

I ring Tamara's doorbell. She knows something. Even if she does live in a big fancy house with a ding-dongy doorbell, and a brass knocker on a giant door.

The door yawns open.

It's Becky in striped pajamas. Behind her, a sparkling chandelier dangles from the ceiling. Wait—why is Becky opening the door? Isn't this Tamara's house?

"What are you doing here?" I demand.

"Shh." Becky steps out onto the porch. "I'm sleeping over."

"Where's Tamara?"

"Asleep." She slides the door half shut, like she's a goddamn guard, protecting Tamara's beauty sleep.

I'm ready to wake the whole house up if necessary. But maybe Becky will tell me what I need to know. "Did you watch the news tonight?" I say.

She nods. The light streams through the door, shining on half of her face. She looks afraid. She should be. I'm ready to reach up, grab her hair, and drag her down the road if I have to.

"Did you see how Johnson's dad basically said Chris is a criminal?"

"Yeah. I don't know why he said that." Her voice is water dribbling down a dry creek bed.

"I know Tamara spray-painted the dealership. Was Chris with her?"

She glances back, like she's afraid Tamara's parents will hear, or maybe it's Tamara she's afraid of. "It was me," she whispers. "I was with her."

"What?" I say, surprised now. "Why did they think you were Chris?"

"I was wearing his hoodie. It was dark. I'm tall?"

And white. "Why would she spray-paint the dealership?"

"Dave had a temper. And he, like"—she laughs uncomfortably—"he had trouble, you know, getting it up sometimes. I think Tamara laughed at him one time? And he punched her hard, like, in her stomach, so no one could see."

I gasp. "No way." For once, I actually feel bad for Tamara.

"She broke up with him after that. This was kind of, like, her revenge."

"Why didn't you say something to the cops?" I ask.

Tamara steps out from behind the door. "I didn't want Becky to get in trouble. She didn't do anything."

Becky gives her a nervous look. "I would've been happy to tell the cops."

"It wouldn't help Chris," Tamara barks.

"Yes, it would," I say. "Right now, they think he's a criminal. They're going to stop looking for him."

She gulps. A black-and-white cat squeezes out past her and walks to me, winds its body around my ankles, rubs itself against me. We all stare down at it. I bend down and pick up the cat, hand it to her. She holds it, strokes its fur.

"Okay, fine," she says. "I'll call the detective."

"Tonight?"

She nods.

And then, I've got to ask. "Did Chris ever ask you out?" Not that it matters, but I heard you did, and I want to know once and for all if it's true. It just seems like she's been hung up on you ever since we've been going out.

"Yeah," she admits. "I said no."

"Why?"

She gives me a small, sad shrug. "I don't know. I wish I hadn't. Maybe he'd still be here now."

1:55 AM Tuesday, garbage

It's the middle of the night and I'm putting stuff in garbage bags, making all kinds of noise, and dragging the bags out to the curb—the garbage pickup is in the morning. Mom is going to be mad, and you know what? I don't care.

I grab a bunch of cords and rope, tangled together. We never use these things. I shove them in a white kitchen garbage bag. Mom would say we should donate them. Or recycle them. But that never happens. Ten bags of garbage. It's still a disaster. And our house would still be condemned.

So Tamara thinks if you'd gone out with her, you'd be here....
Oh god, that thought? It kills me. Because she's probably right.

Everything got screwed up in the last couple months, and it's all because of how I reacted after that scout came in March. I got scared, that's all. But it was wrong, how I acted.

I'm sorry you had to fall for me. I'm sorry I'm a messed-up person from messed-up people. You say everyone is messed up, but some people are more messed up. Like, I'm more messed up than you.

I hear you laughing now, saying, "Wanna bet?"

I would bet my right hand on it. There. I'm challenging the gods. If he's more messed up than me and he jumped in the river, cut off my hand!!

It's still there. Fingers are wiggling. I'm all good. Told you.

The Ball Game, the Beginning of the End

That day in March, when the scout was coming, you asked me to watch your game. You said it would help if I was there, cheering you on. I wasn't one of those girlfriends who automatically showed up for every game. I'd only gone to one game before then, and I nearly died of boredom. Most of the time, the players were just standing around. You didn't even play half the time, since you're a pitcher. I felt like I was just watching people I didn't know.

But I said, "Sure, I'll scream my face off."

"I'm counting on it," you said.

It was a clear day and the field was dry, perfect for baseball. I sat in the clangy metal bleachers next to the moms and dads.

I knew from the beginning of the game you were going to be chosen. You were mesmerizing, like a ballerina, all grace and flow. The whole game, I cheered and whooped and waved my arms in the air; maybe I went a little overboard to show how supportive I was, even though I was actually hoping you'd screw up. But you smiled at me and pitched like that ball was on fire.

At the end of the game, I threw my arms around you and you said my bazongas were distracting when I was jumping up and down in the stands, and I said, bazongas? And you laughed and said thanks for cheering. You said the scout told your coach he was impressed and he'd be in touch, and I said, "I'm so proud of you." And then we kissed.

But inside, my heart was already shriveling up like a prune.

You were too good for me. Nearly straight As. Superstar athlete. Everyone loved you. And now you were going to be famous. What kind of place would I have in this new world? No kind of place, that's what. So I pulled away. I guess that's what I'm good at.

Loving isn't so easy for all of us.

That night, I stood in the shower for a really long time, and I cried. But I never told you how upset I was. I just packaged my heart in bubble wrap. And pretended that everything was just the same.

3:45 AM Tuesday, the phone call

My eyes blur. I'm so tired, baby. I've never been so tired in my whole life.

I drop down on the sofa next to Steph and let my eyes close. Just a little sleep. If I can.

When I wake up, my head is resting on Steph's hip. The laptop is still on my lap, amazingly. I'm momentarily confused. Where am I? Why am I sleeping on her hip? And then I think, Chris is missing!

This is what happens every time I fall asleep and wake up, a forgetting and then a remembering. It's like getting sucker punched in the head.

There's movement near one of the piles. It's a tail. A rat's tail. It disappears around the pile. Before I can stop myself, I gasp.

Steph squints up at me with sleepy eyes. "What?"

"Nothing," I say. "Go to sleep."

She puts her hand on her hip. It's wet. "Did you drool on my butt?"

It's kind of funny, and we start laughing.

My phone buzzes on the coffee table. I rush for it. On the screen, it says: Chris. It's your phone. It's calling me.

Oh my god.

I answer, hopefully, "Chris?"

Silence. The person is breathing on the other end.

"Hello? Who is this?"

"Bitch."

"Where's Chris?" I say. "Why do you have his phone?"

No response. No breathing. But the person doesn't hang up.

I scream. "What have you done to Chris, you fucking sick asshole?"

"Give me the phone," Steph says, reaching for it.

"Answer me!" I yell.

More breathing.

"I have a gun, just so you know. It's loaded." Oh god. I'm so scared. I don't want him to kill you if you're still alive. "Please. I want my boyfriend back. Please let him go. I'll do anything."

The guy hangs up.

"Fuck you!" I scream into the phone. I'm filled with panic. Searching for something to do. Some way to help you. I should have let out a loud scream, broken his fucking eardrums.

My chest tightens around my breath like a fist. It hurts. My whole body is shaking. Steph wraps her arms around me.

"It's okay," she repeats. "It's okay."

Her voice comes from far away. I'm not really hearing her. I'm thinking about how your phone pinged near my house yesterday.

I hold up my hand to shush Steph, and then I walk carefully around the piles to the back door, no time to put on my shoes.

I run outside in my bare feet and through the rusted gate. Steph's right behind me. The gate slams behind her. It's loud. The neighbor's dogs are barking. I sprint. There's a car with its lights on, in front of my friggin house.

The engine roars, and there's a flash of light as they drive fast, away from my house. I fly down my driveway, toward the road. It's a yellow Honda. Dave Johnson's car.

I chase after it, screaming and cussing him out, but he just drives away. I call the detective, can't barely breathe. "The guy just called me from Chris's phone. He called me a bitch. I think it was Dave Johnson. He was outside my house."

"What?" the detective says. "Back up, Jessie."

"Dave Johnson has Chris's phone! I ran outside because of what you told me about Chris's phone pinging by my house yesterday and Dave Johnson was there."

"You saw his face?"

"I saw his car."

"You got the plate?"

"No, but it was him." Why didn't I get the plate?

"Okay, Jessie, we'll get the call tracked right away. Is your mom home?"

I feel hysterical. "She won't help! She never helps."

"You shouldn't be alone right now, love." That word, *love*, stops me, it's so Irish, so kind.

"Steph is here," I say.

"Okay, you girls just stay inside, and lock your door, okay?"

I'm staring at Steph. Too late. We are standing on my lawn. The bright streetlight is shining down on us. And I can't just sit inside and do nothing.

11 AM Tuesday, the police station

The next morning, Josh and I sit across from Detective McFerson on cushy chairs in his relatively bare office. His face looks grim. He asked us to come in. No idea why. And I'm kind of scared.

His office is weird. It doesn't look like the office of a detective who's doing everything to find a missing guy. There's no giant board, like on TV, with all the details of your case. Some files are sitting on his desk in front of him, along with a cup that holds some pens and a gold-framed photo of a blond woman and two little girls.

I try to read the label on the top file, but he flips it over.

The smell of Indian food is wafting in from the hall. I feel hungry and try to remember the last time I ate.

He clears his throat. "I asked you kids to come in because I wanted to tell you that we're halting the ground search."

I jump up. "You can't!"

Josh glances at me, worried.

"Sit down, Jessie," the detective says. I glare at him, and drop down in my chair, clicking my short fingernail on the plastic armrest.

He takes in a heavy breath. "We've been talking to a number of friends and his family... I want to be honest with you, Jessie. We think that there's some evidence he may have taken his life."

"What?" I shout, glancing at Josh. His face has gone white. Did he tell him about the rig? "What evidence?"

"The print, for one," he says. "We got the lab results back. It looks like it could be a match with his running shoes. It's a seventy percent match and indicates a forward trajectory. Whoever belongs to that shoe went into the water."

"Even if it's his print"—I break off, gulping, trying not to cry— "someone could have pushed him in. It doesn't prove anything." You can swim, but the current is strongest now. The rapids are close. I close my eyes. Breathe. I force the words out. "If he jumped, there wouldn't be any print. He'd jump all the way into the water. Maybe they hit him in the head. Maybe he was barely conscious."

"We also have an eyewitness now who saw him on the riverbank, right by where you found that print."

I glance at Josh. His arms are resting by his sides. He looks exhausted. He has no more energy to fight.

"Did the person actually see him jump in?"

"No, he didn't," the detective admits. "The eyewitness was walking across the bridge. He saw Chris standing on the bank. He said he didn't think much about it at the time. But he noticed because it was so late, and he saw a person of color, which isn't so common here."

"Who is the eyewitness?" My voice sounds strangled.

"The person was anonymous. They called in. We don't have a name."

"That's convenient," I say. "What time did he see him?"

"After midnight."

"But you can't see that spot from the bridge, not even in the day."

He raises his big eyebrows. "Jessie, we think he went down to the river earlier, ate those pistachios, thought about it for a while, and then he went back to say good-bye."

"You think he dropped the pistachio packet on the ground? He would never litter. Something had to have scared him." Would you have littered just to get back at me? "What about the phone calls I'm getting? And his phone showing up all over town. And how Johnson's dad tried to pin the vandalism on Chris, even though Becky said she and Tamara did it, and Becky might be tall but she doesn't look like Chris at all. Nope, there's no creepy shit going on. It's just fucking normal that a guy jumps into a river that terrifies him, even though there are a million other ways to kill yourself." My rage is full on now. He lifts his eyebrows. I want to tear those eyebrows right out. "It's hard for you to imagine, isn't it? Those nice white boys hurting him, throwing him into the river. You don't want to see their perfect futures ruined, do you? So of course you say he tried to kill himself. You know what that's called? Racism."

"Whoa." He waves his hands. "First off, I'm not racist, at least no more than anyone else. I try not to be biased." He's gritting his teeth. His cheeks are flushed. He looks real mad. Give me the calmest person and I'll push him to the brink. He goes on, "I do think Johnson and his friends were harassing Chris, possibly for months, and that recently this harassment has gotten out of control. It might have played a role in Chris's depression. But there's no evidence of foul play. None."

"There's no evidence he jumped!"

"Jessie," he says, softly now. "We think his depression may have gotten worse over the winter. It might even have had a seasonal component. And then, it didn't get better. Once the chemicals go off—" He shakes his head.

"What do you mean, his depression?"

He squints at me, and then at Josh. "You don't know?"

"His mom said something," Josh admits.

"What?" I bark.

Josh explains, "I guess he had issues, like, before. In Brooklyn."

My chest hurts. You did mention something. That you were having trouble getting your shit together. That was part of why you all moved to Pendling. More nature, that kind of thing, get out of the big city, but I thought it meant you were in with the wrong people. Yes, like a gang or something. I know that's messed up.

The detective clicks his pen on his desk. "Did you notice anything lately?"

I don't want to admit to anything because then he'll stop looking at Dave Johnson.

Does love have to end in heartbreak?

"A little," I say. "After March, I guess, he acted needier, or he'd space out sometimes."

Josh sighs, heavily.

I add, "But I don't think it means anything."

"The Northwest can be hard on people sometimes with all the rain; seasonal depression can affect some people pretty strongly, and it doesn't always go away."

I just stare at him.

"I'm just trying to sort out the pieces here, Jessie. Sometimes the most obvious answer is the right one. But I'm not giving up. Not by a long shot. We're going to find that phone. And"—he hesitates— "you should know, we're going to search the river tomorrow. We're sending divers in."

"Divers?"

"It's standard procedure when someone goes missing near water."

My heart is a small quivering animal. "I bet you anything they aren't going to find him in there."

Josh looks at me, miserable, and then shifts back to the detective.

"You might be right," McFerson says. "But I learned a long time ago not to make wagers about death."

I don't say anything, even though I know he's wrong. And tonight, I'm going to prove it.

10:00 PM, Tuesday, the bridge

I wait until ten. This is when you were last seen running toward the river. Our last reliable sighting. I need it to be really dark out.

I jump on my bike and ride fast toward the bridge. The rain is coming down in sheets, slapping me in the face, making it hard to see. Cars splash me with pothole water. I'm getting drenched from all sides. But I ride faster, following my light, ducking my chin.

Did an eyewitness really see you in our spot? Did you come down here, think about jumping, and then come back later? Is it really that simple? Then why does someone have your phone? Why are they calling me?

You're running beside me now. It makes me feel a little less alone. You grin at me, dimple and all, and rain water drips down your face into your mouth. You stick out your tongue to catch it. I join you. Did we ever do this? Is this a memory? Or just my imagination? It feels real. You feel so damn alive.

How can they be searching for you in the river tomorrow?

You sprint ahead. Your T-shirt is soaked. Your running shoes kick up muddy water onto the backs of your legs and your white shirt. I chase you on my bike.

I hit the bridge.

My tires buzz on the slick surface.

I jump over the curb onto the sidewalk, and my bike skids out, but I manage to get it back under control. You disappear. I'm disappointed, even though it's just my own damn mind, and I could make you come back if I wanted. I need the real you, not the imaginary you.

Halfway up the bridge, I stop and lean the bike against the railing. I stand there for a minute and scan the surface of the swirling, angry water below. There are no floating bodies. Which is good.

I look toward our spot, or where I think our spot is. Hard to see in the rain.

Beside me, cars are whizzing by. The headlights hit me, but nobody stops. Nobody wonders why a girl has stopped on the bridge with her bike in the pouring rain.

The river hisses below, black and churning. The lights on the bridge shine down on it, shimmer off the surface, like a shield, hiding whatever might be underneath.

I tuck my hands into my armpits. The railing is not high. A person could easily climb it and get on the other side and jump. If it were a high bridge, maybe they'd build a higher railing.

I look at our spot. Mr. Tom, the cedar, blocks the view. The branches swoop down, block even people standing on the bank. The eyewitness couldn't have seen you standing there. That's what I like about our spot; we can see out, but people can't see in. I mean, if he could see you from the bridge, think of all those times we had sex there. Oh god, right? In my brain, I hear you say, *Making love.* Ha-ha. You always say, *making love.*

I walk along the bridge and stop every few feet to look, but it doesn't make a difference. I walk back. Maybe if the person were taller? I step up on the lower bar of the slippery railing and then go higher.

When I'm at the top of the railing, I lean forward, like I'm on the *Titanic.* The cold wind whips my hair against my face, the rain beats down, and I squint, trying to see if there's any way someone could see you. It makes no difference. The guy couldn't have, at least not near our spot. And the rest of the bank is really tough to get down. There's too much shrubbery and trees and moss.

Why wouldn't you just jump in by the Pitt, closer to the rapids, if that was your plan? Maybe you tried, but Johnson and them were there? Your second choice would be our spot.

There aren't a ton of black guys around here so the eyewitness couldn't have seen a different black guy. Unless it was the whistler. Trying to make it look like you killed yourself.

I stare down at the swirling, dark water. The rain is dumping down on me. I'm shivering like crazy.

The whole thing makes no sense. Not to be morbid, but everyone has the one way they'd choose to go, if it came to that, and there's no way this would be yours. You're terrified of the river. I'm terrified of fire. You think I'd light myself on fire? No fucking way. Why would anyone pick the very most terrifying way to die?

The river rages below. The wind blows right through my wet T-shirt. I'm shaking from the cold. I close my eyes and send out another useless brain message. *Hey, baby, give me a sign. Let me know if I need to stop looking.*

I wait. There's no thunder. No lightning. No sign.

11:20 PM Tuesday, researching

On the news tonight, the detective says they are moving into a body-recovery phase. He says there is sufficient evidence to believe you're in the river. I turn off the TV.

Sufficient evidence, my ass.

Body-recovery phase?

Oh god.

Tears drip down my face. I'm a sniveling mess.

If they're sending divers in, I got to be prepared. You know me. I need to learn everything about the science of it. Somehow, it calms me.

I pull out my laptop and start researching, wiping away at my face. Hard to read with all the waterworks going on. If you've been in the river since Friday night, that means your body's been submerged in water for four days. Will your body have deteriorated in the water? Will you be bloated?

Now don't take this like I'm giving up. I know you're not in that river. I know it. With every part of my soul. But I still got to be ready, that's just how I am. So I type into Google: *What happens to dead bodies in water?* This is what I learned, for your information. (You're welcome.)

What Happens to Dead Bodies in Water: An Optional Science Report for Sickos

If you drowned in the river on Friday night, your body would sink as soon as the air in the lungs was replaced with water. Rigor mortis would set in after about three to six hours. Now you'd be stiff, at the bottom, drifting among the weeds. Your body would stay down there until the bacteria in your gut produced enough gas to make your body float back to the top. This would take about a week. After your body floated back to the top of the water, your head, arms, and legs would still hang down because they wouldn't have the gas making them float. A body in water stays pretty intact for that first week of floating, though it gets cracks and blisters. Then fluids from your gut cavity would start seeping out of your nose and ears, and eventually the pressure from the gas could make cracks in your skin for the fluids to ooze out of. Bugs would be attracted to your body at this point. You'd still be identifiable without relying on DNA tests for another week.

Your skin would turn blackish green. That's what it says, but I'm pretty sure they're only talking about white people's skin. So I don't really know what you would look like, if you were in the water. Which you are not.

7:00 AM Wednesday, the river

In the morning, Josh rides by on his bike with Sam, and I follow him on good old Ella, down to the water. I have to ride hard to keep up, but I'm so damn exhausted. Steph came over after work and slept on the sofa. I crashed out for a while, but mostly, I just did YouTube research, watching people searching rivers for bodies.

My breath wheezes out of me. God, my legs are aching.

It's weird following Josh when I normally follow you. I'm used to staring at your back muscles in your gray T-shirt as you run.

Then pop! There you are. You're jogging beside me now, looking from Josh to me, your dimple creasing, but you're not smiling. You have to admit, it would be weird for us to go separately.

Josh slows on the trail as he nears our spot. Sam's tongue is hanging out of his mouth. His big lab eyes look back at me.

I call up, "Let's go watch by the Pitt." I can't be in our spot, not now. I'll just keep imagining you jumping in.

Josh rides on.

At the Pitt, there are more beer bottles than last time. There's some charred firewood too. Looks recent. Maybe people were down here last night. I wonder if it was Johnson. How could he have an alibi? I keep thinking about how he couldn't look at me.

Josh and I sit on the bank, and Sam runs around to the water, laps it up, and then climbs the bank by the trees and flops down next to us on his side, tongue hanging out.

The divers are upriver, under the bridge. My stomach turns. Why would they be there? Do they think you jumped from the bridge? You wouldn't need to do that. You could just jump from the side and let yourself drift out to the rapids. I mean, if you didn't hit your head or get sucked under, you could still live, but people die in this river all the time.

Only not you.

Did you know most people don't die when they jump from bridges? Even the big ones? Not immediately. Instead they break a ton of bones so they can't swim and then they writhe in pain, squirming in the water like a spider with its legs plucked off. After that, they drown.

Some people get rescued. That's the good part. I read about one guy who got rescued—he said he regretted it halfway down. Like, in the air. Can you imagine? He was probably screaming and trying to figure out a way to land on the water so he didn't die, pointing his toes, wishing he'd taken those damn cliff-jumping lessons.

Josh crosses his arms in front of his body and stares at the divers, his mouth hanging open, like he can't believe this. I sigh heavily and sit on the grass, pull off my bike helmet, and mess up my hair to get the sweaty itch out, then force myself to look up the river.

Of course I count the divers. There are twenty-two. They're floating below the bridge, in a circle. I wonder how they found that many divers who'd volunteer for this kind of job. Are they the same divers for the brothers who drowned? Where did they learn to dive? On vacation? In Cancun? That's just sick.

They put their mouthpieces in and masks on, and swim away from the bridge, toward me and Josh. Many of them hold metal rods with the hooks on the end. The divers push the buttons on their regulators and go under with their metal rods and their hooks.

Those hooks.

Josh reaches into the pocket of his cargo shorts and pulls out a package of Pop Rocks. He rips the pouch open, dumps a bunch into his mouth, then holds it out to me. His face is more serious than anyone who's ever held Pop Rocks. I can see you with your lips closed gently around the rocks, the shadow of a mustache on your top lip, quivering, your brown eyes widening.

I open up my hand, and Josh pours them into my palm. I tilt my head back and toss them in, like my grandma used to pop pills.

They chatter in my mouth. I hold my lips together. Try to like them.

They stab the insides of my mouth. It's hard to swallow. I don't choke. You'd be proud. Remember you said I'd choke to death if you weren't here? Not choking. Ha. You really want me to like these damn things. You keep making me try them and I don't like them, I just don't, not even now that you're missing.

Maybe these Pop Rocks will increase the possibility of telepathy. I send you a message. *I know you're not in that river. Show everyone I'm right, baby. Come home.*

The surface of the water glints under the sunlight. I can't see anything under it. I wrap my arms around myself. It's chilly in the shade. The last of the Pop Rocks clicks away next to my back teeth.

The divers are passing us now. Behind me, there's a caw. It's Little Man. He flutters over to a low branch on the cedar tree.

I look at Josh. There's something I've been wanting to ask him. "Did you know about the harassment? Like, did Chris talk to you about it?"

He shakes his head. "Nah, I don't know, we don't talk about stuff like that. Tim saw it. That's all."

I tug at some grass by my knee. Thinking about that. You were probably trying to act like nothing was wrong.

"He doesn't really care about fitting in," I say.

"I think he cares."

"Not like most of us."

Josh glances at me. "You care?"

"Totally," I say. "Why do you seem so surprised?"

"You don't act like it. You do your own thing."

"I can't *not* do my own thing. Ever since I was a kid, I didn't fit in. Nobody could ever come over. Our house was too messy. Kids were always pointing at my mom and asking why she was so fat. You know?"

Josh nods slowly, like he gets it. He's so much like you.

"I used to stand as far away from her as I could so people wouldn't know she was my mom." I swallow. It's kind of choking me up talking about this. "She used to make me wear these stupid matching outfits, and I had to let her do my hair in some hairdo she found on YouTube." I gesture at my cutoff shorts and leopard-print T-shirt. "Now she hates how I dress."

"You got your revenge, then," he says, his mouth flickering, his dry sense of humor back, briefly.

I let out a short laugh. "At least I didn't make myself look so weird Chris wouldn't want to be with me."

"He just accepts people like they are."

Behind me, I hear a caw and glance back. Little Man teeter-totters toward me, in a cute, purposeful way.

"He's awesome." The word catches like a shirt snagging on a tree. Gulp. Breathe in. Oh god. It's hard to breathe.

You might be in that water. You might have jumped in. You might be dead.

My eyes are slippery puddles.

Josh rubs his eyes with the back of his hand and looks away, trying to keep from crying in front of me. You never cried in front of me either. A tear rolls down my cheek. Please don't be in that water, baby.

The divers swim up to the boat ramp before the rapids. They swim in, kicking with their fins, regulators pressed, filling their vests with air.

"He'd fight if someone tried to push him in." My words are high-pitched, teary. "Right?"

"I hope so." He wraps one arm around me and pats my back. "It's going to be okay, Jessie. No matter what."

Then, one of the divers shouts out. Like he found something.

I jump up.

Little Man flies a few feet in the air and scurries into the bush.

My hand grips at my mouth, my nails digging into the skin on my face. Josh stands up slowly, squinting, looks like maybe he'd rather shut his eyes.

8:45 AM Wednesday, a discovery

The diver is holding up a dark article of clothing. A T-shirt maybe. A blue T-shirt?

"Is that blue or black?" The words shoot out of me.

Josh shakes his head.

"It's too small," I say. "Don't you think?"

Josh hums. Looks like he's stopped breathing.

The diver holds it in front of his body and slightly out of the water as he swims, like a person holds something that stinks, but maybe it's just easier to swim that way. He kicks to the opposite bank. There's a search and rescue guy in a yellow jacket who takes it from him and puts it in a large plastic zipper bag.

Josh blinks real fast. Sits down. Stares straight ahead.

I sit down too, and now we're silent. Even me.

The pack of divers swim toward the boat ramp, where they tug off their masks, rip open the Velcro on their vests, lowering their tanks, peeling off their wetsuits and flippers. They're talking loudly. Someone laughs.

A search and rescue guy in an orange jacket hands out sandwiches. A diver on the ramp leans his chin up to the sun, like he's enjoying getting a suntan. Really?

Josh lets out a frustrated sigh and picks out a clump of grass in front of him, and then another, until he's made a little pile. I like doing that too. There's something real soothing about pulling out grass and making little grass mountains. I tear out a chunk of grass and start my own pile. The pain in my chest eases.

After another ten minutes, the divers stand, zip up the backs of their wetsuits, then load the tanks in two wagons.

Most of them head around the rapids, but a couple stay behind, along with two men in red SAR jackets. They slide an orange raft into the edge of the water. The two divers climb into the raft. The SAR guys hold on to a rope and let it out. They're yelling back and forth. But I can't hear what they're saying. They're too far away.

They pass a long yellow pole into the boat. Is it because of the T-shirt? Do they think it's yours? Do they think your body is down there?

"I saw this online," I murmur to Josh. "They use the pole when they think a body might be caught in a rock tunnel."

"Why would it get caught there?" he breathes.

"The undertow. It pulls—" I pause. "It pulls anything into the turn."

It doesn't help to research these things, it really doesn't.

The SAR guys swing the long rope around a tree to keep the raft stable. The raft bumps over the rapids, but not in the middle where

272

the dangerous rocks are, closer to shore. One of the divers grabs hold of the pole with two hands and stabs down into the rocks below. Again and again. I flinch each time. Feel like he's stabbing it into my gut, my side, my chest. I am barely breathing.

The men onshore let the rope out and then move down the shore, swing it around other trees, and the diver in the boat stabs it down, like he's killing a wild boar who just won't die.

The diver pauses. Wiggles the long pole around.

"No," I whisper.

Josh gives me a sharp look.

The diver calls out to the men on the shore. They pull on the rope. The raft moves back. Inside my mouth, my tongue claps on the roof of my mouth, repeating silently, Oh no, oh no, oh no.

The diver yells something else. The men on shore release the rope. The boat moves past the rapids. They didn't find you. Not there.

On the other side of the rapids, the divers enter the water. Their tanks sink back under the surface. We sit there until we can't see them anymore.

4:35 PM Wednesday, my floor

When I get home, I decide to make you a present. I know it's not looking good for you. But humor me. I need some distraction.

The divers are still searching, way down the river. Maybe they'll find you. Maybe they won't.

It's killing me, this waiting.

So I sit on my red shag carpet with a pile of magazines, a poster board, and my X-Acto knife. The red carpet pools around my body.

I cut out pictures and glue them to a large poster board with the glue gun. The glue is burning hot. It's maybe not the safest thing to do when I'm this tired.

In the center of the board, I create huge letters made up of small letters from the newspaper, forming the word *dream*.

Baby, I'm trying to be optimistic.

At Bear Lake, back in April, you asked me what my dreams were. You were sitting in front of the fire, turning your hot dog, and I laughed at you. It seemed so cheesy. I never thought about dreams before, really; my whole life has been living from one crisis to the next.

"Dreams are for dreamers." I jammed a marshmallow on a stick and held it above the flame.

"Okay, let's dream." You gave me your big old smile. "Imagine you could do anything. What would it be?"

My stomach tightened. It felt like you were criticizing me, maybe you were thinking I wasn't ambitious enough for you, now that you'd been scouted for a big college and you were going to be a big deal.

I laughed. "Here's my dream: get a driver's license."

"Come on. Be optimistic. You can do anything. You can go anywhere. Maybe we can plan a trip."

"Fine." I gritted my teeth. In that moment, my anger was about a five. You didn't know how close I was to storming off. It seemed like you were putting me down. "I want to see all Seven Natural Wonders of the World." I was overshooting so it would be impossible.

You laughed in that deep, patient way of yours. "That's a lot to cover in one summer."

"Who's talking about the summer? While you're at college, I'm going to put on a backpack and see the Seven Natural Wonders of the World. I'll do all kinds of wild things. You won't believe it."

Your eyes danced with worry. "What are they anyway? The Grand Canyon, the Aurora Borealis, Victoria Falls, the Great Barrier Reef, Mount Everest . . . That's all I got."

"The Harbor of Rio, and Paricutin."

"What's Paricutin?"

I gulped down my wine cooler. "This volcano in Mexico. It grew up overnight, in the middle of this farmer's cornfield. In a week, it grew bigger than any building in town. And then it kept growing for the next year. People came from all over the place to watch it grow, like, right in front of their eyes."

"No way." You were pouring your usual amount of ketchup on your hot dog, about a third of the bottle, dripping down over the sides, a ketchup waterfall. You licked the bun, then your fingers.

I stared. "It's a natural wonder that you can use that much ketchup."

You laughed and took a bite of your hot dog. With your mouth full, you added, "Okay, I'm sold." Like, end of discussion.

"What's sold?"

"Paricutin. We'll go right after graduation."

I've never been on a plane, but I didn't tell you that. "Plane tickets are expensive. And I don't even have a passport."

"We'll make it a road trip," you said. "We can do the Grand Canyon and then head down to Paricutin. Next summer we can go to Everest."

I laughed, which jerked my marshmallow into the flames and set it on fire. I blew it out, ate the ashes, and started again. You were so sure we'd still be together after you'd spent a year away at college being a big baseball star, on TV even, girls circling you everywhere you went. You were lying to yourself.

"If you apply now and rush it, it'll come in time." You looked up at me, earnestly. "Please?"

The smoke drifted from the fire, slid between us. I waved my hand in front of my face, using it as an excuse not to answer. Then, finally, I said, "Okay. I'll apply for my passport."

All around the word *dream* I place pictures of my dreams overlapping with yours. I will fly in an airplane. You will design airplanes. I will see Lady Gaga in concert. You will eat snails in Paris. (Um, yuck.) I will climb the Eiffel Tower. We will learn to rock climb. You will fly in an air balloon. I will create gigantic nature collages that cover buildings. We will go to the Grand Canyon and Paricutin. We will have crows as friends. We will have a chocolate lab. And maybe kids one day.

I love you. Please don't be in the river.

Tears drip down my face. I swat at them.

Your voice echoes in my brain. Pick three things you're grateful for, baby. Every damn night on the phone. Three things. Except for the last month. We were fighting, and I didn't always answer your calls at night. I didn't want to think about three things I was grateful for. All I could think about was how I was losing you.

Number one, I'm grateful for you.

I cut a copy of your graduation picture from an extra missing poster. Your eyes look real sad. Why didn't I notice that before?

Number two, I'm grateful for plants and flowers and crows and birds.

I grab a stack of *National Geographic* and cut out plants and flowers and birds, and I sprinkle them all around the collage, layer them on top of other pictures so that they are flying everywhere.

Number three...

Those eyes. Why didn't I see that?

If you're in the river, right now you'll be drifting through the weeds, through the silty, tannin-filled water, up to the surface.

A familiar pain is stabbing away at the muscles in my chest. It's just anxiety. But it feels like the beginning of a heart attack.

I close my eyes and breathe in for a count of four, hold for four, exhale for four, hold again. It relaxes me, helps me breathe. My counselor in middle school taught me this, and it occurs to me now that the whole time we were together, I didn't need it.

Number three, I'm grateful for you.

You're going to say I already said that. Too bad. Saying it again.

My phone is ringing next to me. It's the detective. I snatch it up. "Hello?"

"Jessie, I have some good news," he says.

You're alive!

"You asked me to call you once the search of the river was completed—and I wanted you to know...the divers didn't find him."

9:45 PM, Wednesday, Chinese food

"Chopsticks or a fork?" Josh says.

We're sitting in his car, which is filled with the smells of Mr. Chinese for once, overpowering the smell of the old running clothes and Red Bull. You could say it's a no-body celebration.

"Fork." I'll probably spaz out with the chopsticks, stab my mouth, and choke, just like your prediction.

After the detective called, Josh texted if I was hungry and wanted Mr. Chinese. I said sure—I've been living on yogurt cups—and he picked it up. When he got here, he called and I came out of the house to eat it in his car. Definitely did not invite him inside, even if he is your best friend, and I've told him about the hoarding. People are always shocked.

He hands me the white box with sweet and sour pork. Yep, I ordered your favorite. I'm feeling a bit more optimistic now. Maybe you'll still show up. Maybe you're alive.

"I always like to open my fortune cookies first." I don't tell him that it's something you and I always do.

"You don't like the suspense?"

"Nah, if I'm going to get food poisoning, I like to know. And with the way things are going..."

"Good plan."

He reaches into the bag for the cookies and we open them. Mine says: *Good fortune comes to those who wait.* Which is good news. I read it aloud.

"Man." He shakes his head and sighs.

"You never know. The divers didn't find him. No dead body, right?"

Josh winces.

I feel bad. I guess talking about a dead body is my way of avoiding the awfulness; I smash my fist up against it. But maybe, right now, I can just shut the hell up about it.

I clear my throat. "What's yours?"

"Invest your money wisely."

"No food poisoning."

"I'd bet there are no fortune cookies that warn of food poisoning." He opens his broccoli chicken and digs in with his fork.

I'm not hungry, but I take a bite of mine anyway. "I can't believe we're graduating on Saturday."

"Me neither."

Then, nope, I can't shut the hell up. "Do you think Chris will make it back in time?"

He pauses with the food in his mouth, and then shakes his head slowly as he swallows.

I stare at him. So, what? He still thinks you jumped? "The fact that they didn't find a body is good news."

He doesn't say anything right away, and then: "I keep thinking about how I shouldn't have gone to the meet."

"You can't blame yourself, Josh. It's stupid." I can't believe he's saying this. "He knows you'd do anything for him."

He nods, real fast, staring down at his carton of food.

"Seriously, Josh, he told me you're the best friend he's ever had."

He looks up at me, finally, and manages a wiggly smile. "Thanks. That means a lot to me."

"He's alive, Josh," I say. "I just know it."

He blinks hard a couple times, like he's struggling to keep it together. Then he dives his fork into his box and starts shoveling food into his mouth. He's eating as fast as he drives. It's kind of mesmerizing.

He chews. Gulps. Glances at me. "Eat."

I shove my box on the dash. "I can't."

"Jessie, we just have to try not to think of it."

My gut tightens. He doesn't know how impossible that is for me, how every waking moment of the day reminds me of you, how I talk to you in my head, like, all the time.

"I can't do anything but think of him."

He nods, and I guess it's the same for him.

His cell rings from the dash and he grabs it. "Yeah?"

Tim's yammering away on the other end. Josh looks worried, as he stares straight out the darkened windshield. "Okay." More talking. "You have to tell the detective," he says.

He hangs up. Stares down at the box of broccoli chicken. The suspense is killing me. Why the hell isn't he saying anything?

"What?" I bark.

"He says he checked the Find My iPhone app and Chris's phone is in the Heights right now."

"It's on?"

"Apparently," he says. "It's by Johnson's house."

"Holy crap. We have to go there."

He's already shaking his head. "Detective McFerson said we need to stay away. Tim's calling the detective. He'll probably send a cop car out."

"You really think they're going to do anything? I mean, why aren't the police tracking the phone? They should have it by now. All they're doing is looking in the damn river."

He's hesitating.

"Josh! Come on." I grab his arm. His arm hairs are extra long and curly blond. Never noticed that before. "Please?"

If you were here, you'd be smiling, even laughing at me. "That's my girl," I hear you say. That's right, baby, I told you I'm not giving up.

Maybe Josh hears your voice in his head too. "Okay, fine."

He starts up the car and shakes his head. "I can't believe I'm doing this."

"I have to get my purse," I tell him.

I run back in the house and grab the large black purse on the hook next to the door, yes, with the gun. I hear your voice in my head telling me to stop. Sorry. I know you don't approve. That's too bad.

10:21 PM Wednesday, Johnson's house

I am creeping up Johnson's driveway. It's so quiet here. No kids crying. No loud music. No tires screeching. No doors banging. Nobody's on their porches smoking. And there aren't any cats either. Isn't that funny? No cats anywhere.

This neighborhood feels dead.

I glance back. Josh is sitting in the car, stewing. He's such a rule follower—he's like you in that way. But it's fine with me. He doesn't know what I have planned. It's better this way.

There are no fences in the Heights, not metal, not wood, nothing; it's like they think nothing bad can happen here.

Johnson's huge white house has those pillar things in front. I even spotted a tennis court by the side yard. It's like a goddamn palace. I need to get closer. Take a good look inside.

The whole house is lit up—every room—like they don't have to worry about an electric bill. I can't see in, though, not yet. The front windows are shielded behind the long, closed velvet curtains. Killer curtains. Some things are creepy, straight up, and velvet curtains are one of those things.

My flip-flops are too noisy, clapping on the wet cement. I slip them off, look back at Josh. He's watching. Looks scared. The house lights shine from behind me, stretching my shadow toward his car, like it wants me to get back in.

I creep down the driveway. It's cold and wet, but smooth. Not a single pebble. I bet they sweep it. Which is classic. Only messed-up people sweep their driveways.

I'm even with the house now. The driveway runs along the side. Johnson's bright yellow car is parked in the back. Through the side window, I can see a girl with long, blond hair, holding a bowl of popcorn: Johnson's sister, looks like.

My purse swings from my shoulder. The gun is growling inside. It's hungry. I know you wouldn't want me to use it, not even if Johnson killed you. But if he has your phone, if he's done something to you, I swear, I won't be able to stop myself.

At Johnson's yellow car, I peer inside. I'm thinking he'd leave the phone in the car. I try the door. It opens. That's how safe this neighborhood is. People leave their car doors open. I slide down into the black leather seat. The car still smells new. It's cleaner than Josh's car, but not as clean as your truck. There's a soda can next to the driver's seat, a baseball jersey shoved in the back. And a black hat with a yellow *Go* on the front. I pick it up. That's funny. It's the same hat that Michael has. Must have bought it at the same store. It matches his car.

I check the glove compartment. He's so organized, which surprises me. Registration and insurance in this pouch, ready to give to cops. Nothing else. There's no phone.

I glance back at the house. It looks like someone's moving around in the far room. I slide out of the car. Leave the door cracked open. Because they'll be able to hear a car door slamming shut.

Are his parents home? Don't see any other cars.

My feet press into the moist grass. The room has a bunch of books. I can see that from my angle. Maybe a study?

I creep across the lawn. My feet are getting cold.

Dave Johnson is sitting at the desk. In front of a computer screen. I reach into my bag. Pull out my phone. If your phone is on, it'll ring.

I call your number.

It's not on speakerphone, but the first ring is loud in the quiet of the yard. My heart thrums. Johnson doesn't move. He's just staring at the screen.

Come on, I urge.

The second ring.

He jerks. Does he hear it ringing on my end? No, he's reaching in a desk. He's pulling out a phone. It's a black iPhone. It's the one I gave you. He's looking down at it. He turns it off. I look down at my screen. It goes to voicemail.

Motherfucker.

I dive my hand into my purse, pull out the gun, click off the safety. It's shaking in my hand. It's up to me now. Nobody else is going to do anything. But I'm scared.

Put the gun down, baby.

It's you. Are you here? Are you watching? I have to do it. You don't understand. He took you from me.

And then something hits me. I'm falling into the grass. The gun flies through the air and lands a few feet away.

Josh is pressing his body into mine. Days-old funk floats off of him. "What the fuck, Jessie?" he hisses in my ear.

"He has the phone. He has the phone. Josh, he has the phone." I can't stop repeating it. I'm all jittery with adrenaline. I can't believe I was right all along, that Johnson did something to you and nobody believed me but I was right, I was right. "He hurt Chris, maybe he killed him, and he's going to get away with it, Josh. Guys like that always get away with it."

"Shhh." He covers my mouth. He's pushing me into the wet grass. I had no idea he was so strong. "Jessie. We need to leave. Now. The police are on their way."

He's talking to me like I'm a crazy person, but I was right all along.

I nod, planning to dive for the gun. But he's faster than me.

He grabs it. I look up at the den. Johnson's still staring at his computer. He has no idea how close I came. And now, there's a picture on the screen. Holy shit. It's a picture of you in a blue T-shirt and black shorts. That's what you were wearing on the day you disappeared!

I roar with anger and run to the den, smash my hands on the window.

Johnson leaps from the chair. He turns and stares at me. His bright blue eyes are on fire.

"You fucker!" I scream.

Josh grabs my arm. And we run.

10 AM Thursday, waiting

The cops are at Dave Johnson's house. I'm sitting next to Steph in my house on the brown sofa with the television blaring, waiting.

We told the detective everything. Except about the gun. Josh made me promise to put it back in my mom's closet. I said I would, but I didn't do it.

Dave Johnson is not getting away with this.

I stare, fuzzy-brained, at the images flashing in front of me. Steph is sitting beside me. She brought over some yogurt. And now, she's shoveling a spoonful at my closed mouth, saying, "Eat." She bangs the metal on my lips. "Open."

I allow the yogurt into my mouth. Has he tied you up somewhere? Or did he kill you? Oh god, please be alive.

The detective said it's impossible to search the entire river. Sometimes bodies show up later. That's what he said.

Tomorrow is floating day. If the divers missed you somehow, you'll be on top of the water on Friday.

4 PM Thursday, a manila envelope

I'm still sitting in front of the TV. Steph went to work. My phone is next to me. My computer is on my lap.

A few people have driven by Johnson's house and texted that the cops are still outside. Josh and I have been warned—if we're seen anywhere near his house, we'll be charged with obstruction of justice.

Slow, heavy footsteps come down the stairs. Mom's breathing is labored, panting. "This came for you." She hands me a manila envelope. Pats my arm. Then turns to go back upstairs. Doesn't ask me how I'm doing. Doesn't ask what's been happening with the investigation.

"That's all?" I say, incredulous.

She turns around. "What?"

"You could ask me how I am." Anger whistles through me. "It's a normal mom thing to do, you know. To check in on your kid when her boyfriend's gone missing. When her boyfriend might be dead. When his killer is being interrogated."

She runs her hand through her greasy hair. "I'm sorry. I never know what to say to you."

"You could try."

"It's just, I've been real tired lately. I don't know. My muscles have been aching me and—"

I jump up. My teeth are clenched. "I. Don't. Care." My anger flings itself at her. "For once," I yell, "this isn't about you. *I'm* the one who's going through a rough time. It's *my* boyfriend who's gone missing."

She hobbles backward. "I—I know that."

"You've done nothing, not one little thing to help me find Chris. You don't even make me meals. I'm not eating, Mom. Do you even care?"

She gulps. "I do care."

"It's so shitty," I cry. "I help you all the time. I do everything." I wave my arm in front of me. She flinches. Like she thinks I'm going to hit her. Doesn't she know I would never? "You can't even clean your own stuff," I sob, even though it's not about the mess anymore. "If I put it upstairs, you put it down here. I have to live in this rat's nest and the thing is, I can't leave, because I got to pay for groceries and help with the mortgage."

"You're right," she says. "I'm sorry, sweetie." Her mouth is quivering, and for real, she does look sorry, but I'm too mad.

"Sorry's not good enough," I say. "Just clean your shit up."

Without saying another thing, she turns and shuffles out of the room. I feel like crap. Man, she can't help herself. Why do I have to attack the people who love me?

I look down at the priority mail envelope.

My heart drums. Could it be something from you? A final note? Please, no.

I stroke the smooth envelope, then rip it open with the tab. I reach inside and pull out another envelope. I look closer. It's from the State Department. It's my friggin passport. Oh my gosh. I nearly had a heart attack. You'd think they'd mark in big letters, PASSPORT, and make you sign for it, but they don't. So, now I'm ready for this trip that we're supposed to go on starting next week. Passport. Check. Boyfriend. No check.

I wouldn't have applied for a passport if it weren't for you.

The truth is I'm not a wild girl. I'm afraid of so many things. I'm afraid of college. I'm afraid of not making it in a big city. I'm afraid of trying to do something amazing and failing. But I'm even more afraid of not trying and being stuck in this crummy-ass town. I'm afraid I'll marry some loser and have babies. I'm afraid of being unimportant, not just to you, but to everyone else, to the whole goddamn world, just living and dying, and making no kind of difference.

The day after I promised you in front of the campfire, I went to the post office with my two passport photos and my ID and I sent the application off. And then I started to look at colleges. I never would have done that either if you hadn't made it seem possible. I wouldn't have thought about how I love nature and I want to conserve it and maybe I should go to school for that. Because of you, I started thinking I could make a difference.

Josh texts: I talked to McFerson

Next text: He says Johnson didn't do anything

No. Oh my god. Panic sweeps through me. I write: What the fuck?

Josh: Johnson says he just found the phone

More typing and then, finally: Detective says they need more evidence to charge him, it won't stand up in court

Me: That's bullshit

Josh: Guess he got a big lawyer

Rage heats my eyeballs. I want to throw things. I want to scream. I want to grab a knife and stab and stab and stab. It's scares me, how crazy I feel inside.

Is Johnson really going to get away with this?

I reach for the first thing I can grab. That damn rabbit bottle, now on the coffee table. And I fling it hard against the wall. It's plastic, so it bounces and falls down into a new random pile of junk. It's not satisfying. I reach down and grab a big pile of laundry and cords and fling it against the wall. Grab more things. Throw them across the room. More shit. The piles transform into lumps. The pathways disappear.

Finally, I'm so exhausted, I collapse on the sofa. This can't be happening.

6 PM Friday, teen night

It's weird to be here, next to my long metal locker, with my bathing suit hanging and my chlorine shampoo and extra-dry hair conditioner standing up on the top shelf, like normal. But I don't know what else to do. Being home is not better. Watching TV is not better. I might as well make money while I'm waiting to find out what's happened. Waiting for you to appear.

Today is floating day. And so far, nothing. You didn't float.

When I walk upstairs to the deck, Michael's got the music blasting, like normal. It's totally weird, déjà vu. Michael's leaning on the glass by the office, looking at his phone, like usual. He says, "Hey, beautiful!" like usual. He gives me one of his warm hugs and smells of cologne, like usual. I pull back, kind of uncomfortable.

He clears his throat. "You okay to guard?"

I nod. "I slept last night." For three hours. My head is foggy. But it's teen night. Nothing ever happens.

"That's great," he says, too enthusiastically. "Um, just a heads-up, I got some stuff to do tonight in the office. Do you want to take first shift?" Usually Michael and I spend the whole shift talking; we don't even take breaks.

"Sure, I can do it," I say.

Then he hurries off. He's acting weird. Maybe he just feels bad because we were dancing and then you saw us and that night, you disappeared. Maybe he feels like it's his fault.

Anyway, I wouldn't be much fun to talk to. All I can think about is Johnson.

I scan the pool. It's dead, as always on teen night. That's why there's only two of us working. The teens are scattered around the deck, but not in the pool.

Some thirteen-year-old girls strut around the deck in pods, and a group of fifteen-year-old boys head over to the hot tub. The boys have one girl with them in a red-and-white polka-dotted bikini. She slides in close to one of the guys. We always got to watch for sex in the hot tub. No joke, the way they do it, the girl "sits" on the guy's lap, like we're too stupid to figure it out. Michael and I normally laugh about it.

Billboard's Hot 100 is playing. You know how much I love dancing to this kind of music. But today, I got nothing. There's no *thump-thump* pumping around inside me, making me want to gyrate. That part of me is dead. The last time I danced with Michael, the *thump-thump* was there. Then you disappeared.

I release a long slow breath out of my mouth, lips pursed, like I'm blowing bubbles in the pool, and I stare at the flat surface of the water.

Your arm reaches up. Why does my mind keep doing that? That's not how people drown, even if they're caught in weeds. And if you were sucked under, you'd just be gone. Nobody would see you. Get it right, brain.

Will I ever be able to guard again without my mind messing with me? I don't know. I guess you better come home. You better be alive.

After twenty minutes, Michael bumps me. "Go relax," he says.

Code for: I don't want to talk.

Man, one week ago, we were dancing on the deck and talking nonstop, interrupting each other, laughing our brains out. Today, everything is different.

Maybe he doesn't want to make me lose my shit on deck. I don't move.

"Any news about Chris?" he hazards.

"Yep, you know that Dave Johnson guy? He had Chris's phone, but the cops aren't arresting him. I guess he got a big lawyer."

"That sucks." Michael stares at the pool. He's quiet for a minute. "But you know, maybe he didn't do anything. Why would Chris go down there if that's where he got beat up before?"

"I don't know," I say. "Maybe he was hoping they'd beat him up again and then I'd have to end this break."

"That would be pretty screwed up," he says. "Like, you know the time I got attacked? I never go near that street anymore."

He doesn't understand. I tell him about the stalking and the phone calls and everything. It looks like he's going to say more, maybe argue with me, even defend Johnson again, but then he glances at me, and maybe he can see I'm getting pissed, so he just pats my arm and says, "Take a break. You need it. Take thirty."

Maybe he thinks you jumped and I'm fooling myself, but he's wrong. Johnson had your phone. Nobody keeps a phone if they're innocent. That's a sick fuck kind of thing to do. He did something to you, I just know it. I don't say another thing to Michael, just stalk off the deck.

9:40 PM Friday, Michael's car

Michael offers to drive me home. Maybe he can see I'm kind of a mess. Maybe he feels bad for defending Dave Johnson. Maybe he wants to make it up to me.

My dad's back for graduation and he was going to pick me up when I called him, but I might as well as take the ride. So I say okay.

When we get in the car, Michael blasts the country music, which is what he listens to when he's not on the pool deck. The convertible top yawns open. Then he hits the gas. With the top down and the music on, it's so noisy it's impossible to talk.

We fly down the road. "Relax," Michael yells.

He looks at me with those blue eyes and smiles, all high cheekbones and sculpted jaw, blond hair tossing around in the wind. He really is like a model. I can't blame you, I guess, for thinking the wrong thing.

I lean back against the seat. My eyes flutter shut. The cold wind whips my hair against my face. The heater blasts hot air against my body. You know how much I love the mix of hot and cold things. It feels real good. But I still feel guilty enjoying anything.

A slow song comes on, a woman's voice, sad and twangy; I never heard it before, but it's kind of beautiful. I'm about to ask Michael who it is when an airy whistle comes from the driver's seat. From Michael. He's whistling, badly.

It's the same whistle.

My eyes fly open. We're not near my house. We're heading out of town.

"What are you doing?" I say, my voice sharp with panic.

He stops whistling. Doesn't say anything. Keeps driving.

"Michael, where are we going?" My hand grips the armrest.

"Relax," he says. "I want to show you something."

Relax? I can barely breathe. My chest pinches tightly inside me. "You don't know how to whistle?" Does he hear the fear in my voice?

"I'm trying," he says. "Everyone should know how to whistle. I figure it's a major defect in a human being to not be able to whistle. You haven't seen me practicing on deck?"

I've seen him do duck lips. But I couldn't hear him. I shake my head and wrap my arms around my body. I'm shaking. He doesn't know that I know.

"What do want to show me?" I say.

He glances at me. "It's okay, Jessie."

"What are you going to show me?" Louder now.

"Relax." His fingers grip tight on the steering wheel. "I just want you to meet my new guy."

"Did you go down by Matheson Trail Sunday night?"

"That was your bike?"

I nod. Oh my god.

"I thought it looked familiar." He gives me a sharp look. "Jessie, stop freaking out.... Like I said, I just want you two to talk."

Us two? What is he talking about?

We're out by Bear Lake. He turns down a road where all the cabins are. Josh's cabin is out here on the other side—I remember the time we stopped by to hang out. He'd just come in from water-skiing.

On this road, a couple cabins have lights on, but most of them are dark. I pull out my phone, expect Michael to rip it out of my hands, but he doesn't stop me. My hand is shaking. I text Josh:

Michael is the whistler, took me to Bear Lake, by cabins

I push SEND.

"Jessie." Michael shakes his head, pissed, like I'm the one acting crazy here. "We've been friends a long time. Don't you trust me?"

I think about that, all the things I know about him, his family, things he's told me while we guarded. But he's the whistler. "I don't know," I say. "You're taking me out to the middle of nowhere. You freaked me out down by the river the other day. Michael, this isn't normal."

He sighs. "You're right."

He pulls to a stop in front of one of the dark cabins. A figure steps out of the shadows. It's Dave Johnson.

10:05 PM Friday, Bear Lake cabins

Johnson takes slow steps toward me. My heart thumps in my chest. I need to get out and run. I need to hide.

Why am I here? How do they know each other?

I look back and forth between the two of them, and suddenly it dawns on me. "You're with him? You're fucking *with* him?"

Michael nods. "It's—Jessie, it's not what you think."

"Did you do something to Chris?" I cry.

"No, no, that's why I'm bringing you out here. You have to talk to Dave, he's real bent-up about this."

"What?" My whole body shakes with rage. *He's* bent-up?

"Give me a chance to explain," Johnson says in his overly deep voice. He moves closer, blocking the door, towering over me. I can't get out.

I spin toward Michael. "Your boyfriend attacked Chris three weeks ago. And he punched the crap out of a girl half his size. What the fuck? You said you liked jerks, but Michael, he's not just a jerk. He's a killer."

"He didn't—"

"Oh my god," I rage. "Michael, I *saw* him. Looking at Chris's phone. Looking at pictures of Chris. And Chris was down there, running, at the same time he was. You're telling me this is all a coincidence?"

"It's not," Johnson spits. His blond, buzz-cut head is so close to mine, his saliva lands on my face. "But you gotta stop this bullshit."

I look into his killer's eyes. He has no problem hurting girls. He lunges toward me, his fist clenched.

I scramble backward. He's going to kill me. I climb over the open convertible top fabric, jump off and bang my knee hard on the bumper. It hurts like crap. I cry out, grab my knee, and stumble to the ground.

"Jessie! He's not going to do anything to you," Michael says, leaping out of the car.

Johnson saunters around the convertible. "Calm down. I'm not going to hit a girl."

"Really?" I jump up. "What about Tamara?"

He rubs his hand over the top of his head, looking uncomfortable. His eyes focus on the trees behind the cabin. "That was a mistake. I lost control. I didn't mean to hurt her."

"Like you lost control with Chris?" I limp a few steps back. My eyes dart to the woods. Maybe I can make it there. But Johnson is fast.

"I didn't lose control with Chris," he says in his lazy, rich boy drawl. "I meant to teach him a lesson. It should have been me getting recruited. It was my fucking time. He sweet-talked the coach."

"Stay away from me." I hobble backward, away from him.

Michael runs his hands through that blond hair, like he's frustrated—with me. "Come on, Jessie, give him a chance. Just listen to him."

They both walk toward me. I feel cornered and look back at the woods. Maybe I can run. But first, I need to know the truth. "What happened on Friday night then? Did you 'lose control' again?"

"No." Johnson shakes his head. "No, that's not what happened."

But clearly something did. I see it on his face.

My phone is in my pocket. Maybe I can record this. I can record it and I'll have proof—if I can get away. I fumble around in my pocket, try to turn it on. "How did you get Chris's phone then?"

"I ducked out on my friends to meet up with Michael—it was after Chris dropped you off—but I left my stuff, because I was planning on coming back. They were so drunk they didn't notice."

I remember Michael talking about meeting his new mystery guy. I teased him about putting on cologne. He said his boyfriend liked it. But Johnson was down by the river, with his friends.

"Your friends know you're gay?"

"What do you think?" Johnson lets out a bitter laugh. "They thought I was taking a piss. A long piss. Michael and I were, um, together and then I look up, and Kirk is standing there, with his fucking phone. I thought he was taking pictures of us. So I took

303

off after him. But he threw the phone at me, said to take it. I just wanted to delete the photos. He told me his password and he said to give it to you when I was done with it. Then he ran off." His eyes are haunted. "I looked on the phone and he hadn't taken any pictures. I didn't know what the fuck to do. I had no idea why he wanted me to give it to you."

"What was the password?"

"0708."

That's your password. Did he beat it out of you? I look at Michael. "You knew this?"

"I didn't know the guy was Chris, I swear—I would've told you. My back was to him. I didn't even see him. Dave just took off." He sucks in a shaky, scared breath. "He didn't tell me who it was. He didn't mention the phone. I had no idea until Sunday. When Dave's face was plastered all over social media, I called him and he told me everything. I said I'd back him up, but the police already suspected him, so he didn't want to tell them about the phone."

Why would you just give this asshole your phone? "Nice story."

"He didn't do it. I'm telling you, there wasn't enough time." His face is solemn. "Seriously, he's been real broken up about what he did to Chris." He looks back at Johnson, who's just staring at me with cold killer eyes. "Tell her."

Tell me what? I look back between the two of them, hot with fury.

Johnson blinks his pale eyelashes. "It was shitty, what I did to your boyfriend. Yeah, he was an arrogant asshole, but I regret it. Especially now."

Asshole? He's the asshole. I'm so angry, I can't even think of my own safety. I just want to hurt him. I fly at him and shove hard at his brick wall of a chest. He doesn't move.

Fury slides over his face.

Then he shoves me. I stumble backward and fall on the ground, scraping my hands on the gravel. He towers over me. "You don't hit me."

"Holy crap, Dave." Michael pushes between us and helps me to my feet. Then he shoves his shoulder against him. "Get back," he grunts.

Johnson pushes him aside. He's way bigger than Michael. He jams his finger at me. "I didn't do anything."

"Why didn't you give me the phone if you're so innocent?"

"I wasn't going to give you shit. You know how many news stories there have been because of you? My life is destroyed. Everyone's saying I'm guilty. The cops have been at my house all week. I've been getting hate messages. Because I got in one fight with the guy three weeks ago. You pretty much killed any remaining chances I had to get scouted for anything. No college is going to accept me. I've been training my whole life for this. You took that away from me, you fucking trash bitch, and now you say *I* killed him? When you're the person who broke up with him? You did this, not me. I didn't do nothing to that fucking—" And then he says it. He says that word.

305

Oh my god. I fly at him and slap his face as hard as I can. My nails rake his cheek.

Johnson winds his hand into a fist and drives it at my head. It doesn't hurt, weirdly, not that bad. Not like you'd think. But I can't hear.

"Stop!" Michael shoves him away from me. They grapple with each other, look like they're wrestling. Johnson's trying to push past him to get to me. Michael shoves him hard. They fall on the ground. Michael is on top of him screaming: "You said you just wanted to talk to her."

"Get off of me!" Johnson grunts.

"We're done," Michael pants. "You hear me? We're done."

"Fine. I was done with you anyway." Johnson jerks away, pulling himself to his feet.

"Don't go near her," Michael says, standing, and blocking him. His chin is bleeding. Weirdly, I can smell his cologne.

Behind us, a car screeches up. I'm hoping for the cops, but it's a familiar Toyota. Josh jumps out. "Get the fuck away from her."

I dive into his car and lock the door. My whole body is shaking. Josh drops back in and takes off, tires screeching. "Holy shit," he's saying. "Holy shit."

I look back.

Michael is getting in his car. Johnson is sitting on the ground. We drive off. Michael follows. We leave Johnson there.

I pull out my phone with fumbling fingers and call the detective. He says he'll be sending a squad car out to pick up Johnson for assault, but he knows everything I'm telling him and they're looking at your phone. "I'll have more news soon, Jessie."

"What do you mean?" I breathe. "Did you find his body?"

"No." He lets out a heavy sigh. "I can't tell you anything yet. But I will soon."

I hang up and turn to Josh. "He says he has news."

Josh grips the steering wheel hard and lets out a groan.

"What?" I say.

"Um, Jessie." He takes in a giant gulp of air and lets it out as he speaks: "I have something to tell you."

11:25 PM Friday, Josh's cabin

I'm sitting in Josh's cabin on his flowery sofa that sags in the middle. Next to me, the lamp flickers. The crickets outside are making a racket.

Josh is pacing, his hands twitching by his sides, like he's had too many of those caffeine drinks. "Jessie, I think he jumped."

"He didn't." My voice doesn't sound so certain, though.

He continues pacing. "I told you about the rig, but I didn't tell you this . . . on the side of the road that day, he told me he wanted to die."

"What?" I breathe.

"I laughed at him. I said, you don't want to die. I punched him in the arm, treated it like some joke. I just wanted him to cheer up. Then, it worked. I mean, he smiled at me. He said I was right, he was fine. And we kept running.

"The next day, when I was driving to Seattle with my dad, I kept thinking about it, how he looked, what he said. I wish I'd told my dad to turn around. I was worried about him all day. Lamed out on my race.

"During dinner, I almost told my dad that we had to go back. But then, I got Chris's call and I listened to the voicemail. He sounded great. So I called him back and even though he didn't answer, I figured he was fine and I went to sleep. But then his mom called in the night—" His face falls.

He runs his finger under his eye. "I just knew. Dad drove me back. He kept trying to reassure me that Chris was okay. I didn't tell him what I knew. I kind of tried to forget about it, you know? I tried to convince myself he was okay."

I speak up. "Josh, if he did something to himself, it's my fault." I blink, but tears are coming anyway.

He stops pacing and sits down beside me on his old sofa. "No, Jessie. Even if you had broken up with him, it's not your fault. On Friday, you guys were waving at each other. He was smiling. It was all good, you know? You couldn't have guessed."

You did seem fine.

"If you're going to blame yourself, I have to blame myself, and I'm not going to." He closes his eyes tight and then opens them, gazing at me with this fierce intensity. "You hear me, Jessie?"

But he doesn't know what you said to me.

If You Ever Left Me

It was last month. You were running your fingers through my hair. Adele was playing on my stereo; we were gazing into each other's eyes. It was a cheesy, beautiful moment and then you had to go and ruin it.

"If you ever left me, I'd kill myself," you murmured, as if that was a sexy thing to say. Your dimple danced on your cheek.

I sat up in bed, shocked. "What are you talking about?" I snatched my black T-shirt up from the floor and tugged it over my lacy pink bra, the one you liked, which I wore for you, even though it had zero support.

"Where are you going?" You sat up on your elbows and the quilt dropped down from your body. Your bicep muscles bulged, your abs tightened.

"You think that's a romantic thing to say?"

You blinked those deep brown eyes with those long lashes that had no business being on a guy. Your face was soft, so easily wounded. "I was just saying it. I didn't mean it. Come on. Lay down."

You acted like I was the one who wrecked the moment.

I picked up my jeans from the floor and tugged them on. "There's no such thing as just saying it. What if I want to break up with you one day?"

"Do you?" Your voice curved up, like a sharp note on a violin.

"What?"

"You want to break up?"

I thought you were suggesting it, but then I realized that you thought *I* wanted to break up. "No, oh my god, no, I mean, one day. Come on, Chris. We're seventeen. You're going to college. I don't know. What are the chances?"

"I think we have a chance," you said, pleading with me. "Please, Jessie. I didn't mean it. I just, sometimes, I don't feel right, you know?"

I paused when you said that. I heard you, but I didn't want to hear you. I've got a mom who doesn't feel right. I couldn't face that in you. It was like you'd vomited by my feet. I couldn't even look at it.

"I'm not breaking up with you, for god's sake," I said. "But when you say shit like that, it's not cool. It's blackmail. It makes me feel like I've got to be with you no matter what."

"I didn't mean it," you said, reaching for me. "Come here. I'm a dumbass."

My voice cracked. "If you ever say that again, I *will* break up with you."

"I won't. Come on." You patted the bed, like it was no big deal, but I could see you were holding your breath, the dimple in your face held rigid.

I forgave you, climbed on the bed, rested my ear on your warm, firm chest, breathed in your sweet smell, and blew out with my pursed lips. The tiny patch of black hairs on your chest waved in the breeze. I told myself you'd never do it. But maybe you did. Maybe you did.

10:10 AM Saturday, the fake funeral

The next morning, all I can do is think of Raffa. If you really did it. If you really swam out into the rapids. She's going to be devastated. I want to write her something. Just as you would have done if you were here right now. I find a paper and a pen, and sit down at the coffee table, and write.

Dear Raffa,

I want you to know how much Chris loves you. He's told me so many times how amazing he thinks you are. He talks about you all the time. Every day, he tells me how cool it is having a sister. He loves your stories; they always crack him up. And he's always telling me some funny thing you did. Like how you hid under his bed and scared the bejeezus out of him. He laughed about that one. You're real good at making him laugh. Every day, he sells me on how

cool it is to have a sister. We don't know what happened
yet, but one thing I know is how much he loves you.

xoxo, Jessie

I fold the letter into an airplane, head outside, and walk to your brown duplex. I can't stand Raffa being so mad at me. She's got a right to be mad, I know that, but I hope this helps her.

I pull open the screen door. My hand wraps around the knocker. I ignore the bell. It doesn't work. I know this and so many other things about you—how can you be gone for good?

I'm about to knock, but then, from inside, I hear Raffa yelling. I've never heard her yelling before. I've never even heard her talk back. But right now, she's screaming at your mom, "I'm not going to his fake funeral!"

"You will go if I say you're going," your mom says.

What are they fighting about? Did Raffa say *funeral?*

"Why are you giving up on him?" Raffa yells.

"Don't speak to your mother like that." It's your dad. He's speaking calmly. "We are having the funeral on Sunday. Unless Chris comes home. End of story."

Your funeral is on Sunday. Oh no.

I bring the knocker down three times.

Inside it's silent.

Then there are footsteps. Your mom opens the door. The smell of chocolate and bacon reaches toward me. She stares at me. Her makeup isn't on today. Her hair isn't done. No pearls. She's wearing sweatpants and a T-shirt. I didn't even know your mom owned sweatpants.

She touches my swollen cheek and clucks her tongue. She knows what happened. Her hand drops.

"I guess you heard that," she says.

"You're having his funeral?" I ask.

"I was going to tell you," she says. "I talked to the elders and it's time. It'll be on Sunday."

"But we haven't found him." I cannot say *your body*. "He might have just taken off. We still don't know. It's not—"

She rests a soft hand on my arm. "I know." The edges of her mouth turn down and her whole face sags.

Most moms know. That's what I hear. Moms are supposed to know.

I look down at my feet. Can't barely talk. "I have something for Raffa."

"She's in the kitchen," she says.

I slide off my flip-flops and follow your mom into the kitchen, where a timer is beeping. The counters are covered with casserole dishes.

Raffa and your dad are sitting at the table, eating eggs and bacon. Your mom turns off the timer and takes some chocolate bread out of the oven. Raffa chews on the edge of a piece of bacon she's holding in her hand. She's not looking at me.

"Raffa?" I say. "I wrote this for you." I hold the airplane out to her.

Her beautiful brown eyes open in surprise. She doesn't move. The airplane shakes in the air. I'm about to drop my hand, but finally she takes it.

I can't watch her read it in case she doesn't like it. I'm not a real good writer. It was hard to figure out what to say, and I knew I could never write it like you do, but I wanted to do something. So I turn to your mom. "Can I go look in his room?"

"You go ahead."

I walk slowly out of the kitchen, down the hallway, and up the stairs. It feels like this might be my last time in this house.

When I open your bedroom door, your sweet body fragrance hits me. Do you know that smell is important for falling in love? There have been studies. I don't like your stinky foot smell or the smell of you after a long workout, but this you-smell, in your natural state, it's like honey. It permeates the room. How do your mom and sister not sit in your room all the time and breathe you in?

"Chris?" I whisper.

I stare at your blue curtains. *Chris, if you're dead, move your curtains.* I look for any little movement. They are as still as curtains can be. It doesn't prove anything except that if ghosts can move curtains, you're not here.

If you're dead, I don't blame you. If I were a spirit, I sure as hell wouldn't hang out in my bedroom. I'd fly through the air like a bird and then I'd flip in and out of the river and I'd circle the Earth and go to the Taj Mahal, maybe freak out worshippers, and I'd definitely open and close drawers in people's kitchens. Johnson's kitchen. Ha. That would be awesome. Please, if you are a ghost, please do that for me.

Oh god, I'm crying now. Please don't be a ghost.

I step out of your room, creep down the stairs. I don't feel like I belong here anymore. My hand wraps around the cold door handle to outside.

"Wait!" There are fast barefooted steps running down the hall toward me and when I turn around, Raffa is throwing her arms around me. I grip her skinny body so tight, it hurts.

4:10 PM Saturday, graduation

I'm standing in a long line by the auditorium, trying to avoid looking at people, so they don't give me their "sympathy" stares. I keep looking at the peach walls instead, and holy crap, they are disgusting. It's like people picked their noses and wiped it all over the wall. Never noticed that before.

I don't know if I can do this. Not without you.

My partner is Samuel Donaldson. He's a nice enough guy, but I've never seen him before. Our graduating class is only four hundred. You'd think I'd have met him before now. Do you know him? Scrawny guy, glasses, bump in his nose. We've said maybe five words to each other in the line. Poor guy to be stuck with me, the girl with the possibly dead boyfriend, who looks like she's in mourning.

Dad gave me a carnation corsage this morning. He showed up, grinning, smelling of Cheetos with that flower in a box. I hate carnations. You know that.

I'm wearing a black grad dress. It was supposed to be a sexy surprise. When I picked it out, I thought it would be perfect. Mom said, "But black is so dreary." I said she was wrong, but it turns out she was right. It looked sexy before I lost ten pounds. You would have loved it. Now it looks like a black mourning dress that I borrowed from an old aunt.

Josh put the announcement for the memorial service on the website. So if you're somewhere following your disappearance, now you know. You can come and surprise the shit out of everyone.

My big goal of the day is not to cry, but that damn Billie Holiday song keeps running through my head. *Take my lips, I want to lose them. Take my arms, I'll never use them.* It's funny which songs seep into my head at different times. Like, why "All of Me," why now?

In the auditorium, I can hear Principal Pesh calling names. The grads go through the double doors in pairs. Parents are cheering in there even though everyone is supposed to wait until the end.

The line circles around at the end of the hallway. Samuel and I are one of the last couples. Josh and Becky are going in soon. They're walking toward me on the other side of the hall. They got partnered together. I never thought about how close their last names are. Josh looks real nice, dressed in a black suit. He gives me a thumbs-up, and I smile at him to reassure him that I'm not about to go all batshit crazy. Even though I am.

The reasonable part of me knows you're probably dead. The other part of me is still hoping.

Chris? Now would be a good time to show up.

I gaze down the hall and imagine you holding my lily corsage, dancing toward me. Snapping your fingers. Swaying in that stiff way of yours. In my mind, I run toward you, push people out of the way, grab you, kiss your lips, and wrap one leg around your hip, try to dirty dance with you right here in the hall. You're laughing. Then, the lights dim and Marvin Gaye is playing and we aren't really dancing. More like, I'm reaching my hands under your blue suit jacket, running my fingers along your pressed white shirt, feeling your muscles through the thin fabric, and then, I can't stop myself; I rip your shirt open. Buttons fly through the air, ricochet above people's heads. I touch your bare chest, run my fingers over your small nipples, your understated six-pack. I press my nose into your neck and breathe in. You smell so good, sweet like your bedroom.

Then, it's like a record screeches. My imagination stops. I'm here in this hall that smells of sweat and perfume and a faint remnant of bleach. We are moving forward like zombies. Samuel Donaldson shuffles along beside me. Every now and then he gives me an awkward glance, like he wants to say something.

If you really did come, poor Samuel Donaldson would have to find another partner because they wouldn't be able to pry my fingers off your arm. I'd have to walk down the aisle and graduate with you. (I'd let you put your shirt back on.)

Tamara is sashaying toward me in her pink, cotton-candy dress. Her partner is a guy from band, big curly hair, glasses. I heard her parents paid for the insurance deductible for the damage to Johnson's dealership and Johnson's dad didn't press charges.

She's staring at me, kind of mean, like she's planning to say some horrible thing. I always feel like I've got to ready myself for the attack. Pull out my blades. Send them slicing through the air toward her, so she doesn't slice me first.

You told me Martin Luther King Jr. said to love the person, not the behavior. You said violence begets violence, and even yelling is a form of violence. I asked you if you thought love begets love and you said you did, and then you kissed me like a crazy man.

Okay, fine, I will beget love. But I'm not doing any kissing. And I don't have a paper airplane for her.

I take in a shaky breath. "Tamara?"

She pinches the side of her cotton candy dress. "What?"

What do you say in a situation like this? I forgive you? Good luck? I settle on my old favorite. "Take care."

She blinks at me. And then says, "Thanks."

"Congratulations." This time, it feels real, like I care.

She squints at me. "Yeah, you too."

Then she walks past. And you know? I kind of feel better, like maybe you were right. Maybe love begets love too. Not that I love her. I mean, let's be real. But, like, if you did come back, I could handle being in the same room as her.

Steph circles around the end of the hall and then glides toward me. Her wavy brown hair is down, and she's wearing a deep green strapless dress. Looks real classy. Glowing.

She steps out of line and gives me one of her power hugs, which nearly does me right in. I guess maybe she sees that I'm missing you. "You okay?" she whispers in my ear.

People are watching us.

I sniff and nod real fast. "Oh my god." I run my forefinger to wipe away tears. "I wish he were here."

She squeezes my bare arm. "Think of shit in a toilet."

I let out a half laugh, half cry. "I thought you were supposed to think of people in their underwear."

She shrugs. "It's not sad. It's not scary. It's just gross." Her line is moving and people are waiting. She returns to her line, and a few minutes later, she's walking through the double doors into the auditorium.

Soon it's my turn. Mrs. Lousteau says my name to confirm it's me and not some other mourning imposter in black, and I hold the inside of Samuel Donaldson's elbow, and we walk through the double doors. Even though it's dark in the auditorium, I see Dad's shiny bald head and Mom next to him, on the aisle. She's hard to miss—her butt is bulging over the seat in her large yellow nylon dress, but for once, I'm not embarrassed that every kid has walked past that. At least she's here. She actually made it out of the house.

She can't turn her head all the way, but she's turning some, in anticipation. A murmur spreads through the crowd and the whispers follow me.

I picture shit in a toilet. It does not help. I want to turn around and run back through those doors. Samuel Donaldson squeezes my hand with the inside of his elbow; he must sense me getting ready to flee. His puny bicep muscle presses against my hand, and I miss you with a sharpness that cuts me.

You were supposed to be here! Just in the nick of time, you were going to arrive and we were going to walk down the aisle like we were getting married.

Tears roll down my face. With my free hand, I try to save my makeup. Samuel guides me to the stairs by the stage. I'm wiping my face with my hand that I should be using to hold my dress.

On the second step, I trip on the fabric and fall straight toward the stairs. Samuel can't do a damn thing to stop it. My body crashes onto the steps. There are gasps. Yes, people, I am DRAMATIC entertainment.

I'm on the stairs. Some survival instinct must have kicked in because I got my hand under me and did not smash my face. The shock of it makes me stop crying. I stare at the dirty step and see a brightly colored Pop Rock. Does Josh have them in his mouth? Is that how he's graduating with you?

Poor Samuel Donaldson is tugging at my arm, trying to pull me up. Slowly, I stand. People clap. It's a rising wave of cheering, as if I scored a touchdown, even though nobody should clap in this situation.

I make it to the stage, shake Principal Pesh's hand, feel pats on my back from somebody, probably the assistant principal. Then the rolled diploma is in my hand and I'm sitting down in the bottom row, in front of Steph. She went to the rehearsal on Wednesday and told me she'd be right behind me.

Samuel Donaldson sits down. "Are you okay?" he whispers. It's sweet because he's so shy, it must have been hard for him to say.

I nod, wiping my eyes with my forefingers. I don't know why I care if I look like a mess, but I do.

"Sorry I let you fall," he whispers, his voice clogging up with phlegm. He coughs. I look at him. His face is red.

"Not your fault." I sniff.

Steph bends forward, kisses my cheek, and passes me a tissue, which I use to wipe under my eyes to clean up the mascara. She must have tucked the tissue in her bra for me when we were getting ready.

I'm grateful for her. That's one. I'm grateful my mom is here. That's two. I'm grateful that I didn't smash my face. That's three. I did it. You'd be so proud.

After the eighteen people behind me make their way up to my row, everyone is allowed to clap.

"Thank you," Principal Pesh says. "Tim Pinochet will now come up and give his valedictorian speech."

Tim edges past people in the back row, pulls index cards out of the pocket of his suit, and walks toward the podium.

He stands there, and for a moment, he doesn't say anything. "I have a speech," he says, holding up some index cards. "But I—" His voice breaks, he sniffs, and he hangs his head down. We all wait for him to continue. My eyes pool with tears. Everyone is blurry. "It's been a tough week. I read this speech to my friend Chris. He laughed." Silence again.

You told me it was hilarious. Tim is trying to pull it together. He holds up the cards and shakes them. "But he couldn't make it here today, so I'm not going to do this speech now. Instead I want to tell you a story about Chris. Last year, I was feeling real down. My grandpa died. He was the chief of the local Lummi tribe. A real amazing man. He taught me everything I know about art; I taught him how to use his iPhone." He lets out a bark of a laugh. "Chris met him a bunch of times, he liked hanging out with him. Talking. My grandpa looked forward to it."

I remember how you said he had a really cool grandpa.

"And then, when my grandpa died last summer, Chris came over to my house every day. I didn't much want to go anywhere. But he gave me this little book of photos he took of my grandpa—I still look at it all the time—and then he just played video games with me. For weeks. Because that was what I needed." He sucks his lip trying to hold it together and finally goes on, "He was the kind of guy who always knew what you needed." A long pause. "Let's do something good, guys. Let's do it for Chris."

My eyes are bleeding tears. Steph is rubbing my back.

Principal Pesh steps back to the mic and clears his throat. "Thanks, Tim. I think we're all missing Chris today. An incredible athlete, a 4.0 student, an all-round kind and respectful kid, he disappeared while going for a run along the river a week ago. He'd accepted a full-ride baseball scholarship at North Carolina State University. I have his diploma here." He holds up the rolled document, shakes it, like he's going to sell it to the highest bidder. I gaze over the heads of all the parents. The back doors crack open. My heart leaps. Maybe you're here!

The principal leans forward into the mic. "His mother, Rosemary Kirk, is here to accept his diploma on his behalf."

The door swings open. But your mom does not walk through the doors. Instead the French teacher, Mrs. Lousteau, strides down the aisle, waving her hands, like, No, she's not your mom. Um, yes, we know that. She goes up the stairs to the stage and hands Principal Pesh a note.

He whispers something away from the mic and she nods. Very serious. What are they talking about? The audience is quiet.

I grip my hands into tight balls so that my fingernails, short as they are, bite into my palms. "Mrs. Kirk has called the school and asked us to hold his diploma for her." He bows his head. What's happening? A hum builds in the audience. I look back, real fast. Josh is sitting with his mouth open. People in the audience are looking at their phones.

Principal Pesh speaks into the mic: "Chris's mom is asking me to invite you all to his funeral tomorrow afternoon at the Jehovah's Witness Kingdom Hall. Now, I'd like to have a moment of silence for Chris Kirk."

Everyone bows their heads. There's sniffling. But I'm not crying anymore. I'm frozen. We don't know if you're dead. Not for sure. It's just a fake funeral.

Steph reaches forward, pinches hard on my shoulder. I grip her hand tight, nearly squeeze it right off.

"Thank you," Principal Pesh says, looking over at us graduates. "Congratulations, everyone. You've graduated."

It's good we don't have caps and gowns at our school because I'm pretty sure nobody would be throwing their caps in the air. The audience claps, a couple parents yell out, halfheartedly, Principal Pesh tells parents to stay seated until all students have exited the auditorium, and we file out in the orderly way everyone else practiced.

I walk down the aisle, numb, gripping my dress. The audience is buzzing. I hear your name.

Out in the foyer, people cheer, not as many as if your funeral hadn't been announced, but it doesn't wreck everyone's day. I'm the twenty-first person out. Samuel Donaldson stands next to me, shifting from one foot to the other, not saying a word.

Where's Steph?

Parents fill the lobby now. People are looking at their phones with sad faces. A group of girls are crying around a phone. One of them looks up at me, like she's scared. What is happening? Mom has my phone in her purse. I need it! Where is Steph? Where are my parents? I turn, searching. I feel dizzy. Panicked.

Josh finds me before Steph. His face is a mess of emotion. He pulls me into a hug, and sobs.

Oh my god. "What happened?"

Josh chokes out, "They found his body."

"Where?"

"In the river," Josh says.

No.

And then the hard, dirty floor is grabbing at me and I'm clawing away from it and then I'm running out of the building and down the street.

your house

Your mom opens the door. Behind her, the house is crowded with church people. Her best friend, Winona, slides up beside her, frowning at me, but your mom waves her back and steps outside.

I'm bawling.

"I'm sorry," I cry. "I'm so sorry."

Your mom just stares at me. "Why are you sorry?" I want one of her hugs, but she crosses her arms.

"It's my fault. It's all my fault."

Her jaw stiffens. "It is not your fault. You shouldn't think—"

I'm hysterical. "It is. If I didn't go on this break, if I didn't fight with him, if I wasn't such an awful human being..."

"Stop it, Jessie!" she yells.

I've never heard your mom yell. My head is pounding and I feel confused and unfocused and half out of my mind, but her voice is like getting splashed with cold water. I blink at her.

"You need to stop it," she says, shaking her finger at me. "Right now. I've had enough, girl. Are you really this self-centered? Do you really think you have that kind of power? To make my boy kill himself?" Her voice breaks.

I step back.

But she's not done. Her eyes are filled with stormy passion. "You do not have that power. You're just a girl. That's it. He dated other girls before you. He had a whole life before you. He has a family and friends who love him. Who are you to say that you are that important? He had all kinds of trials in his life and he made it through. He would have made it through you, too. You do not have the right to claim that kind of power, do you understand?"

I nod, and move numbly backward, down the steps, but she follows me. My vision is all blurry. A scream is building up inside of me.

"He had a mental illness," she says.

I cry, "But if I hadn't—"

"Jessie!" Her hands are clenched, and she bangs them now against the sides of her pants. "I don't want to hear about how sorry you are or how it's your fault."

Tears and snot are cascading down my face, and I'm sobbing even though I hear what she's saying, I do.

She presses her hand over her eyes. "Jessie . . . I know you lost him too."

The front door swings open. Your dad steps onto the stoop, and Raffa eases out behind him. He moves slowly down the stairs and wraps his arms so gently around your mom, it reminds me of you.

"Come on, baby," he says. "Come inside."

"Jessie, you should go home now," your mom says, softer.

I turn and walk slowly toward home.

middle of the night, my bedroom

Cold metal. Thick handle. A switch on the side. All I need to do is flick it and the blade will slide out. My X-Acto knife. Which I used to cut the pictures on our dream collage. Dreams that are impossible now, without you.

I imagine what it will feel like, that sharp metal in my arm. I've never been a cutter. Don't much like blood. But there wouldn't be any cleanup. Just a mattress to throw away. My vision would blur and I'd fade. Like steam drifting out of a person's mouth on a cold day.

I do feel responsible, even though I know your mom is right. I mean, why would I be the reason? You had so much to live for. It doesn't have to make sense.

But still, this world feels totally empty without you. I don't know if I want to live this life anymore.

If I die, will I see you again?

Bleeding to death doesn't seem so hard. Not like the panic of drowning. Unless you hit your head first. Oh god, I hope that's what happened. I hope you didn't suffer.

two weeks later, my bedroom

Hello? Chris? Are you there? It's been a while. I want you to know I understand. I've been listening to all the music you loved, and I want you to know, I get it.

There just aren't enough sad songs.

I gaze at the light drifting through my window, catching on the dust dancing through the air. It's kind of beautiful. *Can you see it? Are you here?*

The neighborhood kids are skateboarding up and down the street. They're laughing. A skateboard crashes.

Mom knocks softly on my bedroom door. "Can I come in?"

She carries in a tray with French toast, sliced strawberries, fresh whipped cream. She's cut the toast into little bites. Maybe she thinks I'm going to choke to death. (That's a joke. Ha-ha.)

Every day, she's been making my favorite meals and in the back of my mind, two questions have arisen: How is she cooking in that kitchen? And who is buying the food? I haven't asked.

She squints at me, worried. I think she gets it. Maybe you have to go through it to know. Now I get it too.

It's a heavy black cloud that feels like it will never go away. Did that happen to you? Is that why you got more desperate? Did you think I could push it away for you? Only I couldn't, no matter what I did.

I finish half of the plate while she watches. "Thanks," I say. "I'm full."

"You're looking better today," she says. "You think you can get up?"

"I don't know."

"I have something I'd like to show you."

I close my eyes in answer and she leaves. I drift off to sleep. Weird thing is I've been sleeping a ton. It's the only way to forget.

Steph yanks the quilt off my body. "Get up!" she says. "It's ten in the morning. You can't lie in bed every day."

I open my eyes. She looks good. Her hair is done, long and wavy down her back like she's just curled it. She's wearing a navy-blue dress suit for her new assistant manager job at the Steakhouse, like a real grown-up.

"I'm not just lying in bed." I'm counting pieces of dust in the air. I'm counting breaths. I'm counting the number of times I blink in a minute.

She bends down and speaks into my face. Her breath smells of coffee.

"Please, Jessie, you have to see something." Her hair falls across my face, smells of her lavender shampoo. Meanwhile, I smell of two weeks of BO.

I'm not ready to leave this room.

Steph tugs at my arm. Her hand pinches my skin like the snake-bites we used to do on each other when we were kids, twisting the skin until the other person yelled uncle.

"Ow." I pull my arm back. "Stop it."

I plunk my head back down, but then, she yanks on my pillow. I grab at it because if she sees the X-Acto knife, she'll flip out.

It's too late. It clatters to the floor. She jumps back, bends down, slowly, and picks it up.

"What is this?" She waves it in front of my face, holding its thick steel handle, like she's going to slide the blade out and slit my neck herself.

I don't answer.

"Why do you have a knife under your pillow?" she asks.

"It's not a knife," I say, finally.

"Are you thinking of hurting yourself?"

"No." I look away. The important thing is I didn't do it. I decided to wait a day. And then I waited another day. And another. It just makes me feel better to have it so close. It's weirdly comforting.

Steph looks sick. Her eyelashes, coated with thick mascara, flutter shut like butterfly wings. "I couldn't stand it if anything happened to you," she says. "You're all I have."

"You have Pete."

"It's not the same."

I look away.

"He's dead, Jessie," she says, softly. "It doesn't mean you are."

"I know that," I whisper.

She walks over to our dream collage. "What about this?" she says, clapping her hand flat on the wall. The sound startles me. "Do you still want to do these things?"

Before you, I never thought of dreams. You taught me to want more. To be more. "I don't know," I murmur. "Maybe."

"Then get up." Her voice shakes, like she's honestly scared for me. She marches across my room, opens my dresser, and tosses my cutoffs and black T-shirt next to me. "Put these on. You stink."

Her cell buzzes and she looks down at it. "Better hurry up," she says. "I'm warning you."

She lifts her chin up at me, like when we were kids and she jumped off the high diving board and she was daring me to do it too. That's how we've always been. One of us steps ahead and pulls the other forward.

I swing my feet over the bed and sit up.

the basement

Mom thumps down the stairs and hurries past my bedroom. "I'll
get it," she calls out, like it's normal for her to get any door. She's
moving fast. How is she going so fast in our house?

"Who is it?" I hiss at Steph.

"Josh," she says. "He's coming in."

I yell out, "Tell him I'm sleeping."

"I don't think so," Steph says.

"What's going on?" I say.

Her jaw is fixed. "You're getting dressed, that's what's happening."

The back door is opening. Crap.

"Oh hi, Josh." Mom is all bright and cheery. "Come on in. She's
in her room with Steph."

Come on in? As if we are a normal family. As if people walk into
our house all the time. As if he's ever been inside.

My old instincts kick in and I yell out, "No!" Oh my god. Josh
is coming into my house. He's going to see how we live.

"Just go into her room," Mom says, in a loud voice, as if she doesn't hear.

"No, wait," I scream. "I'm naked. I have to get dressed." I jump out of bed, feel dizzy from standing up so quickly, and I grip Steph's arm. "I'm going to kill you," I say to her, and then it hits me, what I've just said. "Oh."

"Come on, J," she says, lightly. "It's okay."

Josh and Mom are talking. I wait for her to excuse the mess, claim it's temporary, say we're getting ready for a garage sale, but she says nothing. Maybe he's by the back steps and sound is traveling.

I pick up the cutoffs, which are now on the floor, and pull them over my underwear. They slide down my hips. I run a hand through my greasy hair. I haven't had a shower since graduation. It's pretty nasty. I put on a bra and my T-shirt, and I stumble out of my bedroom, intending to create a human wall between Josh and my house.

I let out one of my horror-movie gasps.

The piles are gone. The concrete floor is clear. The coffee table gleams. The old brown sofa has two new pretty cushions, white with red flowers. The rug with the triangle pattern, which I haven't seen in its entirety for ages, has been shaken out, maybe even vacuumed. How did I miss the sound of a vacuum?

The pictures on the walls are straight. There are two watercolors my mom did when she was younger as well as the posters of van Gogh's *Haystacks* and Monet's *Water Lilies*.

On top of the washing machine, a laundry basket is full of my own clean, folded clothing. And there's the extra remote! It's placed neatly, next to the TV.

Mom's clenching her hands at the sides of her long white shirt, in anticipation, and Steph has a grin on her face. Josh never saw my house before, but he seems to be getting it.

"Holy shit," I say.

Steph laughs. "Your mom and I have been working on this for the last week. This is what I wanted to show you."

Mom smiles. Remember how you said that her eyes were green, just like mine, only dulled with sadness? Today her eyes are bright emeralds.

"I found a new therapist," she said. "It's helping."

"I didn't know you were leaving the house," I say, looking around. "How come I didn't see this?"

"We just finished the hallway."

I shake my head. "Wow."

"Your mom did most of it," Steph says.

They share a look. I remember how Steph used to love coming over and baking with my mom back when the house was just messy, not crazy-person messy. She used to be jealous of my mom, if you can believe it.

I rub my eyes. Feel like I've awoken from a hundred-year sleep and everything has changed. "Upstairs?" I ask Mom.

She makes a face. "Got rid of those garbage bags. Didn't even look in them. Steph took them to Sally Ann's. But the rest—" She sighs.

It would take a day for the mess to make its way downstairs.

"Could you and Steph help me?" she asks.

Whoa. That's new. "I can get rid of stuff?" I say.

"Anything you want. I'll close my eyes."

"No fights?"

"Promise. I want upstairs to look like this."

Josh is looking between my mom and me, as if he doesn't know what to do with my crazy-ass family. His hair is cut. It looks like maybe he's slept, but he's still too skinny, and his eyes are so sad.

"Well," Mom declares, like a normal person, "I'll leave you kids alone." She heads down the hall toward the stairs.

"Mom?" I say.

She looks back, her hand on the doorknob to the stairwell.

"Thanks."

"Sure, honey." Then she hobbles back, wraps her thick arms around me, and kisses me on the cheek. I don't think she's kissed me for years. "I'm glad you're up." It's another normal mom moment. Then she heads upstairs.

Josh opens his arms and raises his eyebrows, hopeful. I step forward and hug his warm, thin body. Steph and I gaze at each other over his shoulder. I didn't know how worried she was about me until this moment. I take in my spotless basement and think about all the hours she must have spent, cleaning it with my mom. I wave her into our hug and she lets out one of her snort-laughs and wraps her arms around us.

Finally, we all step back and look at one another in this weirdly clean space. For once, three people can all sit on the sofa together. And it actually smells better, like roses, due to one of those air freshener thingies you plug in the wall.

"I got something to show you," Josh says, "when you're ready."

"Oh yeah?" That sounds serious. "I'm ready."

Steph squints at me, like she's worried. "Jessie—"

I glare. "You can't just say something like that and not show me. Yeah, I'm ready. Hit me with it."

"You need to sit down," she says.

I sit. Josh drops down on one side of me, and Steph drops down on the other. Josh slides something skinny and black out of his pocket.

It's your phone. Your initials on the back of the case. Just like I ordered.

"His mom gave me this to give you." Josh licks his lips and sniffs. And then he breaks the news. "It has a message for you."

My breath pauses halfway into my chest.

"Are you sure you're ready to read it?"

I gaze into his watery blue eyes. "I'm okay now." My voice is odd. Definitely, I don't sound okay. "I need to see it."

He hands it over. Its surface feels cool in my hand.

I press my fingerprint to open it. My fingerprint still works. My stomach tightens. I haven't even seen the damn message and I want to wail over this one fact. You didn't erase my fingerprint.

"It's in the notes," he says.

I open it. Your message pops up on the screen.

Dear Tangerine Girl,

I'm sorry. I'll love you forever.

Your Loverboy, Chris.

The period at the end of your name. It's so final. You always did that, wrote a period. The date on the note is last Friday. Forever? What does forever mean when you're dead?

A sob builds inside of me and Josh wraps his arm around me and I bury my face in his shoulder. It's different when you know, like, absolutely and for sure, when you hear a good-bye from your boyfriend, in the only way he would say it.

Josh is sobbing so hard, he's shaking, and Steph is there too, rubbing my back, and then we're all crying together, clinging to one another like buoys in the middle of a rocky ocean, until the sobs turn to sniffs and then the only thing we can hear is our slow, steady breathing, inhaling and exhaling, together.

the river

The next day, Steph makes me go down to the river with her. I put up a fight, but she says it's important. She has something to tell me, and we need to go there together. We have unfinished business down there, she says. I haven't gone down there since your body showed up. I haven't even left the house.

We pass the dentist's house and then slide down the slippery path toward the river. My shoe glides on a patch of mud, and I fling my hand out to grab on to a tree branch. Ahead, past the trampled grass and through the trees, I can see the river. I'm afraid. What does she have to tell me? Why here?

I step carefully over the train tracks. A part of me still thinks they're going to electrocute me, an old superstition from when I was a kid.

"Remember Kidnapped Girl?" Steph stands on the tracks and then jumps in the middle. It reminds me of when she was a kid—she always did that and it freaked me out. She puts on her deep voice. "I'll help you, little girl."

"That game was messed up." We used to pretend to be tied up on the train tracks. One of us would go in the woods and then the other would scream for help on the tracks and "the bandit" in the woods would run out and say in a deep voice, "I'll help you, little girl."

That was before we met real creeps, before we knew how awful people could be, before we knew about real danger.

We walk across the long grass field, toward the river.

"We're going to be in trouble when we have kids," she says.

Not something I want to think about. I take big steps over the grass, scanning for snakes.

"Speaking of which..."

I whip my head to look at her. "You're pregnant?"

"No," she says. "But this happened." She lifts her left hand. There's a big old diamond ring. Which, for some reason, I haven't seen on her finger until now.

"What the hell?" I grab her hand and stare at it like it's not a hand, but a claw. "You're engaged?"

"Yep." She grins. "It happened on graduation night."

"I'm so happy for you." I wipe a tear running down my face. "It's beautiful."

"Right?" She gazes at it, all lovesick.

"You're really getting married?"

"Yep."

She always said she wanted babies when she was young. How can anyone be that certain they want to spend the rest of their life with anyone?

"Aren't you worried it's too soon?" I say.

"Nope." Her face is glowing, all rosy cheeked and everything. "I love him. I mean, I know you think we just started going out, but we've known each other for, like, two years, since I started at the Steakhouse."

I throw my arms around her and give her a Steph-quality squeeze. I let go and stare into her face. She's going to stay in this town. I'm going to leave.

"You going to have babies right away?" I say.

She shrugs. "Maybe."

"You'll be a great mom." Even though she's crazy and she drinks too much and she likes to gamble, she's the most loving person I know.

I take in a deep breath and let it out; this is happy news. We keep walking all the way to the edge of the riverbank. I stare out at the swirling water.

"You okay?" she says.

I see your arm slide out of the river. "I keep seeing him, Steph," I whisper.

"What do you mean?"

"I see his arm coming out of the water. Or I imagine him getting sucked under the rapids. At night, when I close my eyes, he's in the water."

"You have to find a way to forget. I mean, it'll get better, right?"

You're unforgettable. Good old Nat King Cole. Played him a lot this week. *Unforgettable. That's what you are. Unforgettable. Tho' near or far. Like a song of love that clings to me, how the thought of you does things to me. Never before has someone been more.*

I nod, gulping. "Why did you want to come here?"

She shrugs. "I don't know. I guess I thought it was important for you to remember the good times, that this town and even this river is, like, the place of our childhood. It's not just a place where horrible stuff happens, you know?"

I can see us as kids, right here on the riverbank. We are making up stories together. She was a river mermaid. I was a grand priestess. She was a bank robber. I was the mastermind. She was a fairy and I was a gnome. So many imaginary games.

"I'm going to let my kids play down here too," she says.

"I can be their aunt."

She laughs. "You will definitely be their aunt." She opens her bag and pulls out the vodka and orange juice. "Let's drink to it."

We choke down the first vodka and orange juice fast, and then she pours another. "You still thinking about applying for that program?" she asks.

"Yeah. Next year."

"I'm going to miss you." She forces a smile. "You're going off to get your degree and all. You'll probably forget about me."

"Oh, Steph." I press my head against hers. "I would never."

She lets out a sad laugh.

"Tell me how he proposed," I murmur.

She goes off on this long detailed story about how he put it in the mud pie that she ordered at the end of her shift and the staff all circled around while he proposed.

"Wasn't the ring goopy?"

"I just licked it off. Everyone clapped. It was super romantic."

I gulp down my sadness. "That's cool." Then I sit up and rummage around in my big black bag, which no longer has the gun, and I pull out my paper airplane, decorated with flowers. I know it was your thing, but it might be mine now. "Here—I made this."

Tears jump to her eyes. "Oh my god." She bites her lip. "Like Chris."

Then she unfolds it. I look away. It's hard to watch. She's quiet as she reads. I just wrote her a bunch of things I was thankful about. She sniffs again. Wraps her arms around me, squeezes my guts out of me.

She pours me another drink, then lifts her cup. "To adventure." I bang my plastic cup against hers and gulp it back. I'm getting wasted, but I don't care.

Soon, we're leaning our heads against the trunk of Mr. Tom, the cedar tree, moss and all. Steph isn't even thinking about spiders in her hair. It's splayed against the wood. She looks like a fairy creature.

"You have the best hair," I slur.

"You have the best boobs," she says, grinning at me.

This has always been our thing—she has the hair, I have the boobs. "You want to do me?" I joke.

She laughs and I snort. We have the same coarse sense of humor. Thank god. I mean, without her, I don't know what I'd do.

the next Saturday, Bear Lake

I'm clinging to the tow rope behind Josh's boat. My water skis are clattering on the surface of the water. I'm holding on and that's a big step. My legs are shaky and my arms feel weak from lack of exercise, but for the first time in ages, I feel alive, really and truly alive.

Josh made me come. Dragged me out of the house. Said it would be fun.

The water is buzzing beneath me. The wind is blowing through my hair. The skin on my hands is burning. But it's simple: all I need to think about is staying up on my skis and holding on.

Then I see you. In the midst of all this forgetting, you follow me. In the quiet, glistening water, an arm reaches up. It distracts me. I hit a bump in the wake. I fly over the water in silence. I grapple with the air. Swing my legs forward. My skis land back on the water. I hold on, somehow.

That Four Tops song you love plays in my brain: *Sugar fly, honey bunch. You know that I love you.* I hear it loud and clear, like someone's playing a record.

Yes, I know it's not *sugar fly*. It's *sugar pie*. You told me that, laughing, and I still sing it my way anyhow. It should have been *sugar fly*. If I wrote that song, it would have been *sugar fly*.

The trees whiz past. Josh is watching me from the boat. Probably expects me to bail. My arms and legs ache. Crazy what weeks of lying in bed can do to a body. But I don't let go. I cling to the rope and gaze at the reflection of trees in the water.

It's so beautiful here. Maybe I can forget about you today. I don't need to bring you everywhere I go. Maybe you'll always be with me, making little appearances, but for now, it's just going to be me, the trees, and the lake.

a week later, the pool

It's my first day back lifeguarding. No phone on deck today. The smell of chlorine is oddly soothing. I'm scanning the pool efficiently, I think. Already had to bandage up a scraped knee. Didn't pass out from the blood. I'm checking all yeses in the normal column.

I'm trying not to think of you too much. Writing to you in my head might sometimes be okay, but not all the time. I need to be here, in real life. That's harder than you might think, since you're the dead person.

When I walked onto the pool deck at the beginning of shift today, everybody greeted me back with hugs, even the cashier. Valerie said she's proud of me and, "Nothing like getting right back up on the horse."

After your body showed up, Michael sent flowers. He's here today. We haven't really talked. He keeps giving me an M&M every time I bump him. These shy, sorry smiles. I guess we all make mistakes, right? Maybe the challenge is to keep forgiving.

He's on break now; Valerie is opposite me. I think she's double scanning into my zones, but it's okay. I'm not offended. I might do the same thing if I were in her shoes.

"Hi," a small voice says.

I look down.

It's Talia. She grins up at me. Her two front teeth are growing in.

"I like your bathing suit," I say. It's new, bright blue with black hearts.

"I'm learning how to swim," she says, proudly sticking out her chest. "My mom put me in lessons on Mondays."

I smile at her. "Yeah? Good for you."

Talia stands there and watches the pool with me for a minute, like she's another lifeguard. "Well," she says, rising up on her tiptoes and teeter-tottering there. "Thank you for saving my life."

It chokes me up. Almost can't talk. Then I nod my head. "You're welcome."

She skips off down the deck and even though we don't let kids skip on the deck, I don't tell her to walk.

end of summer, a final campfire

Josh heads off for college tomorrow, so he invited the whole gang over to his cabin. We're all sitting around roasting marshmallows—Steph and all your friends, even Tamara. Shocker, right? Tim and Tamara are together, like, together-together. She's a lot nicer now. And Raffa's here too. She's pressed up beside me on the low wood stump. Her skinny knees poking in the air. Laughing.

We've been telling stories about you. Funny things you did. Sweet stuff you said to us. Raffa is turning her marshmallow stick slowly.

"That's got to be just about the most perfect marshmallow," I say.

"Chris taught me how to roast them."

"No way. When?" I'm asking because I taught you how to roast a marshmallow, out here, when we camped across the lake. We could have stayed at Josh's cabin that time, but I wanted to wake up with you in the morning in a tent with the cold fresh morning air.

"May? He made Mom get the fireplace cleaned out and then we went to the woods and found some sticks. He cut the ends into these little points and we roasted marshmallows in the house." She glances at me, gives me a shy smile. "He told me you showed him how."

I laugh. But it hurts my chest. Maybe one day it won't hurt. That's what I'm hoping for.

our spot

I'm standing on the edge of the riverbank. Once again, I'm wearing only my pink underwear. Can you see me?

I gaze across the dark water. It looks deceivingly peaceful. You can't see the undertow from here, or the speed of the water. Can't see more than a foot under.

It's a hot, beautiful day in September. No pulp-mill smell. A slow breeze is blowing through my hair. Is that you?

I've got to say good-bye to you now. There's no point writing this letter anymore, not in my head, and not on paper. Letters are for the living, and anyway, this isn't a love letter. I made that clear from the beginning.

I hear a caw and look up. There's a crow on the branch above me. Maybe it's Little Man. He can fly now, of course, but I can't tell if it's him or some other crow. I caw back at him and he looks down at me, cocks his head to one side. I want to think it's him.

Did you see Little Man that day you stood on this bank?

You hid your sadness for so long. Now I remember the times

when you thought I wasn't watching you, when your eyes glazed over and the smile fell from your cheeks and your shoulders drooped and I'd say, "Chris?" You'd turn to me and you'd smile and pretend you were all good and I made myself pretend too.

When I look across the water, standing in this spot where you stood, I can't help but imagine that gigantic step you took into the cold water. Did you change your mind at the last minute? Is that why one foot landed by the edge of the water? And then, you couldn't slow your forward trajectory? Maybe you tried to swim back, but it was too fast. The river is easy to underestimate, especially at that time of year. Did it thrust you toward the rapids? Did you choke? Did you struggle? Did you hit your head early or did you suffer?

It didn't have to end like this.

When you were in the rapids, you must have had a moment of regret. Maybe you wanted to kiss my lips one last time. Maybe you thought of Raffa and her big, trusting eyes and how she adores you. Maybe you remembered your mom, how she'd pat you two times on your back to show she was proud. Or you thought about your dad sitting across from you, playing chess. Maybe you realized Josh was going to have to run alone now. And he does. But every time he runs, baby, you are still running next to him.

Can you read my mind from the land of the dead? I don't know how it works, but I sure hope so. I think you've been with me this whole time. If you have, you can see that I've missed you every day.

We all want you back, but you're gone forever. There's no going back. Not for me, not for you.

Tomorrow I'm leaving on a road trip. I've got my passport. There's this volcano I've been wanting to see.

Josh started college last week. When I get back, I'm going to apply for that conservation program. Maybe being a nature nerd is kind of a good thing nowadays.

No matter what, baby, I promise you I'm going to make a difference, like you would have done if you'd stuck around. Man, I wish you had.

Hoo boy. Deep breath.

We all say good-bye to the people we love one day. I just wasn't ready to say good-bye to you yet. But now I have to do it. That's why I'm here.

In a few seconds, I'm going to do one last brilliant dive through the air, into this cold water. Are you here? Can you see me?

There are so many things I wish I'd done differently. But most of all, I wish I could have been here on this bank when you jumped in. I would've dove in after you and stopped you from swimming out. I would have pulled you back to the bank. I would have loved you back to life. But I wasn't here. I couldn't save you. So now, I need to choose to live or die.

I choose to live.

In loving memory of my friend, Al

Author's Note

When I was eighteen years old, two weeks before my high school graduation, one of my closest friends disappeared while going for a run along the river. He was an African Canadian living in a mostly white mill town in Northern British Columbia. The seed for this story was planted in this experience. However, all of the characters and events in this story are entirely fictional, including Chris, his family, and all of his friends.

But the emotions are real. Sometimes life can feel too painful. I have felt that way myself and I'm here to tell you that it does get better. Often it takes medicine and therapy to make it better. Sometimes brain chemicals go off. If your brain is telling you to hurt yourself or others, please, get the help of a professional. You can call the National Suicide Prevention Line: 1-800-273-TALK. It is anonymous and they can make a big difference.

Acknowledgments

I'm so grateful for my incredible literary agent, Sara Crowe at Pippin Properties, who saw the potential in this book and helped shape it into what it is today. Thank you also to my rock-star editor Laura Schreiber, who blew me away with her amazing feedback. Thanks to Hannah Allaman and Jody Corbett for your sharp edits, and to my publicist Cassie McGinty for all your work to bring this book into the world.

Thank you to the advisors at Vermont College of Fine Arts, where I've been working on my MFA in Writing for Children and Young Adults over the last two years. In particular, I want to thank my semester advisors: Kekla Magoon, Daniel José Older, Amanda Jenkins, and A. S. King. You made me a better writer, and taught me so much about writing, revision, and life. All these lessons have made a huge impact on my rewrites for this book, and I'm sure, my future books. Thanks also to my workshop advisors: Cynthia Leitich Smith, An Na, Nova Ren Suma, Mark Karlins, Tim Wynne-Jones, and Linda Urban. I'm grateful to my fellow VCFA writers, and the Tropebusters, for their enthusiastic support, and all the sparkly, zingy times.

Thanks to my writer friends who read and critiqued this book: Amalie Howard, Jennifer Castle, Amy McNamara, Delina Codey, Anna Van Lenten, Galaxy Craze, Susanna Kohn, Justine Lambert, Adele Myers, Donnaldson Brown, Kris Percival, Susan Merson, Melissa Baumgart, Meg Cook, Jessie Janowitz, Tali Noimann, Jiton Davidson, Naadeyah Haseeb, and Alexei Auld. My writer relatives give me great feedback: thanks to Jake Purcell, Florine Gingerich, and Rachel Purcell.

I also want to thank my extended family, who are always cheering me on. Thank you to my aunt Angela for your poetry and encouragement. You gave me a green leather journal when I was ten, a place to put my special words, my dreams, and my anger, and you taught me that it was okay to write down the things you are afraid to say out loud.

My mom has been one of my biggest cheerleaders, always saying *I believe in you*, and reading my stories. My dad shared his love of nature and answered all my questions. And my amazing sisters, Jenn and Tara, said all the nice things.

Thank you to Adelina for taking care of my kids and our household when I'm writing. You have made it much easier for me to create.

I also want to thank my fourth- and fifth-grade teacher Mrs. Aalto. She put me in a special enrichment class where I wrote a book called *The Mystery of the Poison Ivy.* I was so proud of that book. Teachers can make a gigantic difference.

Finally, thank you to my husband, Gavin, and my two daughters, Madeline and Harper. You are my first readers. You inspire me every day. Your love helps shape every word I write. I love you.